Bruce B

Murder on the Lake

Detective Inspector Skelgill Investigates

LUCiUS

Text copyright 2015 Bruce Beckham

All rights reserved. Bruce Beckham asserts his right always to be identified as the author of this work. No part may be copied or transmitted without written permission from the publisher.

This is a work of fiction. Names, characters, places and incidents either are the product of the author's imagination or are used fictitiously. Any resemblance to actual persons, living or dead, events and locales is entirely coincidental.

Kindle edition first published by Lucius 2015

Paperback edition first published by Lucius 2015

For more details and rights enquiries contact:
Lucius-ebooks@live.com

Cover design by Moira Kay Nicol

EDITOR'S NOTE

Murder on the Lake is a stand-alone whodunit, the fourth in the series 'Detective Inspector Skelgill Investigates'. Chronologically, its events take place a few months after those described in *Murder on the Edge*. It is set primarily in the English Lake District, with scenes in London and the Scottish capital, Edinburgh.

Absolutely no AI (Artificial Intelligence) is used in the writing of the DI Skelgill novels.

THE DI SKELGILL SERIES

Murder in Adland
Murder in School
Murder on the Edge
Murder on the Lake
Murder by Magic
Murder in the Mind
Murder at the Wake
Murder in the Woods
Murder at the Flood
Murder at Dead Crags
Murder Mystery Weekend
Murder on the Run
Murder at Shake Holes
Murder at the Meet
Murder on the Moor
Murder Unseen
Murder in our Midst
Murder Unsolved
Murder in the Fells
Murder at the Bridge
Murder on the Farm

1.
DERWENTWATER

Sunday evening, late October

It might be surmised that Daniel Skelgill is never happier than when he crouches alone, afloat, alert; a trusty rod gripped in the left hand, an oar deftly manoeuvred in the right; another epic piscine battle about to augment his inventory of pike-infested pub tales. Yet the casual observer would not think so to look at him. At this moment of truth – when defeat may be plucked from the fishy jaws of victory – he appears anything but content. In this instant when intuition usurps rational evaluation, when instinct and experience come together in an artful display of predation – a lupine anticipation takes possession of his demeanour. He is a man transfixed. His pale eyes are narrowed to slits. His lips are drawn back over his teeth. A fearsome grimace grips his features. Indeed he might barely recognise himself – a photograph taken now surely challenging even his indifferent narcissism. He stalks his quarry like a half-starved wolf, hostage to adrenaline that – in the event of failure – will abandon him, hollow with loss. Such stakes perhaps explain the lack of obvious joy – even in the event of triumph, when the stampede of his heartbeat is all consuming.

But on this particular October Sunday evening Skelgill has more reasons to be cheerless. An autumn gale – long forecast but promised for the early hours – has swept prematurely across England's western seaboard and is making of Derwentwater a storm-tossed Irish Sea in miniature. White horses threaten to breach the bow. Seeking refuge in the lee of Grisholm – an uninhabited wooded islet whence browning leaves of ancient oaks stream like migrating birds against the lowering sky –

Skelgill wrestles his small bobbing craft into calmer but still choppy waters. He casts about for a likely spot to fish – but darkness advances and he ought to call it a day. Soaked to the skin and not a little hypothermic, only bloody mindedness now drives him on – he has an appointment with a pint and a fishless blank will spoil his chat.

But if it is a yarn he craves, then perhaps all is not lost. As his boat is drawn shoreward by the refracted waves that embrace the isle, a movement attracts his attention. In the gloom, a pale shape weaves amongst the bankside trees. It is the slim figure of a woman, almost ghostlike. The roar of the wind in the canopy drowns out any sound she makes. She has long fair hair, plastered down by the rain; around her is drawn a fawn mackintosh that reaches her ankles. As she picks her way towards him she stumbles on the uneven ground, and clutches protectively at her midriff. Then suddenly she glances across the water, as if she senses that she is being watched. For a few seconds they exchange curious stares, each squinting into the dusk, like the meeting of an explorer and a savage (in appearance, Skelgill fulfilling the role of the latter). The boat washes closer, and at about twenty feet of separation the woman breaks her silence.

'We need help.'

Though she calls out, her voice is weak and tremulous.

'What's wrong?'

Skelgill has no such trouble in projecting his reply.

Still clutching one hand to her stomach, with the other she wipes beads of rain and strands of hair from her face.

'Somebody has died – we have no means of communication.'

Skelgill pushes closer to the bank, but there is an empty clunk as the hull strikes a rock and he is forced to reverse.'

'Who's we?'

'It's a writers' retreat – at Grisholm Hall – there are nine of us. Eight.'

Skelgill evidently decides he has heard enough. Energetically he begins to row away from the shallows. He calls out, not looking at the woman.

'I can't get ashore here – meet me round at the landing stage – you know where that is?'

'Yes.'

'Five minutes max.'

The woman nods and turns and disappears into the darkness beneath the trees. Grisholm is a small oval island, barely half a mile at its widest, with its long axis oriented north to south. The landing stage is located on the west bank, diametrically opposite his present position. Skelgill must battle the breakers that surge around either headland – he sets his course in a clockwise direction, to take advantage of the south-westerly once he rounds the point. Spray and spume and precipitation soak him anew, but he bends his back to the task and reaches his destination in more or less the predicted time. The woman is waiting for him, shielding her eyes from the rain with a deckhand's salute.

Skelgill pulls in his oars and allows the swell to sweep the boat up against the wooden jetty. The woman watches as he leans over the bow and makes fast the painter around a sturdy upright. Then he hauls himself onto the greasy planks and stands beside her, panting from his exertion. He regards her with some surprise – she is small in stature – barely over five feet – and young, too, a girl really: early twenties if her elfin appearance is not misleading. Her skin is fair and – framed by the inverted 'v' of her hair – her features are indistinct in the gloom. He notices that she is shivering.

'You alright, lass?'

'I'm cold – that's all. I thought it worth looking for a boat – before it became too dark.'

She is well spoken, her accent privately educated. She seems quite calm, though her demeanour is rather solemn.

'Well, you were right.'

She does not respond, as if she is waiting for Skelgill to take the initiative.

'I'm Dan, by the way.'

Stiffly she offers a hand in a formal manner, and does not reciprocate his grip.

'Lucy.'

'Where are the others?'

'They're at the house. The majority think we should wait until the morning. Until the storm has died down.'

Skelgill adjusts his *Tilley* hat, pulling it more firmly into position.

'That might be a long wait – this is one of the deepest lows on record.'

The girl looks at him rather blankly, as though meteorology was not included on her finishing school curriculum.

'We should get you inside. Let's head up to the hall and see what's what.'

Skelgill is familiar with their immediate geography. Grisholm Hall, a rather austere Victorian edifice at the centre of the isle, lies chronically vacant and shuttered, a situation that has persisted for the best part of half a century. With no caretaker in residence, the peeling and tilted *'Trespassers will be Prosecuted'* signs nailed around the perimeter held little fear for him and his fellow adventurers, who spent many an illicit hour here in their teenage years. From the mooring a winding footpath climbs through dense woodland to a highpoint, where the property rests in a clearing of lush mossy lawn, though entirely hidden from the lake year-round by a judiciously planted inner ring of conifers. It is necessary to climb one of the fells surrounding lower Derwentwater to discover this hidden mansion from afar.

The girl seems accepting of Skelgill's local knowledge. She walks silently, half a pace behind him. As they move away from the shoreline, rhododendrons close in to banish the wind at ground level. Skelgill tries his hand at making conversation.

'I thought writers were all old wrinklies.'

The girl might be expected to reply to this clumsy compliment with some degree of energy, but her considered answer is rather perfunctory in its delivery.

'Agatha Christie wrote her first novel in her twenties.'

'Shows what I know.' Skelgill tilts his head in a gesture of bafflement. 'Not really my bag, fiction.'

A few more moments of silence pass before the girl responds, more casually now.

'What *do* you like?'

'Well – fishing, believe it or not.' Skelgill hesitates, perhaps weighing the pros and cons of revealing his official vocation. 'Fell running. Real ale. But in my day job I'm a police officer.'

He glances back at the girl, but it is too dark beneath the trees to gauge any reaction. She appears to be concentrating on her progress, as the path takes a sudden upward bound. So Skelgill chimes in again.

'You might say you struck lucky.' He lifts his hat and scratches his head absently. 'Although my boss would probably disagree.'

She treats this self-deprecating remark with the same detachment as his observation about her youth; but perhaps she is just overawed by his seniority. They emerge upon the edge of the lawn, and she quickens her pace and moves ahead of him. Before them looms the imposing form of Grisholm Hall. It is a substantial construction, though not one that is especially easy upon the eye, even with the benefit of daylight. In the advancing darkness the main impression is of unplanned asymmetry, with wing-like structures added on either side of the original house, and numerous dormers and chimney stacks protruding erratically from the roof. There are just-discernable bay windows in both of the main storeys, and an offset porch reached by a broad flight of stone steps. Perhaps the most salient feature, under the circumstances, is the virtual absence of artificial light, either illuminating the route of access, or emanating from within the building itself. The only sound above the wind is the irregular spatter of rainwater escaping from a blocked gutter. The castaway would be excused for thinking there is no one at home.

The girl, Lucy, might not be forthcoming with chatter, but now she leads the way nimbly up to the darkened entrance. She has to lean upon the heavy timbered door, which admits them with a creak of hinges into a stone-flagged hallway, dimly lit and – the noise of the storm now excluded – filled with the steady background hiss of gas lamps – the explanation no doubt for the lack of external lighting: the island has no mains electricity.

Skelgill hesitates for a second and glances down at his sodden walking boots – but they are washed clean as such and the girl is already entering a room at the end of the hall, through one of a pair of double doors. There is the murmur of voices from within, and, as he hurries to catch her up, she makes an announcement to those persons as yet out of his sight.

'The police are here.'

Removing his hat, Skelgill enters the now-silent room to be greeted by half a dozen or so inquisitive faces that have abandoned their conversations to look his way. Despite its size the drawing room is cosy and welcoming, its subdued gas lighting bringing out the best of its autumn colour scheme. The members of the party are seated upon a trio of sprawling country house style sofas set around a broad slate hearth, where a log fire smokes in the grate.

If Skelgill were able to adopt a fly-on-the-wall perspective, he might be persuaded that, in the bemused stares directed his way, there is an element of collective anticipation along the lines that someone else is yet to enter the room. This notion is perhaps confirmed by the first person to break the silence, a somewhat nondescript middle-aged man in shirtsleeves and waistcoat, who sits closest to the fire, and who is mainly distinctive for sporting an extravagant spotted bow tie and a public school accent.

'You couldn't look less like the police, if you don't mind my saying so, old boy.'

Skelgill fixes the man with a polite but steely glare.

'Wouldn't you say, sir – in my profession that might just be an advantage?'

The man does not appear disconcerted by Skelgill's challenging tone.

'You mean you are a plain clothes officer?'

'DI Skelgill, Cumbria CID.'

The girl Lucy takes half a step forward. She begins to unfasten the oversized mackintosh, which, on reflection, she must have borrowed.

'He was fishing – it's a Sunday, after all.'

This little intervention seems to break the ice, and several of the group now rise to their feet, and begin to approach the new arrivals. They all try to ask questions simultaneously, but one woman – a rather voluptuous brunette who might, beneath her extensive make up, be around the forty mark – reaches Skelgill first, and fastens on to his upper arm with both hands. Rather swooningly, in the exaggerated fashion of a player in a silent movie, she begins to regale him with her concerns (in summary, along the lines of having to sleep in the equivalent of a mortuary), and apparently to wreathe him – if his reaction is anything to go by – in the coils of her heady perfume. Not to be outdone by this possessive display, a general clamour breaks out from the remainder of the crowd, who begin to bombard him with more requests and opinions. Skelgill backs away – brunette attached – holding up his free hand in protest.

'Ladies, gentlemen – please!'

He evidently looks suitably disconcerted, for the petitioners seem to realise they have overdone their advances and fall silent, temporarily at least. Into this hiatus, the man who first spoke interjects.

'Why don't I explain the background to the Inspector – then if there are any outstanding issues we can take it in turns? The poor chap hasn't even got his coat off and we're haranguing him half to death.'

There is one disapproving cough, but that may be aimed at the man's unfortunate choice of words – otherwise the company falls in with this request, and even the ardent brunette detaches herself from Skelgill with a sheepish flutter of her surely false eyelashes.

The man with the bow tie seems to carry authority. While Skelgill removes his rain-soaked *Barbour* and zips off his leggings, and drapes them over the back of an antique Windsor chair, he returns to his place and raises a glass from the low table before the fire.

'Why doesn't someone get the officer a drink – what's your poison, Inspector?'

Skelgill raises an eyebrow.

'Perhaps a hot chocolate would do the trick, if you have such a thing.'

'Can't we tempt you with something a little stronger – or are you considered to be on duty?'

Skelgill is again scrutinising his boots, perhaps contemplating whether to remove them. He seems to conclude in the negative, and clumps across to a vacant position beside the fire, opposite the man.

'On and off duty tends to be a bit of a grey area in this part of the world, sir. I generally play it safe – never know when I might have to get behind a wheel to reach an emergency.'

Skelgill sinks into the comfort of the settee. Another woman, a brunette whose hair is streaked with grey, perhaps in her mid-forties and plainer in looks and dress than the others present, approaches the end of the table.

'Do you have any special requests for your hot chocolate, Inspector? We've got skimmed, semi-skimmed and whole milk – long life, I'm afraid.'

'Oh – just the full-fat for me, madam – and three sugars.'

The woman smiles convivially.

'Shan't be two ticks, Inspector.'

As the group settles down and order returns, Skelgill inspects the fire with a critical eye. The logs have been arranged laterally, like a stack stored for seasoning; they are crowding one another out, damping down the airflow. It is clear from his reaction that he can see this build deficiency, and that he has to restrain himself from taking up the long cast-iron poker and tongs in order to improve its function. The man in the bow tie clears his throat and reaches across the expansive coffee table with an outstretched hand.

'Dickie Lampray, Inspector – I can introduce you to everyone when appropriate – young Lucy Hecate, you've met already, of course.'

Skelgill shakes the man's hand and then, as he lets go, indicates with a sweep of his arm towards the shadows of the high, ornately corniced ceiling.

'This place is generally empty.'

'I believe it is available for special hires such as this, Inspector.'

Skelgill nods. The man continues.

'We are on a writers' retreat. A local boatman conveyed us from our rendezvous at Brandlehow Inn on Thursday afternoon. This is our fourth night of a planned seven.'

At this juncture there is fidgeting among the group listening in, as if they harbour differing opinions regarding the idea of seeing out the full week.

'Abel Thurnwyke.'

'I'm sorry, Inspector?'

'The name of your boatman, sir.'

'Ah – I see, Inspector. He was somewhat taciturn, if I may say so.'

'That's him being chatty.'

'Well – it was a rather disconcerting journey, what with all nine of us and the luggage and water sloshing about in the boat – and he let us off at the landing stage and was gone before we knew it.'

'So, is there an organiser here?'

'Well, though it may seem curious, Inspector – there is no organiser – at least not in person.'

Skelgill looks puzzled.

'Don't you have writing classes – that kind of thing?'

'It's probably not entirely odd, Inspector. Naturally there was an outline proposition for how we should spend our time – to which I assume we each individually responded. Wordsworth Writers' Retreats they call themselves. But the agenda was positioned as largely open for interpretation as we saw fit. Six of the party are writers, and there is an agent – myself – a critic,' (he gestures towards a rather severe-looking woman in her late thirties, with tightly drawn jet-black hair and aquiline features, who is perched on the sofa that faces the fire; she inclines her head somewhat haughtily) 'and a publisher.' He coughs discreetly. '*Was* a publisher.'

Skelgill's demeanour suggests he intends to return shortly to this point. Dickie Lampray continues.

15

'The idea is for the writers to gain optimal peace and quiet to write, and obtain informal advice as they might seek it. The, er... *professionals* among us drew up a programme of informal talks for the evenings.'

Ever the pragmatist, Skelgill homes in upon matters closer to his own heart.

'What about meals – cooking? Are there no staff?'

The man shakes his head, though he gives no impression of disapproval.

'The event was advertised as self-catering, Inspector. The kitchen was provisioned prior to our arrival. As it turns out we are fortunate enough to have among our number a chef – she aspires to write cookery books – Linda Gray, who is presently making your hot chocolate.'

'How many people does the building accommodate?'

'Well – there are ten bedrooms, Inspector – so it is more or less full under these circumstances – but perhaps one person did not turn up – or they failed to sell all the places.'

'Or maybe it was intended for a course leader?'

The man frowns.

'Well – I don't think so, Inspector – I'd need to re-read the literature, if I have kept it – and you'd have to ask the others – but I don't believe we were led to expect someone in residence – it was positioned as a communal effort, easy as you go. This is not entirely atypical.'

Skelgill glances around the group, to see that this assessment is met with small nods and gestures of agreement. He returns his attention to Dickie Lampray.

'And someone has died – your publisher person.'

The man nods earnestly.

'You have a mobile telephone, I take it, Inspector?'

'In a dry-bag in my boat.'

Dickie Lampray appears relieved.

'His name is Rich Buckley, Inspector – you may have heard of him – rather a high-flyer in the book trade.'

Skelgill purses his lips, but is non-committal in his response.

'How did he die?'

The man does not reply immediately, but instead raises an uncertain hand to his chin. Just then the drawing room door opens, and he removes the hand to point to the newcomer.

'Ah, Inspector – here's the chap best placed to answer your question.' Now he raises a palm like a diner summoning a waiter, and addresses the new entrant, a tall bowed man of retirement age, whose prominently boned features protrude from the surroundings of a bushy grizzled beard and matching hairdo. 'Dr Bond – this is Inspector Skelgill of Cumbria CID. He was just inquiring about the cause of death.'

A flicker of apprehension seems momentarily to crease the doctor's heavy brow, but he quickly composes himself and with a loping stride crosses to the rear of the sofa on which Skelgill sits in order vigorously to pump his hand.

'Gerald Bond – at your service.' He has a pronounced Yorkshire accent and a bluff manner to go with it. "I'm a retired GP, Inspector – planning to write guide books about walking in the Lake District.'

Skelgill looks alarmed. For a second it seems he might be about to inform the good doctor that he should not waste his energy – that he was beaten to this particular summit by the peerless Wainwright, half a century ago. Sensibly, however, he keeps his own counsel long enough for the man to continue.

'Heart failure appears the most likely cause – he was lying on his bed, fully dressed as though he'd been reading.' He contrives a wry grin. 'No indication of foul play, I'm afraid, Inspector.'

There is a sense of expectancy in the air as he glances around at the semi-circle of silent faces that are turned upon him. Skelgill does not respond to the doctor's little attempt at humorous melodrama.

'What was the time of death?'

Again there is a hint from his demeanour that the doctor is momentarily discomfited. Skelgill has posed the question in the brusque manner he would of his regular forensic physician, demanding a proficient response.

'Er, well – that would be hard to say, Inspector.' He folds his arms defensively. 'I merely confirmed he had no vital signs. He

17

was discovered about an hour ago – but he'd remained in his room all day. There had been a 'do not disturb' sign on the door since this morning.'

Dickie Lampray interjects.

'I ought to point out this has been very much his habit, Inspector. Our rooms are self-contained suites. Rich has not been an early riser – I believe each day so far he has breakfasted in bed in lieu of lunch.'

Linda Gray has re-entered the drawing room bearing a tray at chest height. Dickie Lampray glances at her for confirmation. She nods enthusiastically.

'That's right, Inspector – I've done a continental breakfast – rather like this – for three or four people who've not made it down. Mr Buckley was one of them.'

'And how was he this morning?'

The woman places the tray before Skelgill. He nods with approval when he sees there is a large home-made buttered scone, and assorted single-portion jars of preserves.

'I've just been leaving trays outside the rooms – his was taken inside at some point, but I never saw him. I'm not sure anyone did.'

Skelgill looks back to Dickie Lampray.

'When was he last seen alive?'

'We have discussed this, naturally, Inspector. We believe he was here in the drawing room until approximately two a.m. with myself, Angela Cutting' (again he inclines his head towards the woman he introduced as a literary critic) 'and Bella... er, Miss Mandrake. The actress – you know?' Now he indicates with a palm the woman whom Skelgill had been unable to fend off a couple of minutes earlier. Though Skelgill shows no sign that he recognises either her face or her name, and regards her rather blankly, she smiles coyly in response.

'Who found him?'

Linda Gray, who has lowered herself into the space beside Skelgill, raises a tentative finger, as though about to make an admission.

'That was me, Inspector – I went up to see whether he wanted soup or a cold starter tonight. We were all gathered here for afternoon tea – it's a convenient time to ask – when you know you're not interrupting anyone – and he was the only one of us missing.'

'I take it his room wasn't locked?'

'No, Inspector.'

'And what did you do?'

'When I couldn't wake him I came down here and – well – I suppose I raised the alarm. The others went up again with me and the doctor confirmed that he had died.'

'And you didn't see anything that would make you suspicious?'

She shakes her head vehemently.

'Like the doctor says – you'd just think he was asleep.'

Skelgill has been eyeing his scone, and now – eschewing the selection of spreads – he takes a substantial bite. There is a silence while he swallows and sluices it down with a gulp of hot chocolate. He appears immune to the effects of the still-steaming liquid.

'Well – I suppose I ought just to have a look – then get someone over from the relevant authorities to deal with the formalities.'

Going by the collective body language, there seems to be a little ripple of relief that runs through the group around Skelgill. Dickie Lampray sits up and straightens his bow tie. Skelgill takes another swig of his drink and glances about to seek out the girl, Lucy, who brought him to the hall. She is standing a little aloof from their coterie, over towards a curtained window, one hand resting on an occasional table. She has removed the loose coat to reveal a close-fitting pale-green woollen dress, and apparently little else beneath. He watches her as he speaks.

'Lucy mentioned that you have no means of communication.'

Dickie Lampray follows Skelgill's gaze, and then looks back at him.

'Given the lack of mains services, you won't be surprised to hear there is no landline, Inspector. Moreover, we were requested not to bring our mobiles or laptops. Of course – there is no electricity – so those of us who did bend the rules soon found our devices had run out of charge.'

Skelgill frowns as he pops the last piece of scone into his mouth.

'Not very handy in case of an emergency.'

'It was positioned as one of the benefits of the retreat – no irritating alerts, no facile ringtones, no intrusive email, no distracting internet. Just perfect peace in which to write.'

'Or die.'

Now Dickie Lampray averts his eyes from Skelgill's scrutiny.

'With hindsight, Inspector, you are quite right.'

Skelgill gets to his feet, brushing crumbs from his lap.

'And you have no boat.'

This is a statement of fact – something that was obvious to Skelgill having arrived at the small pier with its empty boathouse.

'Not that any of us would be competent to use one, Inspector.'

At this juncture another of the party, hitherto silent, pipes up.

'I think I could have got us out of here.'

The man, perhaps in his early forties, though of an athletic-looking build with short-cropped salt-and-pepper hair, designer stubble and a tanned complexion, and dressed in slim black jeans and a tight matching t-shirt that emphasises his cut musculature, sits diagonally opposite Skelgill, with legs crossed and an arm casually thrown along the back of the settee.

Skelgill casts a disinterested eye in the man's direction, as a professional might dismiss the ill-informed pronouncement of an amateur. The man does not seem fazed and coolly returns Skelgill's gaze. Dickie Lampray perhaps senses the slight tension in the air, and manufactures a hearty chuckle.

'Mr Boston is our resident action man, Inspector.' He lifts a conspiratorial finger and taps the side of his nose. 'Ex-SAS we suspect, though he is very close. A clue is that he is writing a debut novel about the last Balkan war. At this very moment we might all have been afloat on a raft made from mattresses, if Burt had had his way.' He affects a shudder. 'I use the word *afloat* reservedly, Inspector.'

The man so named as Burt Boston makes a slight shrug of his shoulders, but does not comment. His expression remains impassive. Skelgill's narrowing eyes, however, betray a hint of discontent. Dickie Lampray continues.

'Without your serendipitous arrival, Inspector, the reality is we would have been entirely marooned until we could attract the attention of someone at first light tomorrow.'

Skelgill bends down to retrieve his hot chocolate. He takes a thoughtful pull at the mug.

'There's not many folk on the lake this time of year. Not least in this weather. You might have been lucky to see anyone all day. And there's no road beside the bank down at this end of Derwentwater. Just woods. Wouldn't be of great use trying to signal.'

Perhaps Skelgill has already reached the conclusion that a raft would have been their best bet – a competent outdoorsman could surely fashion a seaworthy means of escape and an improvised life vest. It would only take one person to raise the alarm – there would be no need to risk the lives of the entire group.

'Well, as I say, Inspector – we are indebted to your dedication to angling under such adverse conditions.'

Skelgill shrugs modestly.

'Call it pig-headedness, sir. I'm meeting a couple of pals later in the pub – I've got a bit of a running bet concerning a particular size of pike I've been hoping to catch from Derwentwater.'

Dickie Lampray nods sympathetically and checks a worn silver fob timepiece that he extracts from the watch pocket of his waistcoat.

'Well – I hope, at least, we shan't keep you from your appointment, Inspector – it is not yet six p.m.'

As Skelgill begins to make his way between the coffee table and the sofas, the one woman to whom he has not been introduced, directly or indirectly, rises to let him pass. She is a striking redhead of just over medium height in her early thirties, her slim figure accentuated by ochre stretch jeans and a close-fitting floral sleeveless top. She has electric-blue irises and high freckled cheekbones that combine to give her a rather wild-eyed look, and she returns his inquisitive gaze with a defiant appraising stare of her own. Dickie Lampray seems to notice this frisson, and intervenes with a diplomatic *ahem*.

'I ought to introduce you to Sarah, Inspector – she is popularly known as Xara Redmond – as author of the *Chief Inspector Frances Furlough* mysteries.'

Skelgill and the woman exchange polite nods.

'Until your arrival, Inspector, I was beginning to think we had a plot in the making for Sarah's next bestseller – but perhaps, all the same, you could give her a few tips that might be of local literary interest?'

Skelgill grimaces and then grins apologetically at the woman.

'I struggled to get beyond *Swallows and Amazons,* I'm afraid, madam.'

2. THE PIER

Sunday 6pm

Skelgill picks his way gingerly through the intense darkness of the woods towards the landing stage. In the hour he has spent indoors dusk has slipped into the wings and night's curtain has fallen. The gale is still tearing at the treetops high overhead, and heavy drips splatter continually upon him. It is by tread alone that he can tell he keeps to the damp mulched path. As such, his progress is slow – nobody at the hall owns so much as a pocket torch; a provisional search has revealed no oil lanterns to hand, and – while there are candles aplenty in all of the rooms – a naked flame would not survive the inclement conditions. When fishing earlier, the advent of the rain prompted him to secrete his mobile phone and flashlight with other sensitive items in a large dry-bag stored in a compartment beneath the rear thwart of his boat: thus he has no means of creating artificial light until he reaches the craft.

His superficial examination of the body of Rich Buckley, and an equally cursory inspection of its surroundings – a well-appointed suite with bathroom facilities and an adjoining sitting room and writing desk – has produced nothing to raise any suspicions. The dead man was wearing corduroys and a loose-fitting designer label shirt beneath a silk dressing gown – as though he had been lounging about his quarters – and exhibited no marks of anything untoward having befallen him. Dr Gerald Bond, who – along with Linda Gray accompanied Skelgill – indicated such signs as might point to sudden cardiac arrest (frankly, it must have seemed to Skelgill, by a process of elimination of other possible diagnoses). Linda Gray, meanwhile, drew attention to a copy of a hardback business book, *Damned Publishers*, that she had picked up from the floor on entering the room, and had placed on the bedside table prior to attempting to raise him.

Skelgill then held a brief audience in the drawing room. He explained that under such circumstances it was necessary for a practising doctor to certify the death, and that he could probably organise for the said official to arrive in a covered motor launch that would be more suitable than his rowing boat for conveying those present to a temporary refuge on the 'mainland', so to speak. It was his view that the body could probably not practically be removed until tomorrow, when the relevant undertaking services could be mobilised. Then there was the matter of contacting next of kin, the property owners, and other formalities. There had ensued among the delegates a rather fraught debate about what they ought to do – whether the retreat should be abandoned in its entirety as the Inspector seemed to be suggesting, or whether to continue, perhaps at another venue – that is, if they could contact the organisers, Wordsworth Writers' Retreats. The spectrum of opinion ranged from Bella Mandrake's dramatic reiteration that she could not be expected to spend a night on a secluded island in the same creaky old house as a corpse, to the phlegmatic Burt Boston's stance, who was all for remaining at Grisholm Hall. This point of view was supported by Dr Gerald Bond who, rather in keeping with his county stereotype, was quick to point out that the place was booked and paid for, and – after all – that people die in adjoining rooms in hotels all the time — it is just that the staff do not make a song and dance about it; a fact to which he is privy, having often been called to such incidents, both on and off duty. Skelgill had left them with the discussion still in full flow.

Now, as he suddenly comes upon the jetty, he must realise, however, that the debate's outcome is academic: *for his boat is gone.*

Though it might be dark – albeit less intensively so than beneath the woodland canopy – there is sufficient contrast between the various shades of charcoal for him to discern its absence. In any event, he would expect to hear the gunwale grating against the timbers of the small pier, as the craft is rocked by the heavy swell. He approaches the sturdy upright mooring post and, on bended knee, slides his hands down its circumference, feeling for the painter. There is no trace of the rope.

He rises and stares into the blackness of the gale that rages across the lake. Wind and rain lash his features, but he ignores any discomfort, his arms hanging loosely by his sides. Perhaps he is replaying in his mind the moment he tied up the boat, under the watchful eye of the silent girl: she may be able to corroborate his version of the knots. Or maybe he is considering the limited range of scenarios, one of which must have occurred during his absence. The jetty faces due west, and the storm is blowing up from the south west. Had the boat somehow become free of its own accord, it ought still to be pressed into the little rocky inlet, either against the pontoon or even to have been driven into the ramshackle boathouse at the foot of the pier. At the very worst it might have been sunk on the spot by the wash. If so, his dry-bag may be recoverable.

Cautiously he makes his way back along the slippery boards, and passes into the pitch-black entrance of the boathouse. The clean splash of the waves tells him it is vacant, as it had been on his arrival. He begins to feel his way along the rough planks of the adjacent wall. He dislodges a polystyrene lifebelt from a bracket – carefully he weighs it for efficacy. Slowly, he moves on – and then lets out a little grunt of satisfaction. He has found what he seeks: a wooden boat hook, damp and slimy and somewhat warped, but about ten feet long.

Now, like a gondolier trying to divine a safe course, he begins to prod into the water, methodically covering the surface as far out as he can reach, beginning in the boathouse, and gradually working his way along the jetty. But he draws a blank – all he encounters is the jarring rocky bottom and, in places, yielding patches of mud. The depth ranges from about three feet inside the boathouse, to perhaps six or seven feet off the end of the pier. He does not attempt to replace the long pole upon its fixings, but instead slides it inside the boathouse, against the near wall.

A little more purposefully, he returns to the very end of the pier. There is a second mooring post here, cut off at about waist height. He places the heels of his hands upon it, and leans over the water, like a forlorn figurehead adorning the skeleton of a wrecked ship. While there is little to see, he seems to be listening to the rush of the tempest. He knows the lie of the land, the curvature of the island's shoreline beyond the inlet. It would just take one good push to propel a small boat past the little point, whence it would be picked up by the wind and surface current and be carried into the open reaches of Derwentwater, perhaps to sink, perhaps to come to rest on some distant shore.

Of course, a simpler explanation is that someone rowed it away.

*

'Gone – it can't be gone!'
'I'm afraid so, madam.'
'What about your mobile phone, Inspector?'
'I'm afraid that's gone, too.'
'But how?'

Skelgill shrugs his shoulders. There are dark patches around the collar bones of his jacket, where the wax proofing needs to be restored and water has soaked through. Methodically he begins to unfasten the brass press-studs, biting one side of his lower lip as he does so.

'That's what I'd like to know, madam.'

The woman, Angela Cutting, stares accusingly at Skelgill as though she suspects him of some subterfuge. Yet she herself poses conspiratorially beside a rather dumbstruck Dickie Lampray, who is in his original position beside the hearth. They are the only two persons remaining in the drawing room, caught in confab by Skelgill upon his somewhat ignominious return. Skelgill runs his hands restlessly through his damp hair.

'Is everyone still here?'

Blinking, Dickie Lampray rapidly shakes his head in the fashion of someone recovering from an unexpected clip around the ear. He sits forward and straightens his bow tie, as if this act will restore his powers of speech.

'I believe some of them are packing, Inspector.' He rises mechanically to his feet. 'I'll go and round them up, shall, I?'

Skelgill nods.

'I think – just to be on the safe side – we should do a roll call, sir.'

Dickie Lampray squeezes past Angela Cutting, patting her lightly at the top of one arm, in a reassuring gesture. Rather short in stature, and plump around the midriff, he has a queer gait, and leaves the room with a series of small steps that seem to articulate at the knees. For a moment or two there is an awkward silence, but then the woman's severe demeanour seems to soften, and she leans back against the sofa, crossing one leg over the other, causing her midnight-blue satin pencil skirt to strain against her sheer stockinged thigh.

'Why don't you reclaim your place, Inspector?' She gestures regally to the position more or less opposite her, where Skelgill sat earlier. 'This fire gives out so little heat, you ought to take priority, since you are the one who has been braving the elements.'

Skelgill, under close scrutiny, has now finished removing his outer garments for a second time. He raises a quizzical eyebrow, but nonetheless, he complies with her suggestion.

'Don't worry, madam – that's top of my list to sort out.'

Indeed, he reaches for the heavy poker, and with a couple of heaves he separates the logs, skilfully racking them into a more open lattice. Immediately, the fire responds – first with a rather ominous billowing of smoke, but then with a sudden burst of bright orange flame. The woman claps her hands together gleefully, and slides sideways to be closer to the grate. Her dark eyes glint as they reflect the growing blaze.

'What a relief to have a man about the house.'

She says this rather musingly. Skelgill seems unprepared for the compliment.

'I thought your Mr Boston was a Special Forces trooper, madam?'

She seems entranced by the flames that lick and leap about the woodpile, but now she flashes him a dismissive sideways glance. Her response, however, is somewhat oblique.

'I haven't felt properly warm since we arrived here on Thursday.'

'It has been rather autumnal, madam.'

Now she considers him more resolutely.

'You *are* allowed to call me by my name... *Inspector*.' She smirks as she emphasises the enunciation of his title. 'To my friends I'm Ange.'

Skelgill hesitates; he seems unsure of how to respond to the woman's self-confident manner.

'Sorry, madam – er, *Ange* – it can be tricky when there's a whole crowd of new people and I've not quite taken in their names.' He pulls at the knees of his jeans as if to restore non-existent creases. 'Plus I get the feeling I'm now definitely on duty, given the latest development.'

The woman, her torso twisted towards the fire, languidly raises a shoulder and turns her head to face him. 'Well, at least you can call me Ange in private... *Inspector*.'

Skelgill's high cheekbones have acquired a reddish tinge – it may be the extra warmth of the fire, or perhaps the heat subtly applied by his companion. He inhales as though he is about to reply, but as he does so the door of the drawing room swings open and people begin to enter. Angela Cutting uncrosses her legs and demurely tugs down the hem of her skirt.

'In the meantime,' (she speaks quietly, as if for Skelgill's ears only) 'let's see if we have a missing castaway.'

Skelgill glances at her; she returns his gaze with a shrewd narrowing of her eyes. But now he watches with care as the members of the retreat file into the room; he seems to be counting them in, perhaps rehearsing their names and occupations – something that he has a better memory for than he is prepared to admit.

Angela Cutting, literary critic – already seated opposite him.

Bella Mandrake, aspiring writer (actress – resting?) – wearing an elaborate ball gown that emphasises her bosom, she glides theatrically over the carpet and is quick to nestle in beside Skelgill.

Burt Boston, aspiring writer (and ex-SAS man?) – he occupies the same position as before, diagonally opposite Skelgill, on the same settee as Angela Cutting.

Sarah (aka *Xara*) *Redmond*, successful writer – she also resumes her former seat at one end of the cross-bench sofa.

Linda Gray, aspiring writer (and chef) – she takes the other end of the aforementioned sofa.

Dickie Lampray – literary agent – he pushes ahead of the two people yet standing to commandeer the space between Burt Boston and Angela Cutting; though it is noticeable he settles closer to the latter.

Dr Gerald Bond, aspiring writer (and erstwhile GP) – awkwardly he squeezes past those already seated and lowers his lanky form between Linda Gray and Sarah Redmond, facing the hearth.

Lucy Hecate – aspiring writer (and perhaps too young either to have completed or failed in some other career) – she hangs back rather reticently, and requires encouragement from Dickie Lampray to take the remaining empty place beside Bella Mandrake. Skelgill watches as she alights, his eyes sliding down her bare calves, and lingering upon the toes of her dainty green ballet pumps, which are still stained with dampness from earlier.

Even if Skelgill has not indeed been counting, the fact that each of the three-seater sofas has its full complement of backsides tells him that all eight people who could come, have come. He makes nine; one more would have been a crowd. It must be evident from the anxious faces around him that Dickie Lampray has conveyed the headline news about the missing boat. Accordingly, Skelgill gets straight down to business.

'Ladies and gentleman, as I see it we have three options.' He coughs to clear his throat. There is a mood of hopeful expectation as they – the majority, at least – surrender themselves to his capable expertise. 'The first, and simplest, is to stay put. Batten down the hatches, and wait until morning. The storm will ease, and once it is light we may be able to attract attention. If my boat is found drifting, there will be search activity out on the lake.'

A little murmur ripples around the group. Perhaps it is the morbid realisation that a believed-drowned fisherman might ironically bring help their way. Skelgill continues.

'Secondly, we try to signal.' He holds up a palm to silence some questioning words. 'As I have already said, I don't hold out much hope in that regard. It's now pitch dark. There's a mist in the rain – I doubt if a light on the island is visible from the shore – even if there were anyone about to see us. We also lack the means of flashing an SOS.' He raises his hips from the seat cushion and digs into a back pocket. He produces a small orange item and holds it up. 'A mountain whistle is useless in these conditions – I've tried it – you can barely hear yourself think out there.'

'What about an explosion?'

Suddenly all heads turn towards Burt Boston. He has adopted what appears to be his customary pose, legs crossed (in the male fashion, one ankle upon the opposite knee), an arm trailed casually along the back of the settee. Before Skelgill can respond – or is willing to do so – Dickie Lampray pipes up.

'Burt, my good man – what do you mean *an explosion*?'

Aware that the spotlight has switched to him, Burt Boston uncrosses then re-crosses his legs. He gestures loosely with one hand in the direction of the exit doors.

'There's a reserve gas cylinder in the courtyard outside the kitchen door. We could lug it down to the northern tip of the island. I could rig up a detonator with materials I've seen about the house.'

The audience is silent. Some are open-mouthed. The man's features take on a hard set, as if he is imagining himself back in the bedlam of a Balkan warzone. Then, without warning, he clicks his fingers loudly.

'Boom. Big bang. Big flash.'

Bella Mandrake, beside Skelgill, starts and clutches fretfully at his sleeve.

Burt Boston folds his arms and tilts his head to stare at the ceiling. Meanwhile the faces turn back to Skelgill, anxious for his reaction.

'Fine by me.'

Skelgill seems unfazed by the apparent usurping of his authority. However, Angela Cutting does not appear content with this state of affairs. She leans forward, her tone regaining something of its critical edge.

'Wouldn't that be rather dangerous... Inspector?'

Skelgill shrugs nonchalantly.

'I'm sure Mr Boston knows what he's doing... madam.' There is the hint of a raised eyebrow. 'I'd say the main risk is to the gas supply.'

Dickie Lampray looks a little alarmed.

'What do you mean, Inspector?'

Skelgill, perhaps conscious that, with his implied objection, he has now drawn the attention of Burt Boston, keeps his eyes steadily fixed upon Dickie Lampray.

'An explosion would last – what? – a second or two – depending how the gas ignited. If nobody saw it in that one moment – well, there goes our spare gas. As for the sound of the blast – even if it were heard over the noise of the storm – without anyone seeing the flash there would be no way of knowing where it came from. And Grisholm wouldn't be your first guess.'

Dickie Lampray is nodding.

'So we'd be rather pissing into the wind, in your view, Inspector?'

This remark raises a titter from more than one person present.

Skelgill glances at Burt Boston, who returns his gaze.

'Don't get me wrong – it could work – there are three marine flares in my boat – I was thinking along similar lines – if I had no mobile signal. Irrelevant, now, of course.'

The group is silent for a few moments as they digest the pros and cons of the signalling option. It is Linda Gray who speaks first.

'I think the gas pressure is already falling – I noticed when I put on the soup earlier. The cylinder that's connected could be about to run out.'

Dr Gerald Bond leans back and pats his stomach with the palms of both hands.

'We wouldn't want still to be stuck here with no means of cooking – we've food enough for good dinners and a full English breakfast every morning.'

'And we would have no lights!' This outburst comes, somewhat unrestrainedly, from Bella Mandrake.

'There are plenty of candles, Bella.' Sarah Redmond makes a mischievous spell-casting gesture with her fingers. 'Even more atmospheric than the gas, don't you think?'

'I'm terrified enough as it is.' She shudders emphatically. 'Just how scary do we need this place to be?'

As if he detects that the conversation is taking an undesirable course, Dickie Lampray clears his throat authoritatively.

'Inspector – so what is the third option?'

Skelgill leans back and intertwines his fingers upon his lap.

'I could go for help.'

'But, how, Inspector? Build a raft – in the dark? It would be impossible. And in these conditions – you would capsize.'

Skelgill shakes his head. His features are set grimly.

'I could swim.'

There is a collective gasp. Dickie Lampray is first to summarise the general air of alarm.

'Inspector – surely that wouldn't be safe – the water is freezing – and what about the waves – you would drown?'

Skelgill is impassive.

'I've dealt with worse conditions. There's a kind of triathlon I do every year. Not a dissimilar swim.'

As Skelgill glances about, he can see that Burt Boston scrutinises him through narrowed eyes, while Bella Mandrake has hers screwed firmly shut, her small fists balled at her sides. Angela Cutting and Sarah Redmond share an expression that perhaps contains a mix of intrigue and admiration. Lucy Hecate is turning up the toes of her pumps and looking at them critically.

Now Dr Gerald Bond intervenes.

'Inspector – I have been on first-aid duty at such events. The participants wear wetsuits, and there are always safety boats.'

'Aye, well – beggars can't be choosers, sir.'

The doctor is shaking his head.

'You would be at severe risk of cold shock, Inspector – anything below sixty degrees Fahrenheit and the human body is vulnerable – you could succumb within minutes.'

This statement appears to be too much for Bella Mandrake, who throws up her hands and bursts into tears. She begins to wail about being left alone without police protection. Then she postulates Skelgill dying and that they would be at the mercy of... of... *evil forces*. It is difficult to determine just how much of her histrionics are genuine, but certainly no one seems to want to offer a comforting arm around the shoulder. Skelgill, closest on one side, looks decidedly uneasy, though he does fumble in his pockets as though he is trying to locate a handkerchief, while Lucy Hecate on the other sits in a state of rigid diffidence. However, as Bella Mandrake continues to sob, Burt Boston rises decisively to his feet and crosses to a drinks trolley that stands between the two curtained bay windows. He decants a stiff brandy and brings it back to the group. Sarah Redmond takes the glass from him and presses it upon the near-hysterical woman. Almost magically, the strong spirit has the desired effect. The sobs quickly subside into a succession of choked coughs, although to Skelgill's evident dismay the woman lurches back on the sofa and flops sideways against him.

'Why don't I go?'

The voice is that of Burt Boston, and once again all eyes fall upon him.

Again Dickie Lampray assumes the role of inquisitor.

'What do you mean?'

'I could swim it – instead of the Inspector – then Bella would feel safe, with the police here.'

Skelgill is shaking his head. This time he directly countermands the man's proposal. He rises, perhaps relieved to escape the attentions of Bella Mandrake. He holds out his hands in the manner of a negotiator.

'I can't let you do that, sir – it would be more than my job is worth.'

Dickie Lampray takes a grip of the lapels of his waistcoat, and plays devil's advocate.

'But why not, Inspector – if he is volunteering?'

'Sir – with the greatest respect – I have taken an oath to protect the public – there's too much risk of swimming the lake. When all we need to do is wait here.'

'Yet you were prepared to try it, Inspector. Surely you have a duty to protect yourself, too?'

For a moment Skelgill appears to have no answer to this. Then in rather bashful schoolboy fashion, he hooks his thumbs into his pockets and with the toe of a boot taps an errant log back into place in the hearth.

'Aye, well – as my boss is always telling me – I'm my own worst enemy – so I don't have to worry on that score.'

This somewhat cryptic statement raises a chuckle around the room. It provides a face-saving exit that, without need for further discussion, leads to an unspoken consensus that the sensible thing is to follow the first option: to ride out the storm.

3. DINNER & AFTER

Sunday 8.30pm

'But, Inspector – surely the obvious explanation is that the mooring rope was worked loose by the action of the waves?'

Skelgill glares at the indistinct form of Dr Gerald Bond. The Yorkshireman has pronounced the word 'worked' as *wukt*, and his forthright delivery makes the question sound a little accusatory. Skelgill, for a rather terrible second, looks like he might want to throw a punch – though the distance of separation is too great – but then he seems to remember he is a guest of sorts, and recovers his composure. Glowering disagreeably, he scrutinises the contents of his plate. Thankfully, candelabra set at the centre of the circular dining table render it difficult to see much beyond the bright golden flames, and it appears his reaction goes largely unnoticed, although on either side of him Angela Cutting and Sarah Redmond pause in their movements, as if they have detected the tension coiled within his frame. The party – having migrated across the shadowy entrance hall to the equally ill-lit dining room – is arranged in approximate male-female order, though for the lack of one man Bella Mandrake and Linda Gray are juxtaposed. Burt Boston, who is next to Sarah Redmond, reaches for the claret, and casually tops up her glass and that of Lucy Hecate to his right. Then he proffers the neck of the bottle to Skelgill.

'What knot did you employ, Inspector?'

Skelgill gladly accepts the offer of a refill, and perhaps the question, too.

'Clove hitch.'

Anyone with an understanding of boats would know a clove hitch is a good quick mooring knot, albeit not one that can be relied upon unless constant pressure is maintained on the line. Burt Boston purses his lips and nods. However, Skelgill has not finished.

'Then a double half hitch. Tied off with an overhand knot.' He gestures across the table with his fork. 'Lucy watched me do it.'

Lucy Hecate looks uncomfortable as faces turn to her for confirmation. She glances at Skelgill and then down at the table.

'It seemed very secure.'

'So how did it come undone, then?' Dr Gerald Bond seems determined to keep worrying at the issue. 'Like I say, there must be an explanation.' He brays out the 'neigh' in the word.

'How do we know the boat is really gone?' This is Sarah Redmond; she flashes a mischievous sideways glance at Skelgill. 'We have only the Inspector's say so. How do we even know he is a real policeman? What if he is some local lunatic who prowls the lake in search of victims? Who plans to slit our throats in our sleep with his filleting knife?'

She raises her glass in a mock toast. Angela Cutting seems entertained by the idea, and there are some smiles around the table, although Bella Mandrake is far from amused; affectedly she shakes her shiny coils of hair and makes a grab for her wine glass, greedily downing its contents and holding it out to Dr Gerald Bond, who obliges her with a refill. The rather censorious stares she attracts from the other women suggest a suspicion that she continues to play for the sympathies of certain males present.

For a short while attention switches to the dinner. To follow the soup course – a hearty vegetable broth – Linda Gray has produced steaming dishes of Lancashire hotpot, borne to the table by the evening's volunteer kitchen assistants, Lucy Hecate and Burt Boston. They have explained to Skelgill that they are operating a rota system, although to date it has been the 'aspiring writers' who have tended to fulfil this role, while the 'professionals' have been waited upon. Skelgill reacted to this information as though he considered himself in the latter category, and now sets to work upon his generous helping of lamb stew. To his left, and in stark contrast to his own robust method, Angela Cutting eats sparingly; though there is something sensuous about the way she savours each mouthful, her eyes mere slits, and her lips gently caressing one another. Next to her, Dickie Lampray consumes swiftly, taking small amounts in rapid succession; indeed his cutlery and jaws appear to be in perpetual motion. He has his napkin tucked into his shirt collar, which appears a wise precaution. In contrast, further round the table, after Bella Mandrake and Lucy Hecate, Dr Gerald Bond seems permanently poised above his plate like a praying mantis, swooping only occasionally for large forkfuls, which disappear into the shadows of his beard, and probably not without leaving trace of their passing. It is after one of these moments that he resumes the conversation concerning the boat.

'Of course, if it were still there, we could go down to the jetty and see it.'

Sarah Redmond is quick to gainsay this proposition.

'Ah, but Doctor – he may have moved it to a secret harbour. He has expert local knowledge, remember.'

'There is nowhere else.' Lucy Hecate quietly interjects. One might wonder if she considers Skelgill her discovery, and that she wants to argue his corner, though her voice is entirely matter of fact in tone. 'I've been right round the island. It's all too rocky, apart from the inlet with the pier.'

'Well, what about his warrant card?' Dr Gerald Bond, regardless of the fact that Sarah Redmond is joking, seems to be firmly drawn into the fantasy. 'That will prove once and for all he's a policeman.' He refers to Skelgill as though he is not present.

Dickie Lampray breaks off from his busy undertakings.

'Inspector, I have often wondered – is it necessary to bear one's credentials at all times?'

Skelgill leans forward so that his craggy features become contrasting highlights and shadows in the candlelight.

'It depends on which force you are in, sir. Ours recommends you carry it at all times. Naturally, for a plain-clothes officer, there are occasions when it's the only way to convince a person you represent the police.' He glances about the table. 'Exactly like now, you could say.'

Sarah Redmond's shock of fiery hair has taken on an ember-like hue, and her bright blue eyes seem to flash with a light of their own. She turns to Skelgill and addresses him with an ingenuous curiosity.

'So, Inspector, where *is* your warrant card?'

Skelgill is manifestly expecting the question. He inhales deeply, like a reformed smoker still in the habit.

'With my flares, my phone, my wallet, my car keys...'

There are sympathetic nods around the table, though Sarah Redmond has a roguish smile playing at the corners of her mouth.

'In which case, Inspector, how would you go about convincing us? A hidden tattoo, perhaps? I've heard they're increasingly popular among the police.'

Angela Cutting chuckles throatily. Her reaction seems to unnerve Dickie Lampray, who is quick to quash any line of inquiry that might see Skelgill removing his shirt.

'Oh, I would wager the Inspector could regale us with tales that would persuade us he is a bona fide policeman.'

'Tales of murder and mayhem in the Lakes, perhaps, Inspector?'

Though Sarah Redmond is eager to prolong the provocation, and Skelgill seems not averse to her coquettish joshing, he notices that, across the table, Bella Mandrake is showing continued signs of distress. At the mention of murder she has visibly flinched.

'Oh, it's pretty quiet round here. I doubt it's the stuff of your detective novels, madam.' He lays down his fork and runs his fingers through his hair, a displacement action that reveals an underlying evasiveness. 'Unless you want to write about badger-baiting, or bare-knuckle fighting, or disgruntled farmers dumping manure outside their local bank.'

Sarah Redmond now addresses the group as one.

'I'm sure the Inspector is being diplomatic. Doesn't Cumbria have its robbers... prostitutes... *killers* – just like anywhere else?'

But before Skelgill can respond, Dickie Lampray again interjects.

'You *are* secretly plotting your next novel, aren't you, Sarah?'

Sarah Redmond ostentatiously picks up her wine glass and retreats behind it, with arms folded across her breast. She contrives a hurt expression, as though Dickie Lampray is spoiling her fun.

'It is rather a golden opportunity.' Briefly she glances sideways at Skelgill. 'A writers' retreat is one thing – but how often do you have a night marooned on a remote island with a real detective inspector?'

The question is interpreted as rhetorical, and there is a moment's silence. Angela Cutting, with a feline movement, draws her wine glass towards her over the tablecloth. From beside Dickie Lampray there is an audible gulp as Bella Mandrake takes another draft of claret. Then she raises the glass with the bulb between two hands like a fortune-teller determined to wring some response from her crystal.

'Evil forces took the boat – I know it.'

Her voice is beginning to carry the effects of the alcohol, and there is a slurring in her words. But Dickie Lampray, who appears to bear the office of moderator, makes light of her remark.

'Bella, I think it rather more likely that a beaver chewed through the rope than there was some supernatural intervention.' He turns quizzically to Skelgill and asks, apparently in all seriousness, 'I take it you have beavers in the Lake District, Inspector?'

Skelgill looks uncertain as to how to interpret this inquiry – wild beavers last roamed Britain in the eighteenth century, something that he would expect to be common knowledge.

'There's some up near Bassenthwaite Lake, sir.' His answer is uncharacteristically diplomatic: the beavers to which he refers are tame residents of a visitor attraction. 'Perhaps you were thinking of otters?'

Dickie Lampray looks a little anxious, as if he suddenly realises he lacks knowledge of the distinction. Burt Boston seems to detect this failing and, though serious in demeanour, chips in with a healthy dose of irony in his tone.

'Do you have Bigfoot in the Lakes, Inspector?'

The remark raises smiles, and even Dickie Lampray grins as he realises he is the butt of the joke. The claret is oiling the ceased-up cogs of conviviality, and there is clearly an underlying desire to take the conversation in a more light-hearted direction, despite Bella Mandrake's misgivings. Skelgill is quick to oblige.

'Bigfoot? Aye, she serves behind the bar in the Queen's Head at Cockermouth.'

The group laughs, perhaps with exaggerated relief, and Skelgill beams, quick to garner the credit for their collective mirth. Meanwhile, Linda Gray pushes back her chair and rises to her feet.

'Speaking of serving – would anyone like seconds?' Though she phrases the question with a broad cast, she directs her gaze pointedly at Skelgill, who has been the first to finish. 'Inspector, how about you?'

'Don't mind if I do.' He taps his fork approvingly on his empty plate. 'It's a cracking good hotpot – make sure you put this one in your cookbook.'

Linda Gray simpers bashfully; for a moment she places her hands on the table, as though the compliment has disoriented her and rendered her a little weak at the knees. Watching closely, if surreptitiously, the eyes of the other women reflect curiously in the wavering light – could it be a flicker of envy, that so easily has the Cinderella of their little coterie apparently managed to win over their prince? Of course, if they only knew Skelgill, they would understand that, while his stomach is certainly a short-cut to his heart, it is a route that requires no special emotional dedication or cordon bleu qualifications, and at best is a temporary diversion from whatever destination drives his sensibilities at the time. Nonetheless, Linda Gray pulls herself together and bows graciously to Skelgill, before turning her attentions to Dr Gerald Bond, seated beside her.

'Will you take some more, Dr Bond?'

The man pulls a disapproving face, which has the effect of drawing his features into their bushy surroundings. He hunches up his shoulders.

'Under protest, I might be persuaded.' Now he lifts an admonishing finger. 'Much as it pains me – on the day of the week that we ought to be enjoying Yorkshire pudding – to yield to Lancashire hotpot.'

There is a chuckle from around the table, as those present decide to interpret this 'Roses' belligerence as an attempt at humour. This does not go down entirely well with Dr Gerald Bond, though still he raises his plate for Linda Gray.

Burt Boston and Dickie Lampray both replace their cutlery as if they, too, will take second helpings, and the latter raises his glass in a toast.

'Three cheers for Linda! Once again you have done us proud, young lady.'

As the oldest of the women present, Linda Gray seems a trifle embarrassed by this remark, and the congratulations that ensue.

'Well, Lucy has to take some of the credit – she helped me to make it – and she found the chanterelles this afternoon – that's what's given it such a rich flavour.'

Now Lucy Hecate's pale cheeks seem to colour in the candlelight as she rises and circles clockwise to collect the plates of Burton Boston, who nods his assent, and of Skelgill. Linda Gray meanwhile takes those of Dr Gerald Bond and Dickie Lampray; the remaining women present, it seems, are watching their figures.

While second helpings are being assembled in the kitchen, and thus two of the group are absent from the table, the conversation fragments. Burt Boston rather fawningly plies a bored-looking Sarah Redmond with an elaborate question about theming her novels. Dickie Lampray begins to regale Bella Mandrake with an exposition on the particular variety of Bordeaux with which she has become so well acquainted, and indeed has her rather belatedly tasting its characteristics. However, both Skelgill and Angela Cutting silently twist the stems of their wine glasses, as though each is waiting for the other to speak. It is the latter that finally does so, turning conspiratorially to Skelgill, such that Dr Gerald Bond, who ruminates in silence opposite them, is unlikely to overhear.

'The boat, Inspector – what do you *really* think happened to it? Now that you have had time to consider.'

Skelgill opens his palms in a non-committal gesture. He is evidently still reluctant to countenance the idea that his knots had some part to play in the craft's disappearance. However, his eventual reply ostensibly contradicts this position.

'Looking at it logically – most likely it worked itself loose.'

It appears that, despite Dickie Lampray's best efforts to hold her attention, Bella Mandrake is eavesdropping, for her dark eyes glint searchingly at those of Skelgill, as if she is trying to discern his true belief within.

*

'*Nephron*? My good man – I must challenge you. What in this world is a nephron?'

After dinner the group has retired to the drawing room. Amidst the break resulting from the need for clearing the table and washing up – Burt Boston and Lucy Hecate completing the final phase of their assigned chores – Skelgill set about restoring the blaze in the hearth to its former glory, while Dickie Lampray took charge of dispensing liqueurs and suchlike from the amply stocked drinks trolley. In due course the party has reconvened upon the sofas, in considerably livelier fettle than at any time to date. This heightened state of banter owes itself largely, no doubt, to the stack of empty bottles that has accumulated in the scullery. Indeed, the casual observer would be shocked to discover that, lying 'at rest' only feet above the heads of this joshing throng, is the dead body of one of their number.

To complement the alcoholic liberation from their plight, which has lowered inhibitions and salved reservations, there is now the added distraction of what is evidently the regular *Scrabble* challenge. There being three teams, and this the fourth night, it has emerged that the scores are tied at one game apiece – and thus tonight's contest might be the decider. The teams' composition has required revised seating arrangements, with Dickie Lampray, Linda Gray and Sarah Redmond occupying the cross-bench sofa, Dr Gerald Bond, Lucy Hecate and Burt Boston on the left wing, so to speak, while, on the right, Skelgill is sandwiched between Bella Mandrake and Angela Cutting, the latter closest to the fire. Skelgill is, in an unfortunate sense, playing as substitute for the permanently absent Rich Buckley, and has already several times pointed out that the English language is not his strong suit – "Just ask one of my *subsidiaries*."

His apprehension perhaps stems from the fierce spirit of competition that clearly exists between the three sides: as is now reflected in Dickie Lampray's challenge to Dr Gerald Bond's placement of the word *nephron*. His concern may be heightened by the revelation that, while it is a team game, each individual member takes a turn at leading, on a rotating basis. Not surprisingly, therefore, many of the words placed to date have reflected the particular expertise of the participants. Burt Boston, for instance, has provided 'mortar' and 'hijack', Linda Gray 'dough' and 'stovies' (she maintains, a kind of Scottish stew made from leftovers), and indeed Skelgill himself has contributed the word 'arrest' – a particularly low-scoring effort, until Angela Cutting diplomatically 'noticed' that they did in fact have the spare letters 'e' and 'd' – enabling the past participle to qualify for a fifty point bonus. That she has managed somehow to pin the glory for this impressive achievement upon Skelgill (insisting that only he would have spotted the word *arrest* in the first place, recognition that he took in his stride) has not gone unobserved by certain of those others present. Meanwhile, no doubt in furtherance of her ongoing devilment, Sarah Redmond has patently eschewed longer, higher-scoring words in favour of 'ghoul', 'stab' and 'terror'. And, now, proceedings have drawn to a temporary halt by the dispute over the word 'nephron'. Dr Gerald Bond rises to the challenge.

'Dickie, surely a chap with your extensive vocabulary would have heard of a nephron – indeed would know what one does?'

Dickie Lampray looks mildly inebriated, and might well have made the challenge out of mischief. He glances about with glassy eyes and waves a dismissive hand.

'I have heard of nephew, Nefertiti and of being nefarious – ha-ha – but never nephron.'

'It's connected with the kidney.'

This composed intervention comes from Lucy Hecate.

Dr Gerald Bond, who has taken to wearing a pair of half-moon reading glasses for the purposes of the game, regards her with what would appear to be undue scepticism, given that she is advancing his case. He frowns over the top of the spectacles, as though he is about to rebuke a patient who has had the temerity to suggest they know their ailment before the good doctor has pronounced. However, on this occasion he breaks into a rather macabre grin, and nods slowly several times.

'Thank you, Lucy – I am glad there is at least one scientifically educated person amongst us, since we don't have the benefit of the requisite dictionary.'

'But Dr Bond – Lucy is on your side – surely we should have independent corroboration?'

Angela Cutting smirks as she says this; though the game is being taken seriously it does appear that she is merely winding up the pompous Yorkshireman.

'That's all very well, Ms Cutting –'

'Angela, please.'

'Angela, then – but what I'm saying is, when the only knowledgeable person is on your own team, it's hardly fair to penalise for that.'

Now Dickie Lampray butts in.

'Oh, Angela, darling – I think we ought to let them have it – clearly young Lucy is as honest as the day is long.' He winks across at her. 'Besides – it's only eight points.'

Angela Cutting takes a long slow sip of her martini, and narrows her eyes in a serpentine manner. She has kicked off her heels and has her feet drawn up beneath her, their soles resting against Skelgill's thigh.

'Very well, Dickie – if you insist.' She moves sinuously and slides her free hand over her calf and ankle, and then she drums her fingers over the fabric of Skelgill's jeans. 'All the sooner for our turn – it's you to go for us... Inspector.'

Skelgill has evidently been waiting, and hoping for a space to remain clear, for he eagerly gathers up five of the tiles.

'There's no holding back the Inspector.'

Dickie Lampray makes this remark, but he – and several of the others suddenly fall silent, open mouthed, even. For Skelgill has put down the word *bumfit*.

Now, if this were only admissible, it would be a humdinger of a score, with forty-eight points to begin with (landing a double letter score for the 'f' and a triple word score for the word itself), plus another thirty-three points for converting 'plum' into 'plumb', with the 'b' landing on the triple word square. A grand total of eighty-one points. If it were only admissible.

However, for a terrible moment there is an awkward silence, with all eyes seemingly glued to the board. Who will take on the embarrassing task of querying this apparently new and rather rude-sounding addition to the English language? Skelgill, meanwhile, sits back, folds his arms and looks very pleased with himself.

Perhaps not surprisingly, Dr Gerald Bond – guided by Yorkshire plain speaking, and thus bound by fewer courtesies than others of the group (and perhaps encouraged by the malt he is drinking) – sallies forth with an objection.

'Inspector – so what have we got here?'

Skelgill, tilting his own glass to his lips, raises a poker player's eyebrow.

'Fifteen.'

Bella Mandrake pitches forward; she manages to shoot out a hand to prevent herself from toppling onto the table, but not without revealing just how drunk she is.

'It's lots more than fifteen – it counts as two words *and* it's on a triple word score!'

Skelgill throws her an appreciative glance.

'No, love – it *means* fifteen. Bumfit.'

Several of the audience are looking at Skelgill as though – having referred earlier to *Swallows and Amazons* – he has now reverted to the use of some correspondingly strange childhood backslang, and is trying to inveigle it into the contest. He serves only to amplify this impression when he begins to recite a curious string of lyrics.

'*Yan. Tyan. Tethera. Methera. Pimp.*'

'Pimp?'

Dickie Lampray seems half hypnotised as he repeats the final word. But Skelgill continues.

'*Sethera. Lethera. Hovera. Dovera. Dick.*'

'Dick?'

Now Dickie Lampray *is* entirely bamboozled – reciting his own diminutive has him gazing at Skelgill in a cross-eyed fashion.

'What is this, Inspector – *pimp... dick... bumfit* – some kind of code used by your Vice Squad?'

Now several of the group burst into laughter. Dickie Lampray remains bewildered, while Skelgill simply appears perplexed. But as the hilarity subsides, it is the quiet voice of Lucy Hecate that speaks first.

'There's an English opera called *Yan Tan Tethera*. We performed it at my school. It's about shepherds and the devil.'

There follows another moment's silence. Glances are exchanged. Mention of the devil seems to have Bella Mandrake all of a quiver. Then Skelgill elucidates.

'Lucy's right. It's how shepherds count their sheep.' He points a gunfinger at Dr Gerald Bond. 'I'm surprised you don't know it Dr Bond – given your interest in writing about the fells.'

Dr Gerald Bond looks a little – well – actually, *sheepish*, and shrinks into his seat. Skelgill's chest seems to swell in inverse proportion.

'It's widespread across the northern uplands of England – speak to any shepherd. There are variations in most of the dales – I learned the Borrowdale version from a farmer called Arthur Hope when I was knee-high to a grasshopper. In Borrowdale two is *tyan* not *tan*. It's Cumbric – a relic of the Celtic language – not so different from Welsh.'

Dickie Lampray takes a large gulp of his Benedictine and appears to wink at Skelgill.

'Well, Inspector – you amaze us all – and you have independent corroboration,' (he scowls at Dr Gerald Bond) 'from an unimpeachable source and not just a scientist, it seems. Rather a fount of knowledge. I should not wish to go up against her on *Mastermind*.'

Lucy Hecate lowers her eyes modestly. Though she like the others has apparently been drinking steadily, her role has been as an undemonstrative member of the group. However, while she might be shy, and perhaps a little in awe of the brash worldliness that threatens at times to swamp her, she has surfaced confidently to present an opinion – or, rather, a fact – as the opportunity arises.

Dr Gerald Bond harrumphs – but he realises he can't have his cake and eat it too; the rules are the rules. Dickie Lampray, on the other hand, despite being on the end of a good thrashing, seems jubilant.

'Well, Inspector – it looks like you have your *bumfit!*' He leers drunkenly across at Skelgill. 'And if we hear you talking like that in depths of the night, we shall know you are merely counting sheep.'

Skelgill grins ruefully.

'Not usually one of my problems, sir, getting off to sleep – just tend to be woken by the slightest sound.'

As if to illustrate his point, Skelgill is suddenly overcome by a great yawn. This clearly takes him by surprise, and for a moment he appears quite disoriented.

Dickie Lampray seems concerned.

'Perhaps we are keeping you up, Inspector – after all, we have rather burdened you with our plight – and I don't doubt you were out fishing with the lark, if you will excuse the mixed metaphor.'

Skelgill continues to yawn. He shakes his head in protest, but it is clear to all that he would willingly exchange his place on the sofa for a cosy bed: they ought to pack him off upstairs, especially since he is to engineer their rescue in the morning.

However, a closer examination of the semi-circle of concerned faces would perhaps reveal a less unanimous determination: among some present, there are hints of curiosity, disappointment, and perhaps even intrigue.

Burt Boston springs to his feet.

'Why don't I show the Inspector the spare room?'

He does not wait for assent, and strides purposefully around to the rear of the right-hand settee and pats Skelgill amiably on the shoulder.

'At least come and see your billet before it gets too late – you can always wander back down and join us – you've killed us with your last two scores, anyway.'

*

Skelgill's allotted bedroom is in what might be described as the 'Men's Wing'. Grisholm Hall is arranged around three sides of a square courtyard. The original house – across the upper floor of which are laid out four suites – has a perpendicular wing appended on either side, and each of these holds three more bedroom suites (though of inferior grandeur), making ten bedrooms in total. In the 'Women's Wing', on the left-hand side, entered from the main landing by a swing door, are quartered Bella Mandrake, Linda Gray and, at the far end next to a stair and fire exit, Lucy Hecate. Across the centre of the house, in the 'VIP' rooms, are the 'professional' members of the retreat: from left to right, Sarah Redmond, Angela Cutting, (the late) Rich Buckley, and Dickie Lampray. Through a corresponding swing door the right-hand wing houses Burton Boston and Dr Gerald Bond; Skelgill is to have the empty room at the end of this corridor, also – mirroring the left-hand wing – next to a stair and fire exit.

It has earlier been agreed – largely for practical purposes, but somewhat to the relief of Bella Mandrake – that Rich Buckley's room should be locked, and that Skelgill should hold the key for safe keeping. The property has a rudimentary system of gas central heating, and Skelgill had both turned off the radiator in this room, and opened the main window, in an effort to keep the ambient temperature – and thus the body – as cool as possible.

Now he pads erratically about his own room wearing only his boxer shorts. It would be his custom to familiarise himself with escape routes, fire risks and power sources, along with the general amenities, but there is no doubt that he is flagging fast and he makes only a cursory inspection of his surroundings. He is in any event hampered by the fact that he has been left with a single candle, one that Burt Boston collected from a niche in the stairwell en route. And, though the said former SAS trooper was enthusiastic in volunteering to show Skelgill to his quarters, the invitation ended there, and it was with seemingly indecent haste that he sidled away to rejoin the party in the drawing room.

Skelgill gives the impression that he is about to do something, but then stops dead in the centre of the room, as if he has forgotten what it is. In the absence of inspiration, he climbs into bed. His room is cold and beneath the unwarmed sheets and blankets he shivers for a minute or so. At first his eyes are closed, and as the shivering subsides he appears to have fallen asleep. But suddenly his eyes jolt open, as though he is resistant to the act – perhaps while the party might still be going strong below. Then he gazes rather forlornly across the room – he, or rather Burt Boston, has left the lighted candle on an occasional table beside the door. He makes half a move as if to get up. But he seems to have neither the will nor energy to exchange the chill of the room for the growing comfort of his bed. His eyelids slide shut, and his head sinks into his pillow.

Some time later, Skelgill's bedroom door – unlocked (perhaps unlike many of the others in the house) – silently opens by a few inches. No light is cast from the unlit corridor beyond, and in the flickering shadows a hand reaches in and, with a just audible hiss of momentarily boiled saliva, pinches out the candle flame. There is no further movement for almost a minute. The room is pitch dark. Then comes a faint squeak of an unoiled hinge as the door is pushed wider, and a click as it is shut, and finally the lightest footfall upon the carpet. These gentle pads approach Skelgill's bed, and pause beside it. His breathing, regular and slow, is suggestive of a deep sleep, and – despite his boast of a little earlier – he has not yet been disturbed by the 'slightest sound'.

And now there is the soft rustle of his bedclothes being lifted. And next the louder creak of weight pressed upon the mattress springs. And only now does Skelgill show any signs of wakefulness – a confused murmur that is almost instantly suppressed.

4. GRISHOLM

Monday 7.30am

'**G**uv! Guv – wake up! Come on, Guv – rise and shine!'
'What the – what's going on?'
'Guv – it's me, Leyton.'

That DS Leyton has to state (or, rather, shout) his name is indicative of the torpor in which he finds his superior officer – a first attempt at rousing him some ten minutes ago having failed, beyond him rolling over and beginning to snore. At last, now, Skelgill struggles urgently into a semi-upright position, pale-faced and blinking and swallowing and clearly alarmed by the presence of one of his detective sergeants in his bedchamber. He casts about, but it takes some moments before his surroundings appear to make sense. In a minor panic he makes to throw off the covers – but a sudden knocking from the corridor causes him to hesitate.

'Leyton – chuck us those boxers, will you?'

DS Leyton regards the crumpled shorts with suspicion, but nonetheless picks them from the carpet and hands them over at arm's length. Skelgill wriggles into them beneath the topsheet and, modesty preserved, stands up – then promptly sits down. His fingertips fly to his temples.

'Aargh, Leyton – get me some paracetamol.'

DS Leyton regards his superior with limited sympathy.

'I expect DS Jones'll have some, Guv – I'll go and ask her.'

'Jones?'

'Guv?'

'What's she doing here?'

'She's in with the doc, Guv – with the dead woman.'

Skelgill glances up, though he winces into the brightness of the window at DS Leyton's back.

'Man.'

'Come again, Guv?'

'Dead *man*.'

DS Leyton shakes his head.

'It's definitely a woman, Guv. Bella Mandrake they told us she's called.'

*

'Okay, so let me get this straight – Harry Cobble found my boat drifting near Portinscale at six this morning and he dialled 999?'

'That's right, Guv – having kittens, I was, when I got the call – thought you were a gonner in that hurricane.'

DS Leyton glances sideways at DS Jones – the pair sit opposite Skelgill at the unvarnished oak kitchen table of Grisholm Hall. The detectives have commandeered the room – with its burnished log-fired *Aga* by some degree the warmest in the draught-ridden house – for a rather unconventional exchange of information. But at this moment it is an expression of relief that is fleetingly traded between Skelgill's subordinates.

'Leyton – that wasn't a hurricane – it wasn't even above force eight hereabouts.'

DS Leyton shrugs, as though the distinction is academic.

'All the same, Guv – what with the boat having all your gear on board.'

'So what did you do?'

'I phoned your mountain rescue team – to get their boat out as soon as. By luck the chap that answered was your pal Woody who you were supposed to meet in the pub last night.'

Skelgill, who has been furnished – to follow up several rounds of toast and honey – with a bacon sandwich and a second mug of tea, chews and slurps and nods and indicates that DS Leyton should continue.

'He knew you'd be fishing down this end of the lake – he reckoned if you had fallen overboard and survived then you'd be stranded on an island – because if you'd swum to the shore you'd have got help from a farm or hotel.'

'So you came straight here?'

'More or less.' DS Leyton grins sheepishly. 'You know me, Guv – any longer on one of those boats they had out looking for you and I'd have been proper tom and dick. Ground bait, I believe you fishermen call it.'

Skelgill's countenance is beginning to suggest a degree of disapproval. At the best of times, expressing gratitude to his subordinates is not one of his strong suits. Evidently, now, the notion that he – one of Lakeland's most experienced anglers and boatmen – might have got into trouble does not sit comfortably with him. And perhaps the knowledge of what actually did occur gives him an unreasonably biased perspective. Notwithstanding, on the basis of limited information, his deputies could be excused for thinking they had seen him alive for the last time.

'It was just precautionary, Guv.' DS Jones intervenes soothingly. 'We guessed you'd be fine – but the Chief was down on us like a ton of bricks wanting to know what action plan we'd implemented.'

Skelgill scowls rather ungratefully.

'Why's *she* getting her knickers in a twist?'

DS Jones patiently brushes a strand of hair from her face.

'I think she mentioned something about a valuable senior officer, Guv.'

'Miracles never cease.'

Now DS Leyton clears his throat.

'But since you're safe she wants a report by ten, Guv – before any of this leaks out and awkward questions start being asked.'

Skelgill makes an ironic hissing sound.

'Cancel the miracle.'

DS Leyton shakes his head and chuckles.

'So, Guv – if you weren't pulled overboard fighting a giant sturgeon – what did happen?'

Skelgill again scowls.

'Shove over that teapot, Leyton.' He tops up his mug and stirs in several spoons of sugar. 'We don't have wild sturgeon in Britain. It was a pike I was after. I've bet Woody I'll have a twenty-five pounder out of Derwentwater before the month's up.'

'So you're running short of time, Guv – how much did you bet?'

'It's not the amount, it's the odds, Leyton.' For a moment he appears unwilling to expand upon the details of the wager, but then he relents. 'Tenner – at a hundred to one.'

'Cor blimey, Guv – you're talking a grand.'

'Aye, well – the ale was talking a grand.'

DS Leyton vigorously scratches his head, as though it might help to free up an idea. He appears perturbed by his boss's costly predicament.

'Can't you catch one out of your regular lake, Guv? Ship it over?'

'A bet's a bet, Leyton.'

Skelgill's features are set uncompromisingly. However, with the deadline only four days away, the suggestion of a Bassenthwaite Lake ringer must have growing appeal, and perhaps there is the faintest Machiavellian glint in his eye. Nonetheless, he opts not to become sidetracked.

'And if it weren't for that, we wouldn't be here now. I was fishing close in to the island and I spotted one of the writers – the young girl, Lucy.' He glances up at DS Jones, who averts her gaze and studies the list of names in the notebook that lies open before her. 'It was just getting dark and she was calling for help. They'd discovered Buckley dead about an hour earlier, and they had no communications. I came ashore at the jetty, got the lie of the land, went back down to the boat about an hour later and it was gone. By then it was pitch dark. Considered various impractical options – ended up staying the night. Planned to signal for help this morning – if you didn't find us first.'

'Which we did, Guv.'

Skelgill shoots DS Leyton an irritated glance for stating the obvious. Perhaps there is an element of frustration that he has been thwarted in completing his 'rescue' of the writers' party.

DS Leyton tries again, along less contentious lines.

'I take it no one half-inched your boat, Guv?'

'I wouldn't say that, exactly.'

'Meaning what, Guv?'

'Meaning it didn't blow away.'

Skelgill stares hard at his sergeant, biting his lower lip. But he opts not to elaborate.

'Let's park that for now – tell me what you know that I don't.' He reaches again for the teapot.

DS Leyton nods to DS Jones, who, by dint of her vastly superior admin skills, when present is relied upon as chief note-taker. She flips back a couple of pages, but after a cursory glance she recites from memory.

'We landed at about seven-fifteen, Guv. The front door was unlocked and I recognised your boots in the hall.' (Skelgill raises an eyebrow but does not comment.) 'No one was up, so we started going round the bedrooms. DS Leyton found you. I discovered the dead woman. Some doors were locked. That's why we didn't know about Buckley until you told us.'

'We just thought he'd had even more sauce than you, Guv.'

DS Leyton intends his quip to be light hearted, but he receives a withering look from Skelgill for his trouble. DS Jones quickly continues.

'Dr Herdwick was working an early shift and when he heard you were missing he volunteered to come out with us.'

Skelgill folds his arms and shakes his head, as insult is heaped upon the injury.

'And what's the old vulture saying?'

'He's referring the deaths to the Coroner, Guv.'

'On what grounds?' There is an antagonistic note in Skelgill's question. 'I thought we were looking at a heart attack and an accidental overdose of sleeping pills?'

Now DS Jones refers to her notes.

'Several technicalities, Guv – cause of deaths unknown, or at least, uncertain – deaths sudden and unexplained – no known visits by a medical practitioner –'

'Apart from the quack.'

Skelgill's rather scathing interjection refers to the Yorkshireman and former GP, Dr Gerald Bond, of whom he has plainly not become enamoured.

'Added together, Guv – plus the fact of two deaths in two days among a small group of people – Dr Herdwick says he can't just sign them off.'

'He was joking about quarantining the lot of you on the island, Guv – spin it out longer, or something like that.'

DS Jones laughs involuntarily at DS Leyton's remark, although it is not quite clear to her colleagues why this might be. Under critical scrutiny she resumes her more serious demeanour.

'So is he talking autopsies?'

'Some preliminary tests, at least, Guv.' DS Jones glances at her notes. 'Obviously it looks fairly certain the Mandrake woman ingested medicines plus alcohol, but we've also found various prescription drugs among Buckley's possessions.'

There is another round of silence as each person perhaps attempts to piece together a coherent picture of events. Although the circumstances are unusual, on the face of it they appear to be the product of a string of coincidences. Certainly Skelgill's involvement can be nothing other, while the concurrence of two accidental or even natural deaths is perfectly feasible. For sergeants Leyton and Jones, arriving 'cold' to the scene (with Skelgill's safety their overwhelming preoccupation at the time), the facts are such that undue suspicion need not be aroused. Skelgill, however, has undergone a more qualitative experience, and his intuition is informed accordingly. He consults his wristwatch; the time is approaching ten o'clock.

'I'd better call the Chief.' He holds out a hand to DS Leyton. 'If you could lend me your mobile.'

DS Leyton obliges.

'What do you reckon, Guv – gut-feel-wise?'

Skelgill screws up his face in an unbecoming rodent-like manner.

'Not a lot we can do without something to go on from Herdwick.' He drains his mug and takes care to place it quietly upon the table top. 'Better have a quick word with everyone – get their details in case they decide to scarper.'

DS Jones is nodding.

'From what I can gather, Guv – that appears to be the general consensus.'

'Last night, they were all for seeing it through to the end of the week.' Skelgill purses his lips. 'Except Bella Mandrake.'

*

'How's the head now, Guv?'

Skelgill is checking that his mobile phone is none the worse for its ordeal afloat. Given that he has gained access to a fishing website, it seems all is well. Without looking up, he grips his temples between the thumb and fourth finger of his right hand.

'As my old ma says, there's not a lot in there to damage.'

DS Jones chuckles. She scoops a spoonful of froth from her cappuccino and snaps her full lips over it, rather in the manner of a frog devouring a fly. Then slowly she pulls out the spoon and dips it back into the coffee.

'I get the impression it was a bit of a wild night.'

'I was first to bed – can't think why I had the worst hangover.'

DS Jones watches him for a moment, but there is apparently little to glean from his concentrated features. She drops a hand to her side and taps her attaché case.

'I've got plenty more paracetamol if you want some, Guv?'

Skelgill shakes his head, though somewhat gingerly.

'Just shoot me next time I pick up a glass of red wine.'

'I'll make a mental note, Guv.'

Skelgill puts down his handset and glances suspiciously about the lobby. They are seated in comfy armchairs in a medium-sized hotel at Portinscale, beside the northerly tip of

Derwentwater, and close by the spot where his boat was recovered. He has negotiated temporary mooring facilities, and has retrieved his belongings. He has yet to recover his car and trailer from the public slipway at Keswick – and indeed is still to engineer a change of clothes from those in which he set out to fish yesterday morning. DS Jones has volunteered to chauffeur him for the present, while DS Leyton has returned to police HQ, assigned to coordinate the contacting of next of kin, and as bearer of the bad tidings to Wordsworth Writers' Retreats.

'What did you make of them, Jones?'

'On the island, Guv?'

'Aye.'

DS Jones places her elbows on the arms of the chair and interlocks her slender fingers. Her nails are neatly manicured and Skelgill, looking at them, self-consciously folds his own weather-beaten hands into his armpits.

'I can't say I've met any writers before, Guv. They all seemed well educated – law-abiding.' She unwinds her fingers and inspects her nails. 'Though definitely idiosyncratic – take the James Bond character. Smooth talker. Suave. Very self-confident.'

She refers to Burt Boston. Skelgill is instantly disapproving of her assessment.

'If he's ex-SAS I'm a monkey's uncle.'

DS Jones seems surprised by his vehemence, and edges back in her seat.

'What makes you say that, Guv?'

Skelgill turns and gazes out over the water, which laps close to the rear lawn of the hotel. The weather has indeed improved and, though there is still a swell rolling up the lake, the sun now glints benevolently off the corrugated surface, and Tufted Ducks bob contentedly between dives.

'A few things.'

'Such as, Guv?'

Skelgill appears reluctant to elaborate, as though telling her will force him to abandon an as yet incomplete edifice in his mind. But then he looks her in the eye and begins to count out on his fingers.

'For one, he had no torch with him – basic piece of kit, especially for a trip to an island with no electricity. For two, he knows nothing about knots – he was nodding away when I said I'd moored with a clove hitch. For three – and you're right, he has been watching the *Bond* films – he started talking nonsense about blowing up a propane cylinder.'

Skelgill might add that, though Burt Boston had offered to swim for help in his stead, he had not pressed the point when Skelgill objected on the grounds of his duty to protect the public. DS Jones, looking just a hint chastened, raises a hand in the direction of the lake.

'It's not going to be great PR for this writers' retreats company, Guv – two people dying on one of their courses.'

Skelgill takes a gulp of his coffee and wipes his lips with the back of his hand, which he then rubs with the heel of the other to disperse the chocolate powder mark.

'Eighty per cent survival rate – that's better than climbing Everest.'

DS Jones grins obediently at his rather ghoulish joke.

'That's including you, Guv.'

Now Skelgill blinks self-effacingly.

'My mental maths doesn't extend to seven out of nine.'

'I guess it's an even less flattering figure, Guv.'

'Anyway, there were ten of us – I was an honorary member for the night. Did I tell you I blitzed them at *Scrabble*?'

'You did mention that, Guv.'

'Aye – happen I did.'

There is a shelving unit beside their seats, containing the usual hotel collection of forsaken paperback blockbusters and bulk-buy second-hand hardbacks that could only have been produced without reference to publishers or readers, in a time when it was fashionable to write with absolute and totally uninformed self indulgence. DS Jones is glancing musingly along the top shelf, and she pulls out what appears to be a detective novel.

'I can't help thinking of that Agatha Christie story, Guv – where a house-party get stranded on an island and one by one they start dying off.'

Skelgill appears only vaguely engaged by this allusion.

'Aye – but this crowd are unconnected.'

DS Jones drums her nails on the clothette cover.

'So they were in that story, Guv.'

Skelgill shakes his head dismissively.

'Aye, well you know me and fiction, Jones.'

5. DR HERDWICK'S REPORT

Monday 2.30pm

'Sorry to keep you, Leyton – got a bit tied up over at Portinscale – what with sorting out the boat and one thing and another.'
Skelgill, finding DS Leyton waiting in his office, is economical with the facts, having cajoled DS Jones into a pub lunch at a nearby watering hole. His motives were a little less than altruistic, as he admitted when supping thirstily on a pint of strong ale: there had to be some way to shift his limpet-like hangover. However, given that the 'hair of the dog' has still failed to flush away all vestiges of discomfort, his politeness is somewhat uncharacteristic. DS Leyton, unused to apologies from his superior, looks rather discomfited, and jumps to attention before sidling out into the corridor, offering to fetch them teas from the machine. DS Jones, meanwhile, is consulting with the police pathologist, Dr Herdwick.

'Here we go, Guv.' DS Leyton slides a polystyrene cup carefully across to Skelgill's side of the desk. 'How was the boat?'

Skelgill shrugs, nose already in his tea. He swallows and smacks his lips approvingly.

'Shipshape is probably the word. But there is one annoying detail. Harry Cobble can't remember if the painter was on board or trailing.'

'That's like the tow-rope, Guv?'

Skelgill grins.

'In a manner of speaking.'

'How is that significant, Guv?'

Skelgill puts down his drink and makes a little church with his fingers.

'If it were on board, I'd know for sure it was cast off and shoved out into the lake.'

DS Leyton nods.

'You still thinking that's a possibility, Guv?'

Skelgill glowers.

'Leyton, I've never had a boat work itself loose in my life. And how many others blew free last night?'

DS Leyton looks unconvinced.

'Thing is, Guv – it *was* a storm and a half.'

Skelgill shakes his head.

'In a teacup, more like – I've experienced much worse.'

DS Leyton ponders for a moment.

'Why would someone untie your boat, Guv – when you're the one who can raise the alarm?'

Skelgill crafts a wry grin.

'Well, if it were deliberate, Leyton – you just said it.'

DS Leyton looks a little nonplussed.

'What – to *stop* you raising the alarm?'

Skelgill smiles and opens his palms in a helpless gesture.

'Unless someone decided I would be such scintillating company that they felt compelled to keep me for the night.'

'So, what are you saying, Guv?'

'Join the dots, Leyton – what happened last night?'

'You got a bad hangover, Guv.'

'Ha-ha, Leyton – now be serious.'

DS Leyton shrugs.

'The Mandrake woman died.'

'Correct, the Mandrake woman died.'

'Accidentally, though Guv.'

Skelgill stares at DS Leyton, his countenance hardening. But then there is a gentle knock and the door opens; DS Jones enters bearing her notepad.

'Maybe Jones can enlighten us, Leyton.'

He indicates that she should be seated. He leans back in his own chair and awaits her news.

'Just provisional results at the moment, Guv.' She glances between her two colleagues. 'But if you want it in a word – it's *inconclusive*.'

Skelgill tuts and swills down the last dregs of his tea.

'That's Herdwick's middle name.'

DS Jones, undeterred, flips open her notebook and reads verbatim.

'Bella Mandrake almost certainly died from an overdose of sleeping pills combined with excess alcohol. They're both muscle relaxants and can kill within a few minutes by causing sleep apnoea. The lungs are deprived of oxygen. Alcohol can amplify the effect of the drug.'

'What about Rich Buckley?'

DS Jones nods and taps the notebook with her pen.

'He died of heart failure, Guv – Dr Gerald Bond was right.'

Skelgill scowls disparagingly.

'However – preliminary investigation shows very few indications of a predisposition – Buckley's heart and arteries were in pretty good shape.'

'So what caused it?'

'That's the more interesting aspect, Guv.' Now DS Jones pauses, perhaps for dramatic effect. 'His blood sample contains residues of cocaine – and atropine, among other things.'

Skelgill and DS Leyton remain impassive, until the latter asks the question that his superior may be resisting.

'What's atropine when it's at home?'

DS Jones refers to her notes, as if she senses she should not overplay her hand.

'It's the poison found in Deadly Nightshade. It kills by stopping the heart.'

'Stone the crows!' DS Leyton starts, and his seat scrapes sharply against the floor tiles. But Skelgill is unmoved.

'Deadly Nightshade doesn't grow around here.'

'There's more to it, Guv – apparently it's used in surgery, and in small doses in lots of prescribed medicines – including the anti-diarrheal tablets we found in his room.'

Skelgill ponders for a moment.

'These pills – were they strong enough to kill him?'

DS Jones shrugs.

'Dr Herdwick says cocaine's more likely to have caused a heart attack. It's well known for it.'

DS Leyton punches a fist into the opposite palm.

'Cor blimey, Emma – you build us up for a poisoning and then let us down.'

'Sorry about that.' DS Jones grins ruefully. 'I should add that the doctor also says that about a third of deaths from sudden cardiac arrest can't be explained by observable medical conditions. They call it *unremarkable*.'

DS Leyton begs to differ. He is shaking his head in exasperation and his fleshy jowls respond a fraction behind time.

'I call it flippin' remarkable – in this day and age. So where does this leave us?'

DS Jones glances apprehensively at Skelgill, but he nods to indicate she should enlarge.

'The deaths could be natural, accidental or by misadventure. But technically we can't rule out one hundred per cent that one or both of them were deliberate. Dr Herdwick's admitting that much, at least.'

Skelgill folds his arms and rocks back in his chair in order to regard the ceiling.

'If we're not just going to put this to bed, we need something to make us suspicious. A reason to investigate. A *desire* to investigate.'

DS Jones gestures to her notebook.

'There's the cocaine, Guv – Dr Herdwick says for it to have been in his blood he would have to have taken it while he was on Grisholm. That's surely grounds enough?'

'Plus your boat, Guv?'

Skelgill is still stargazing.

'Aye – the cocaine is categorical – the boat we can't prove a thing – except it bugs me the most. But it's not an easy sell to the Chief – she's narked as it is – apparently the head of Cumbria tourism sits on the board of the Police Authority – and now I've landed myself in the middle of a bad case of public relations.'

DS Jones is nodding in sympathy, but DS Leyton begins to fidget uncomfortably.

'Thing is, Guv – on that score – I've not had chance to tell you –'

Skelgill snaps forward in his chair, rather exaggerating his reaction and causing DS Leyton to look alarmed. The latter clears his throat nervously before he speaks.

'This company – Wordsworth Writers' Retreats – I've had two DCs working on it since I got back this morning – so far, there's not a trace of it.'

Skelgill's features take on a rather cynical cast.

'How hard have they tried?'

DS Leyton reaches for his own notes, which are perched on the tall cabinet at his side. He flicks through several sheets until he locates the page he is looking for.

'Nothing online, Guv – just doesn't come up at all. The nearest was something in Canada a few years ago – no connection. Then we've been on to a couple of trade bodies – the Society of Authors, and *The Bookseller* magazine – they've not heard of it, though they're asking around.'

'What about the people who were on the retreat?'

DS Leyton is already nodding.

'Thing is, Guv – they're all in transit. Plus most of them didn't bring their mobiles with them, like they were asked. We got hold of the Lampray geezer – he's on the train to London – he's plugged his phone in – but he says he can't remember any details and needs to check what info he's kept at home.'

'When will that be?'

'He reckons before close of play – but he's already delayed – apparently there's wildcat tube strikes in London all this week. It's holding up some of the mainline trains.' DS Leyton taps the page with the back of his hand. 'We're keeping trying the others, obviously, Guv.'

Skelgill nods pensively.

'Wordsworth Writers' Retreats. Sounds like it ought to be a local firm.' He glances at DS Jones. 'What do you think, Jones – you're the big bookworm?'

DS Jones seems unsure as to whether this is a compliment or a ham-fisted slight.

'Maybe it was just a one-off event in the Lakes? It's a good name really – it links the Lakes and the poet, and it says 'words worth' – clever idea when you think about it – whoever came up with it.'

Skelgill appears unconvinced.

'Should have been held at Grasmere – though there's no islands there, if that's what they wanted. Or Cockermouth, come to that.'

Though he may not be of a literary bent, he refers to the illustrious bard's locus of best-known domicile, and birthplace, respectively – no local lacks this knowledge of Lakeland's most famous son. DS Leyton, who still employs the incomer's pronunciation of Cockermouth (and, indeed, has his own Cockney rendering), chips in with a light-hearted contribution.

'Don't quite have the right ring to it, though, Guv – Cockermouth Writers' Retreats. Sounds like a cross between a cock-up and putting your foot in your mouth.'

DS Jones looks suitably amused, but she is keen to add a serious suggestion.

'What about the owners of Grisholm Hall – surely they'll have an address?'

DS Leyton slaps his hands onto his ample thighs in a gesture of frustration.

'One step forward, two back. We've been on to the estate office – they don't know much about it. Apparently bookings are handled through agents in London – we're waiting to hear from them.'

Skelgill folds his arms and, yawning, stares out of the window at the darkening sky.

'They must have liaised to organise all the provisions, get the place ready, arrange for the boatman – probably had to pay something up front – plus the hire of the property.'

'I reckon so, Guv, but – these agents – it's one man and his dog and the dog's in charge of the admin.'

'Well, get them chased up. We're not going to look too clever if Wordsworth find out first and start kicking up a fuss – dog or no dog.'

'Will do, Guv.'

DS Leyton inhales as though he is about to say more, but then he hesitates and frowns at his notes.

'What is it, Leyton?' Skelgill's tone suggests he suspects there is more incomplete news to follow.'

'Er... the deceased, Guv – next of kin.'

'Aye?'

'No problem with Rich Buckley – his office in London was open so we've got his wife's number – that's being dealt with. Bella Mandrake, though, Guv '

'Aha?'

'She's not what she seems.'

'In what way?'

'Well, Guv – among her personal effects – there's not a lot – but there's a credit card – in the name of Ms J Smith. Nothing else to indicate she's really Bella Mandrake.'

'What about an address?'

'Nothing, Guv. We're waiting on the credit card company to get back to us – that should do the trick, obviously.' He scratches his head and frowns. 'Unless it's not hers.'

DS Jones sits forward.

'Maybe it's a pseudonym, Guv?'

Skelgill juts out his chin and rubs the weekend's stubble broodingly. DS Leyton looks inquiringly at DS Jones. She elaborates.

'A pen name – like *George Orwell* and *Mark Twain* – it was a fiction course, after all. And didn't you mention, Guv, she was supposed to be an actress?'

Skelgill nods, but does not comment. DS Jones continues.

'Bella Mandrake does sound a bit theatrical, when you think about it. Maybe some of the others, too?'

'Burt Boston.'

Skelgill says this through clenched teeth. DS Jones nods. Skelgill taps the surface of his desk with both palms.

'Let's wait and see if any of them *has* given us a false name – then we might have reason to get a bit hot under the collar.'

6. TRAIN TO LONDON

Monday 5pm

As it turns out, it is not a false name that prompts Skelgill to experience a rise in temperature, but a small item of health information relating to the late Rich Buckley. Via his wife, the investigating team have reached his GP, in order as a matter of protocol to report the death and obtain for the Coroner relevant details of the deceased's medical history. During this exchange it has emerged that Rich Buckley was not in receipt of anti-diarrheal medication, nor was he known to suffer any form of chronic ailment that merited such a prescription. The tablets that could, in theory, have brought about his death may not have belonged to him.

Of course, there are other possible explanations for his possession of the drug. He travelled widely, speaking at conferences on a global basis. The identical medicine is available, for instance, in the United States, where he had most recently attended a major international book fair – and he could have obtained it privately, if not indeed on the same basis in Great Britain or elsewhere. Nonetheless, as Skelgill put it, there were simply 'too many straws in the wind' – the wind, from his perspective, also being one of the straws.

Thus by late afternoon on Monday, Skelgill and his two sergeants – all travelling for austerity purposes on second-class tickets – are seated, upon Skelgill's insistence, in an empty first-class carriage, that rattles down the West Coast Line through indistinct countryside and enfolding dusk towards England's sprawling capital.

While it might have seemed sensible, in hindsight, to detain the retreat's seven surviving participants in Cumbria – indeed on Grisholm – to facilitate convenient interviewing, Skelgill has identified that the scenario is more complex. (Not least, there is no obvious crime, and no obvious suspect.) In any event, to discover much about Rich Buckley it will be necessary to visit his London office and speak with the staff; there is also his wife, and potentially his GP; and then the agents that handle the rental of Grisholm Hall. Moreover, as has already been recognised, the members of the retreat had little with them in the way of reference information that may be of practical use to the police. And although Dr Gerald Bond and Linda Gray, who both live in Cumbria, and the successful author, Sarah – aka *Xara* – Redmond, is based in Edinburgh, four of the seven – Dickie Lampray, Angela Cutting, Burt Boston and Lucy Hecate – reside in the Central London area. Finally, less tangibly, there is the view that Skelgill has iterated to his own superior: that if anyone has anything to hide they are less likely to be on guard on their home turf.

Skelgill's request to pursue the investigation south was thus approved, though not without reservations on behalf of his boss. The rationale for 'foul play' of some kind is very much a matter of conjecture, and seems dependent upon a healthy dose of intuition on Skelgill's part – not a quality that generally carries much weight with the powers that be. Indeed, there is a strong case to be made that Skelgill's personal embroilment in the events (albeit not comprehensively reported) renders him too close to the situation to conduct an objective investigation. Countering this, however, is the argument that he has obtained an insider's insight into the characters concerned, and indeed the minutiae of events as they unfolded. From this perspective he is uniquely placed to move matters forward with greatest haste.

Perhaps this latter point was the clincher, given that there is a desire on high to see the mystery untangled, and its threads neatly wound up, with maximum speed and minimum fuss. However, it is only on the proviso that he achieves these goals that he has been cleared to proceed. He has thus rallied his troops, called fleetingly at home to shower, change and pack an overnight holdall, extend the boarding arrangements for his dog, and rendezvous at Penrith railway station just in time to jump aboard the departing 4:50 express for Euston. Thence, it is not long before trouble arrives in the shape of the conductor.

'This is a second-class ticket, I'm afraid, sir.'

Skelgill nods. His jacket lies on the spare seat beside him, and he reaches into the pocket to retrieve his warrant card, now restored to his possession. He brandishes it at the railway employee, an underfed and rather lopsided young man burdened by an unfashionable hairstyle and a permanently harried set to his pale and pinched features.

'It doesn't make any difference I'm afraid, sir – we're a private company these days.'

Skelgill takes back his card and patiently stows it away. He squints at the man's identity badge.

'Are you a taxpayer, Norris?'

'Of course, sir.'

'And serving the public – if not by name a public servant?'

'In a manner of speaking, sir.'

'We're travelling south to investigate a very serious case. We need to discuss our plan – it'll take us an hour or so.' He lowers his voice conspiratorially. 'It's a double murder.' The ticket inspector's eyes widen. 'At the moment we're on contracted time – but we can't conduct the meeting in second class because it's packed full and people will overhear. If we have to wait until we reach London we'll need to do it tonight and the taxpayer will be charged overtime. Think how much that will cost.'

'I see, sir.'

The conductor takes a half step backward and glances up and down the carriage. Skelgill casts an arm about the four-seater section they occupy.

'I notice these seats are not reserved.'

'That's correct, sir. It's not a popular service, this time of day – at least not for business travellers.'

'So you could do both us and the taxpayer a favour if we were able to use them.' Skelgill grins in a friendly manner. 'Naturally we'll move if the carriage begins to fill up – but I wouldn't have thought there's much chance of that this side of Manchester?'

'It's Warrington we go through, actually, sir.'

Skelgill beams.

'There you go then – one-horse town – no danger of getting busy, eh?'

'Probably not, sir.' The man frowns, however.

'Excellent – and when do we get the free buffet service?'

The conductor hesitates for a moment, as though he is having second thoughts. But then he sighs and his shoulders droop – lopsidedly – by another inch or so.

'It'll be along in about twenty minutes, sir.'

'Perfect – thanks for your cooperation, Norris – we'll keep you posted on our progress as the journey goes on.'

'My shift ends at Warrington, sir – that's... where I live.'

'Good for you, Norris.'

Skelgill settles back and folds his arms, as though the matter is closed. His two sergeants, somewhat embarrassed, tender their tickets for clipping, avoiding eye contact. The remainder of this operation is conducted amidst an awkward silence, until finally the man shambles swaying along the aisle and disappears from their carriage with a swish and a clunk of the automatic door.

'Fair enough, don't you think?' Skelgill addresses his subordinates, seeking approval. 'No point having all this empty space – never mind good food going to waste.'

DS Jones grins at her incorrigible superior. DS Leyton shakes his head.

'I think you nearly blew it, slagging off Warrington, Guv.'

Now Skelgill paradoxically disagrees. 'Nothing wrong with Warrington, Leyton – I was best man at a wedding there once.' He falls silent, and appears to be replaying an old memory, for the hint of a smile creases his lips.

'Anyway, Guv – it did the trick – we might be stuck on here for a while if there's a knock-on effect from the tube strike.'

Skelgill breaks off from his reverie. 'All the more reason to be comfortable, Leyton.' He activates the recline position of his seat and places his hands behind his head. He nods to DS Jones who has arranged her notebook and documents on the table before her. 'Give me a shout when the trolley dolly turns up.' And he promptly closes his eyes.

*

'Beats me how you can solve those things, Emma – does my head in, even the easy ones.'

They have been given complimentary newspapers, and DS Jones is steadily working her way through the cryptic crossword of the *Daily Telegraph*, while DS Leyton peruses the pages of a less cultured journal. Skelgill is perhaps sleeping, although at intervals during the journey so far he has surprised them by suddenly chipping in with a contribution to their conversation, despite his lowered eyelids and sporadic snores. DS Jones smiles at her colleague.

'Oh, well – a... friend... showed me how to do them when I was at uni – half the battle is cracking the secret code that the compiler uses. If you can work out what the clue means the answer's usually staring you in the face.'

DS Leyton puts down his own newspaper and glances across at her half-completed grid.

'Give us an idea, then.'

DS Jones taps her pen on the folded broadsheet.

'Ok – take this one – I've already solved it. The clue says, *"Go without love, with girls getting visual aids"* and it's seven letters long.'

DS Leyton puffs out his cheeks and stares vacantly at the page, and then hopefully about the carriage, as if they are playing a game of I-spy and the item is close at hand, if only he can spot it. But after a few moments he shakes his head and concedes defeat.

'That's just double Dutch to me, Emma – it might as well be written in French.'

DS Jones smiles patiently.

'Let me show you. There are a couple of encrypted elements in here.' She writes out the clue along the foot of the page, spacing it into three distinct phrases. 'See this last bit, *"getting visual aids"*? The word *"getting"* is telling us that the answer is something that means *"visual aids"* and the first parts of the clue will resolve to make this word.'

DS Leyton scratches his head.

'Visual aids? What – like for a presentation when you hold up crime-scene photos?' He counts on his fingers, silently mouthing letters. 'How about *'example'* – that's got seven letters?'

DS Jones nods encouragingly.

'It could be – but if we work out the rest of the clue, it will tell us.'

'Go on then.'

'Well, there's another coded phrase: *"go without love"* – that means the letter *"g"* – because *"love"* is usually code for an *"o"* – so *"g"* is the first letter of the solution."

'Bang goes my example.' He puffs out his cheeks. 'What about *'gadget'* then?' He counts again. 'Cor blimey – not enough letters.'

She chuckles.

'And lastly we need another word for *"girls"* – because the clue is telling us to put "g" with girls.'

'Lasses.'

They both glance up, for this submission comes from the 'slumbering' Skelgill. It is a word from his regular northern lexicon.

DS Jones writes down *"lasses"* – and then with a flourish inks the letter *"g"* in front of it.

'Glasses?'

DS Leyton looks crestfallen – as though her little exercise has been futile – he puts a supportive hand on her arm, as though to share some of the burden of her failure.

'Specs – you Cockney oik.'

Despite Skelgill's disparaging remark, DS Leyton's face suddenly lights up.

'Stone me – *that* kind of visual aids!' He claps his hands together joyfully. 'That's brilliant, Emma – mind you I still don't reckon I'd get anywhere near it on me Tod Sloan.'

Skelgill, having apparently returned to his siesta, has a contentedly smug grin spread upon his countenance, as though he considers himself solely responsible for solving the clue. DS Jones glances sympathetically at DS Leyton. She places the newspaper on the table and rests her pen on top of it.

'Actually, I was on a training course in September. One of the sessions was really fascinating. They had this guy who works in advertising as a Creative Director. His job is to invent ideas for campaigns. He showed us how he uses cryptic crosswords as a kind of brain gym to practise what he called *slow thinking*.'

'Sounds like that's right up my street, Emma.'

DS Jones laughs.

'Actually, he made solving an advertising brief seem just like solving a crime. You have all these pieces of information – first you have to decide which ones are important – and then discover how they fit together. He believes there's always a perfect solution.'

DS Leyton grins disarmingly.

'I would have been rubbish at advertising, as well.'

Skelgill, like some malevolent serpent, opens a reptilian eye – it appears he is tempted to bite, cruelly – perhaps that therein lies the explanation for stasis at the rank of sergeant; but DS Jones continues before he can intervene.

'It's not something you can force. It's like the difference between an ordinary crossword and a cryptic crossword. In an ordinary crossword the clue might say *'solid fuel'*, four letters. And you just go, *'coal'*. It's linear thinking. But in a cryptic crossword the clue has two or three parts, so you have to kind of half-solve them individually and then dump them into the mixer and let your mind churn out the connection in its own time. That's why it's called *slow thinking*. You can't do it to order.'

DS Leyton scratches his head and grimaces ruefully.

'Thing is, Emma – you see these detectives on the telly – like Sherlock Holmes and Poirot – and they've got brains the size of planets – and they get the solution, like that.' He snaps his fingers. 'So, when something gets lost round our house, 'cause

I'm a copper the missus expects me to be able to deduce where it is!'

DS Jones is amused and smiles attractively, her full lips parting to reveal her even white teeth. She touches the tip of her nose with a finger.

'I'd say Inspector Morse is closer to the real thing – he's always charging up blind alleys – thinking he's got the right answer. It's like that with cryptic clues – you convince yourself you're there, but something still niggles. And then when you do get it right, the logic of the clue smacks you between the eyes.'

Skelgill adjusts his seat into the upright position and stretches his arms above his head. He rubs his eyes and yawns.

'Half the crimes I've solved have only made sense afterwards.'

DS Leyton suddenly seems perturbed, as though some long-standing belief in a magic quality possessed by his superior has been dispelled; for a second he has the demeanour of a child recognising for the first time the fallibility of a parent.

DS Jones, on the other hand, looks engagingly to her boss.

'I'll send you the slides from the course, Guv – if you like? The idea was called *The Eye of the Brainstorm* – he describes how you retreat into this quiet place in your mind, metaphorically in the eye of the hurricane, where it's absolutely still and silent,' (she raises both hands and makes the shape of a cylinder in the air) 'and you're surrounded by these towering black walls of cloud, with all this storm debris spinning around – and from this position your subconscious can identify the pieces that are important, and what they make when you put them together.'

Skelgill's reluctance ever to be told of a better way to do anything is perhaps tempered by some subliminal sense of recognition in what she says. Notwithstanding, he manufactures a rather cynical scowl.

'I find it best when I *don't* put my mind to it.'

But DS Jones is undeterred.

'That's exactly it, Guv – it's when you're *not* trying that the answer comes – so long as you've got all the information you need. The guy running the course said he solves crossword clues when he stops thinking and looks out of the window – and that he has his best advertising ideas when he's doing his ironing.'

Skelgill chortles.

'That definitely rules you out, then, Leyton.'

Despite this blatant case of the pot calling the kettle black, DS Leyton phlegmatically hunches his shoulders, guilty as charged.

*

'So where now?'

'It's two stops on the Northern Line, Guv – jump off at Tottenham Court Road, then Charlotte Street's just around the corner.'

As DS Jones says this she glances back at DS Leyton, who lags a couple of paces behind herself and Skelgill. They have succeeded in riding the entire journey in first class, and so are among the most forward to alight upon the platform at London's Euston station, walking with the slightly apprehensive gait of people who have dismounted from an escalator. However, the train has arrived almost an hour behind schedule, and hurrying hordes from second class begin to pour from their carriages, swarming past them with rumbling trolley cases and skyscraping rucksacks and protesting children who point out the fast-food outlet signs with plaintive cries of futile optimism. DS Leyton scurries to catch up, and calls out to make himself heard.

'Or we could just walk, Guv?'

'I thought you Cockneys went everywhere sitting down? Tube, taxi, bus.'

DS Leyton frowns rather defensively.

'The underground might be chaos, Guv – what with the strike.'

Skelgill watches as part of the crowd veers off for the exits marked Northern and Victoria Lines.

'Looks like it's running – it's always a novelty for me.'

DS Jones seems still to have half an eye on DS Leyton. Her brow creases and she turns to Skelgill with sudden vehemence.

'Actually, it's less than a mile, Guv – the fresh air will do us good after all that time sitting down.'

Skelgill shrugs and continues straight ahead. He casts a rather longing glance at the display counter of a snacks stall, and bumps heavily into an elderly gentleman, who immediately apologises.

'Seems I'm outnumbered – though since when there was fresh air in London, I don't know.'

His colleagues grin obediently. DS Leyton appears relieved. As they reach the street, DS Jones indicates with a hand that they should cross and then head west along Euston Road. It is after eight p.m. and the day's workers are long gone, so once they have cleared the immediate vicinity of the station they find the broad pavements largely empty, and they are able to stroll three abreast. The traffic, however, offers little reflection of the time of day, and grumbles past them, honking and choking the six-lane urban highway, and filling the senses with diesel fumes and the distinctive squeal of taxi brakes at each set of lights. The Post Office tower stands sentinel over the area, providing vertigo-inducing glimpses as they proceed from block to block. Skelgill cranes his neck, but overhead the clouded sky is a nondescript haze of reflected neon and offers no clue as to tomorrow's outlook. Right now the weather is substantially milder than that they have left behind in Cumbria and, though they walk into a light breeze, they have their overcoats draped on crooked arms. Presently DS Jones swings left at Tottenham Court Road, and then right into Grafton Way, which elbows ninety degrees onto Fitzroy Street, whence their lodgings are some eight hundred yards ahead. Skelgill squints at the nameplate, which has a small 'W1' in one corner.

'So this is the West End, is it?'

DS Jones looks a little puzzled – she knows the district well, her first-year university hall of residence standing only yards away – but then she nods.

'I suppose so, Guv – but this is called Fitzrovia.'

Skelgill ponders for a moment.

'Sounds made up – like a rogue state in a spy film.'

DS Leyton does a quickstep to get alongside them.

'I believe it is made up, Guv – my old man was a cabbie – he always reckoned it never existed when he was a nipper.'

'Gives them an excuse to charge more for the property, I suppose.'

'They don't need no excuse, Guv – wait till we pass an estate agent's – you can't pay as much for a house in Penrith as what you'd need for a bedsit here.'

Skelgill raises his eyebrows.

'Don't you wish you'd kept your place?'

DS Leyton shakes his head.

'Wasn't an option, Guv. To start off we lived at my old ma's gaff – after that we were just renting – crippling it was – I don't know how young 'uns can afford it.'

DS Jones is nodding.

'Most of my friends who got jobs in London have to live in the suburbs – though they still seem to spend all their wages on rent, and commute for three hours a day.'

Skelgill hunches his shoulders and glances about disparagingly.

'I'm beginning to wonder what's the attraction.'

Though this is a statement rather than a question, DS Jones evidently feels obliged to supply an explanation.

'I suppose it's the buzz, Guv – music and media and fashion – and if you work in the creative industries – advertising, digital and so forth.'

DS Leyton chips in.

'Seems like all the publishers and their cronies are down here, too, Guv.'

Skelgill ponders for a moment.

'Sarah Redmond's in Edinburgh, mind.'

They walk on for a while before DS Jones remarks upon this apparent idiosyncrasy.

'I was reading how there's a lot of crime fiction writers based in Scotland – a *murder* they call themselves – like a murder of crows.'

Skelgill tuts.

'The raw material must be better up there.'

DS Leyton pretends to be offended.

'I'd have thought my old manor would win the gold medal for that, Guv – the good old East End.'

DS Jones grins.

'That's *true crime* – it's a different genre.'

And now Skelgill offers a wisecrack.

'Aye – there and the City, eh?'

This raises a chuckle from the two sergeants, and Skelgill joins in, happy to amplify the response to his own joke. The atmosphere around them is picking up and they seem in good spirits, despite their long day. They are now passing hostelries and restaurants, and there are more people about, young couples and small groups, some in casual wear, others still business-suited, though not yet thinking about heading home. Skelgill and Leyton find their progress interrupted by the sound of a football match being shown inside a pub – the doors are open and a sudden cry of frustration goes up. The place is packed with a standing audience, mostly males and many of them wearing England shirts. DS Leyton takes a couple of steps closer and rises upon tiptoes. Apparently he is unsuccessful; he taps one of the smokers crowding the entrance on the shoulder and asks him a question. The answer is curt, and he nods and returns to his colleagues and they begin to move on.

'Nil-nil, Guv – qualifier for the Euros – over at Wembley – I'd forgotten that was tonight.'

'Who are we playing?'

'It's a real banana skin, Guv – Fitzrovia.'

'Ha-ha, Leyton. Who is it really?'

DS Leyton grins. 'Estonia, Guv.' Then he gazes skywards rather philosophically. 'Think England'll ever win the World Cup again, Guv?'

Skelgill puffs out his cheeks, and pulls an anguished face, but before he can answer DS Jones draws them to a halt.

'Guv – I was thinking we could eat here.' She gestures to an inauspicious-looking Thai restaurant. 'It's been going for years – it's good value and the portions of noodles are legendary.'

'Music to my ears.' Skelgill immediately makes for the entrance, though his colleagues hang back.

'Shouldn't we check in, Guv?' DS Jones points with a finger of the hand that holds her overnight bag. 'The hotel's only five or six doors along.'

Skelgill frowns and beckons them with a toss of his head.

'Come on – my hangover's gone at last – the drinks are on me.'

Despite being well acquainted with the fallibility of this figure of speech, obediently they follow him inside – though they each would perhaps rather freshen up and divest themselves of their trappings. Skelgill, however, is on a mission, and orders three beers before they are even seated. They are shown to a round table at the centre of the dining area. The restaurant is small and, though basic in its decor, it has a cosy ambiance – and there is sufficient background chatter overlaid by piped *luk thung* for them to converse in effective privacy. DS Jones appears to have near-photographic recall of the menu, and her male colleagues are content to delegate to her the task of a communal order – Skelgill's only request being that she should select starters that will come quickly; however, a large bowl of spicy rice crackers soon provides satisfaction in this regard. DS Leyton munches thoughtfully; his eyes wander amongst the clientele. Then he shakes his head and intones somewhat ruefully.

'I get out for more meals with you guys than I do with the missus.'

Skelgill conjures an expression of masculine wisdom.

'There's some would say that's no bad thing.'

DS Leyton is not convinced, and does not respond to Skelgill's attempt at humour.

'I ought to make the effort – but it's difficult, what with the kids, and trying to find babysitters and whatnot.'

DS Jones looks at him sympathetically.

'I could sit for you sometime – you should just ask me – if I'm not on a late shift it's no problem.'

DS Leyton appears surprised, and holds up his palms as though he is backtracking. 'It's kind of you to offer – you might regret it though, couple of little terrors, they are.' He frowns resignedly. 'Last babysitter we had phoned us after twenty minutes 'cause they'd locked themselves in the bathroom and overflowed the bath – there was water pouring through the ceiling and the electrics exploded. By the time we got back there was a fire engine outside and a crowd of spectators in the street.' As his colleagues look increasingly amused, he shakes his head at the memory. 'Funnily enough – that was a Thai meal we were supposed to have.'

Skelgill points at his sergeant with the neck of his beer bottle.

'Sounds to me like you should stick to takeaways, Leyton.'

'I reckon you're right, Guv – though it's her birthday coming up – I'll have to think of something.' However, he shrugs off the awkward prospect and reaches for one of the fast-disappearing crackers. 'So this was a regular haunt of yours, Emma – back in the student days?'

'Not so much when I was a student – we couldn't often afford to eat out.' She appears a little guarded, as though she is reluctant to elaborate. 'After I graduated I used to come down to London – to visit...'

A plate of sticky chicken and ribs floats between them, its aromas punctuating DS Jones's sentence and causing a momentarily distraction. Skelgill swoops as it lands, though DS Leyton offers the dish to his female colleague before he avails himself.

'You still in touch with them, Emma?'

Skelgill is hunched over, already preoccupied with a pork rib, his teeth bared – though he flashes a glance at DS Jones as she replies.

'Not lately.'

She seems unsure of what to say next, and instead takes a hurried bite of chicken and has to lift up her napkin to wipe sauce from her chin. Ostentatiously, she raises her eyebrows at her clumsiness. DS Leyton, who looks like he was expecting a more comprehensive response, nods pensively. Then he re-starts the conversation from a slightly different angle.

'I never came out West very often – I'm an outsider here in town as much as the next man.' He points with a thumb over his shoulder, in what is in fact an easterly direction. 'Course, we've got all our relatives – that still brings us down – though half of them have emigrated to Essex these days.'

Skelgill looks up from his plate and raises a stripped bone in a pontificating manner.

'The way I see it, we're better off up north – I mean, give me one good reason to live in this urban jungle.'

'The aqueduct?'

'What?' Skelgill is taken aback by DS Leyton's apparently nonsensical retort.

'Sanitation, Guv?' DS Leyton breaks into a grin. 'The roads...'

Skelgill suddenly gets the joke.

'Very funny, Leyton – but the roads are nothing to write home about, that's for sure.'

DS Leyton nods.

'Tell me about it, Guv – when we come down to visit the in-laws we spend more time on the M25 than we do with them.' He lifts his beer and takes a sip. 'Which has its compensations, mind.'

The others grin, and their conversation continues in this vein as the meal progresses. Though DS Leyton and DS Jones have their respective associations that bind them to Western Europe's greatest metropolis, ultimately their colours are pinned beside Skelgill's on his rural Cumbrian mast: DS Jones, like him, being a native, and DS Leyton now firmly embedded with a young family whose accents edge further north by the day. So there is little real argument over the issue and as Skelgill, in appeasing mode, points out: it's all England, anyway – a perspective that is reinforced as a group of football fans passes the restaurant tunelessly singing *'Keep St George in my Heart'*, a drunken pursuit that is no doubt being repeated up and down the country, from London to the Lakes. Reacting to this cue, DS Leyton confesses that he ought to go and telephone his wife before it becomes too late. He offers to register them and obtain their room keys, and meet them for a nightcap in the hotel bar – a proposition that Skelgill accepts without protest. Thus DS Leyton departs, leaving Skelgill and DS Jones alone. It is ten p.m. and diners in the restaurant are thinning out – a Central London phenomenon, as last buses and tubes are sought, and unoccupied taxis become like hen's teeth. The pair is silent for a while – Skelgill is looking tired again, while DS Jones seems to be waiting for him to make the running. However, after a minute or two, she leans forward, placing her elbows on the table and pressing her palms together in the manner of prayer. Her arched brows gather with concern.

'Guv – I wondered – if you knew about DS Leyton – what happened on the London Underground?'

Skelgill folds his arms. Her tone of voice has told him that it is not some humorous anecdote she is about to relate.

'What are you talking about, Jones?'

'Earlier on, Guv – when we arrived at Euston – I noticed he wasn't keen to take the tube – then I remembered what a DS from the Met told me on a course I was on – she'd worked with him previously.'

Skelgill is implacable. DS Jones continues.

'It's going back over ten years – when they were both constables on the beat – there was a fire at a tube station – in north London somewhere.'

'So what happened?'

'They were the first on the scene – by then there were clouds of smoke billowing up from the tunnels – but the station staff thought everyone was safe – so they were guarding the entrance to stop anyone going inside.' She pauses to brush away strands of hair that have fallen across her face. 'Then someone said there was a tramp left behind on the platform – he was disabled and probably drunk.'

An expression of alarm fleetingly crosses Skelgill's intense countenance.

'So Leyton went in for him?'

DS Jones nods, wide-eyed.

'He saved him, Guv.' Suddenly her eyes flood with tears and glisten as they reflect the flickering tea light on their table. 'He carried him up something like fifty steps because the escalators had been switched off. They were both in hospital for a month. DS Leyton received the Queen's Medal, Guv.'

Skelgill is chewing his lip vigorously – it looks painful and he clearly cannot be aware that he is doing it – such is the reassessment that must be running through his mind. After a minute he reaches for his beer bottle, though he merely contemplates the label.

'He's kept that quiet, hasn't he?'

DS Jones concurs.

'So I think that's why he's not keen on the tube, Guv.'

Skelgill nods pensively.

'Well – thanks for telling me – saves me putting my bloody great daft foot in it.'

DS Jones grins.

'Oh – I think he's thick-skinned enough for you not to worry, Guv.'

Skelgill scowls; perhaps he registers the implied if unintended criticism in this statement. Nonetheless, he sets his jaw determinedly.

'I'll tell him we'll all be using taxis tomorrow – and to hell with the taxpayer.'

7. DICKIE LAMPRAY

Tuesday 9.30am

'I don't particularly recall going to bed last night, Jones.'

Skelgill utters these words with uncharacteristic formality, and DS Jones glances at him with apparent concern – though it may just be the slanting rays of the low autumn sun that cause her to squint. They walk steadily, side by side, along a chequered suburban pavement. The day is bright and mild, with a forecast of seventy degrees Fahrenheit – something only Londoners can aspire to in late October.

'DS Leyton helped you to your room, Guv.'

'Right.'

'You were a bit groggy. We were just saying at breakfast – we thought you were looking tired, on and off, during the day.'

Skelgill frowns reproachfully, though his reply indicates that his frustration is directed at himself and not his sergeant.

'I don't know what's been wrong with me – I mean, what did we have – a couple of beers and a whisky in the hotel bar?'

DS Jones perhaps refrains from commenting that this might be something of an under estimate, at least as far as her superior is concerned.

'It was a long day, Guv – on top of your night on the island.'

'Not as long as it was for you guys.' He shakes his head obstinately. 'I don't get it.'

'How do you feel now, Guv?'

Skelgill shoots DS Jones a quick sideways glance, as if to check whether she is covertly assessing his state of health.

'Right as rain – I walked halfway round Hyde Park this morning.'

'Really?'

'Aye – I was wide awake at five – once those bin-men came past clanking and yawping.'

DS Jones appears satisfied with this response.

'You did well to find it, Guv.'

'It's hardly rocket science, Jones.' Skelgill's tone carries a friendly reprimand. 'I might be a country boy but I can deal with *turn right on Oxford Street and your destination is ahead*.' He imitates a satnav voice by way of explanation.

DS Jones grins, admonished accordingly.

'True enough, Guv. How was it?'

'Almost deserted – surprisingly peaceful.' He scratches the back of his head. 'Could have sworn I saw a pelican flying over – but it wasn't properly light.'

'There used to be some on the lake in St James's Park, Guv – they were quite a tourist attraction. Maybe they're still around.'

Skelgill purses his lips.

'Aye, well – it would be a relief to know my mind's not playing tricks on me.' He watches a flock of pigeons as they cross low over the rooftops not far ahead. 'Pelicans, though – they eat fish by the bucket load – can't be all that popular – there's supposed to be big pike in the Serpentine.'

DS Jones looks surprised by this idea.

'But people swim in there, Guv – there's a famous club – they have races every Saturday.'

Skelgill must be reminded of his outstanding bet, for his grey-green eyes glaze over – an effect unlikely to be caused by concern for bathers – until he dismisses the recalcitrant thought with a shake of the head.

'I was tempted to have a fish – I've got a travel rod – should have packed it.' He shakes his head regretfully. 'Don't know how I would have landed anything decent, mind.'

DS Jones grins, perhaps amused by the idea of her superior officer wrestling bare-handed with a great snapping and flailing pike pulled unwillingly from London's historic recreational lake, much to the amazement of early-morning inline skaters and horse riders. Nevertheless, just as she is well informed about the

87

existence of the Serpentine Swimming Club, Skelgill's knowledge of the water's piscine population is correct: the lake holds good numbers of large bream, carp, roach and – indeed – pike to thirty pound plus, a lesser-known fact that, if broadcast widely, might deter the more apprehensive among the goose-greased doggy paddlers.

'So what did you do for breakfast, Guv?'

'Came across a café in Soho – it was full of Polish builders – I took that as a good sign – pint mugs of tea and bottles of *HP* on the table. Went for the full English.'

'How was it?'

Skelgill tilts his head from side to side.

'Not up to Gladis's standard – but not a bad second, all things considered.'

'The hotel food wasn't so clever, Guv – I just had the continental buffet, so I was fine – but DS Leyton was a bit disappointed with the fry.'

Skelgill is pensive for a few moments before he next speaks.

'Think I handled the taxi business okay?'

DS Jones nods vigorously. Skelgill refers to a short briefing before they divided into two asymmetrical 'teams'. He had recapped upon their interviewing plan – that he and DS Jones shall visit the members of the retreat, while DS Leyton will investigate the contacts his unit at HQ has opened up. Furthermore, since it is clear that their various ports of call are only loosely serviced by the London Underground system, they should use whatever means of surface transport is most *time*- rather than *cost*-efficient. That said, the 'teams' having gone their separate ways, that comprising he and DS Jones had promptly descended into Tottenham Court Road station, whence the Northern and Piccadilly Lines brought them to Baron's Court in West Kensington. Dickie Lampray resides in the adjoining district of Fulham, and it is just a half-mile walk from this station to his home.

Indeed, closing in, they swing into a residential road just one street removed from the great meander of the Thames that delineates the area and makes it two-thirds an island of the venerable flower. The narrow thoroughfare is tree-lined (though these are now largely bare), with mainly empty residents' parking bays marked at intervals. The houses, which date from the Edwardian era, are unassuming in size and built in tightly packed terraces punctuated only by side streets, though they possess a certain flamboyant charm. There are ornate timbered half-gables above deep bays that extend down to the ground floor, multi-paned sash windows with leaded glass, and red-ochre tiled skirts and porches that contrast nicely with whitewashed harling elsewhere. Each property, which is about a room and a half wide, achieves a semblance of privacy through a small front garden hemmed in by a matching wall of red brick and dressed white chalk.

But, despite the pleasant nature of the neighbourhood, Skelgill has the look of a disenchanted tourist.

'This can't be right, Jones?'

DS Jones is tracking their progress on her mobile. She glances at the handset.

'It's definitely the correct address, Guv – Tummel Road. The house should be near the end on our side.'

'Surely he lives somewhere grander than this?'

DS Jones notices an estate agent's *For Sale* sign that has a quick-response code printed on it. She stops and scans the symbol with her mobile. Then she scuttles to catch Skelgill, watching the screen as the details appear. She emits a little whistle of astonishment and holds the handset for Skelgill to see.

'It might not be grand, Guv – but if he doesn't have a mortgage he's comfortably a millionaire.'

Skelgill takes the device for a moment, as if he needs to hold it to absorb the information. He shakes his head disbelievingly.

'I'd settle for the balance, *less* a million.'

*

'Whoops, here comes Gypsy – do you mind dogs, Inspector – I can send him upstairs if you prefer?'

The canine to which Dickie Lampray refers is in fact an elderly chestnut-coloured spaniel, and despite an initial flurry of enthusiasm in welcoming Skelgill and DS Jones, it quickly settles into a gnawed wicker basket. They have been admitted through a panelled entrance door decorated with Art Nouveau glass into a tiled hallway. Where there might be expected to be a whiff of dog, the air is filled with the artificial scent of roses, which emanates from a plug-in device beside the creature's bed. The walls are decked with professionally taken framed photographs that would appear to relate to literary award ceremonies, judging by the evening wear of their subjects (each grinning group including a dinner-suited Dickie Lampray, sporting various colourful variations of his trademark bow tie).

'It's no problem, sir – I have one myself.' Skelgill bends down to stroke the hound behind an ear; it gazes up with soulful, sticky red-rimmed eyes. 'King Charles, is he, sir?'

Dickie Lampray appears pleased by Skelgill's accurate identification.

'Quite right, Inspector – I'm a man for proper dogs – I cannot abide this nonsense of these outrageously priced and frankly ridiculous crosses the breeders are cashing in on these days.' He gestures loosely towards his pet. 'Only this morning I was walking Jip beside the Thames and we were ambushed by a *Morkie* and a *Schnoodle* – what will they come up with next? I dread to think what they'll call it if someone mates a Shih Tzu with a Dachshund – although perhaps they already have. What kind is yours, Inspector? I would guess a pedigree Bloodhound – ha-ha.'

Skelgill grins rather sheepishly.

'She's a Bull... terrier.'

'Excellent, Inspector – and, of course, they are a much friendlier breed than their ferocious reputation suggests.'

He turns to lead the way, and DS Jones flashes a surreptitious grin at her superior, acknowledging his white lie (for Skelgill's somewhat unconventionally acquired pooch is a Bullboxer). They enter a front parlour, though the narrow house is knocked through into an adjoining living room and kitchen all the way to a small conservatory at the rear, creating a telescopic perspective with a view upon a shadowy courtyard that ends abruptly in the high brick wall of some other building. The whole effect is rather claustrophobic, and gives the impression that the walls are slowly but surely closing in. The succession of spaces is furnished in a masculine style, with leather sofas and easy chairs, and dark mahogany furniture. The various alcoves created by the alterations are lined by bookshelves, neatly stacked with mainly modern fiction hardbacks, arranged in size order from the centre of each shelf outwards.

'Please be seated officers. Is filter coffee acceptable? Custard creams?'

'Very kind of you, sir.'

Dickie Lampray has a tray already prepared, which he collects from the kitchen area. Though his lively manner seems unchanged from that encountered by Skelgill previously, his dress (casual dog-walking clothes, carpet slippers, and no bow tie) renders him a subdued and domesticated version of the urbane character that had seemed so well suited to the imposing surroundings of Grisholm Hall.

'Do you work from home, sir?' Skelgill gestures towards the nearest shelving unit.

'Oh, absolutely, Inspector, most agents do – commercial leases in London are entirely unaffordable in my line of work – keeping up this place is hard enough, as it is – heaven knows what will happen once the hawks at the Bank of England start hiking the base rate.'

Skelgill nods but does not appear to be particularly engaged by this prospect, and instead gets down to business.

'You might wonder sir, why we've come all the way to London to collect a document you could email to us – in fact, I believe *have* emailed to us.'

Dickie Lampray rather obediently fashions a slightly bewildered expression.

'Well, er... yes, of course, I suppose I did.'

'We have a number of calls to make, sir – I thought it might be best to see you first, as you seemed to be unofficially in charge of proceedings.'

'Oh, well – I wouldn't say that, Inspector – and certainly before poor old Rich died, he was rather, the, er... well, top dog, you might say. Ha-ha.'

Dickie Lampray's laugh is tentative, but Skelgill nods encouragingly.

'What it is, you see, sir – the deaths have been referred to the Cumbria Coroner – largely as a result of technicalities, such as being sudden, and of unknown cause – but that obliges us to investigate, in order to satisfy the inquest that there are no suspicious circumstances.'

Dickie Lampray is nodding.

'Of course, Inspector, I understand perfectly.'

Skelgill is holding a biscuit, but he seems to realise he cannot at this moment begin to eat it and he replaces it upon his saucer.

'And one aspect that is baffling us – indeed is going to make us look a bit amateurish if we can't get to the bottom of it – is that, as you are aware, we've so far been unable to locate the company that organised the retreat.'

Dickie Lampray lifts an index finger, and then rises and shuffles his slippers across the carpeted floor with his odd short-stepping gait. He crosses to an open bureau in the living room section. He retrieves a sheet of A4 paper and brings it back to the coffee table.

'This is a printout of the email I forwarded last night, Inspector – I am afraid I did not arrive home until after seven.' He rotates the page through 180 degrees and hands it to Skelgill. 'I think the only information of use will be their email address – it had not really struck me until now that I have no other contact details.'

'We can't a find a website, or a postal address.' Skelgill looks inquiringly at the agent. 'Would you say, sir – in your experience of these things – is that unusual?'

Dickie Lampray, who sits upright with his fingers interlocked and held against his breastbone, alternates his grip and gives a little shake of his hands.

'Well – it is rather curious, with the benefit of hindsight – though if all had gone smoothly I don't suppose I should have noticed.'

'Had you heard of them before, sir – Wordsworth Writers' Retreats?'

Now Dickie Lampray seems somewhat pained.

'Well, the thing is – it sounds like the sort of organisation one has encountered many times – but in fact it is a clever combination of words – it has a familiar ring to it, when actually it appears the opposite may be true.'

Skelgill glances at DS Jones, perhaps acknowledging her matching assessment.

'What made you go on the retreat, sir?'

'Well, to be perfectly frank, Inspector – it was the fee.'

'The fee?'

'That's correct, five thousand for a week's work – free board and lodging – and not much work at that.' He gestures to the sheet that Skelgill holds. 'It is all detailed in the email.'

Skelgill glances vacantly at the page of text and hands it to DS Jones.

'And have you received the fee – if you don't mind my asking, sir?'

Dickie Lampray shakes his head, and rather dejectedly he turns out his bottom lip before he replies.

'No – it was to be invoiced upon completion of the course.'

Skelgill remains silent for a few moments.

'What are you thinking, sir?'

'Well, obviously, Inspector – the course was not completed – but that aside, I am now rather wondering whether my fee – or even some proportion of it – will ever be forthcoming.' He shakes his head unhappily. 'I mean – if this company has disappeared off the police's radar, I don't fancy my own chances too strongly.'

Skelgill looks to DS Jones – who has finished reading the email – for her input.

'Mr Lampray, it invites you as a highly regarded practitioner to provide advice about getting the best out of working with a Literary Agent?'

'That is correct, sergeant.'

'Wouldn't this suggest that they knew who you were – it mentions your reputation, and details about your agency and its achievements?'

Dickie Lampray makes a waving gesture with both hands, as if to say 'not necessarily' and rises again from his seat. Once more he visits the bureau, and this time returns with the current edition of the *Writers' and Artists' Yearbook*. There are several pages marked with slips of paper, and he flips open the hefty tome at one of these and lays it on the table before them.

'Our industry bible.' He points to a small entry, three-quarters of the way down one page. It is headed 'Lampray & Associates Literary Agency' and comprises a couple of paragraphs of small text. Then he flicks through some of the adjoining pages. 'There is a whole section here – most British agents are listed – everything you really need to know, in a nutshell.'

'So you might have been selected at random, sir?'

Dickie Lampray nods.

'Quite possibly, sergeant.'

He looks anxiously to Skelgill, who has been taking the opportunity of DS Jones's questioning to dunk and devour custard creams. Skelgill swallows and clears his throat to speak.

'You seemed to be familiar with the other members of the retreat, sir?'

'Well of course, I do know – at least I *knew* Rich – and Angela, and naturally I have heard of Sarah Redmond and have been at several events at which she has appeared – but I would be able to say the same of almost any random combination of publisher, critic and established author that you would care to choose – it's a small world in the book trade and we many of us are connected for business purposes. I can't claim to be acquainted with them any better than I am with several dozen other people who equally well might have attended. The budding authors, however, they were all complete strangers to me.'

'What about the remaining professionals like yourself – how had they been enlisted to participate?'

Dickie Lampray frowns.

'I really couldn't say, Inspector – it wasn't something that came up in conversation – I imagine I'd supposed they had been recruited in the same manner that I was – and you understand how people like to keep mum about their earnings – one never knows if a would-be author is a taxman in their day job – ha-ha – just joking, of course!'

Skelgill evidently decides not to react to this remark, and continues to gaze at Dickie Lampray as though he expects him to continue. After a slightly awkward moment or two his silent treatment pays off.

'I must confess, Inspector – I *was* rather surprised to find Rich there – I shouldn't have thought the money would have been a factor – I rather wondered if it was because he knew Sarah Redmond would be attending.'

Skelgill pauses, a biscuit hovering midway twixt cup and lip, which is akin to a sudden pricking of his ears.

'Why is that significant, sir?'

'Ah, well, Inspector – book trade gossip, you see.' Dickie Lampray taps the side of his nose. 'Rumour has it that she is in the market for a new publisher – that she has rather outgrown her Scottish outfit – so it would have been quite a coup if she'd gone to Rich Buckley.'

'Did you know she would be there, sir?'

Dickie Lampray shakes his head.

'No – I had no knowledge of my fellow delegates until we assembled at the waterside rendezvous.'

'I see, sir.' Skelgill looks thoughtful. 'You mentioned a moment ago about Mr Buckley being 'top dog', as you put it – what did you mean by that?'

'Ah, inspector – the pecking order of the publishing business.' Dickie Lampray shakes his head ruefully. 'Although the digital revolution has rather put the cat among the pigeons, for the time being the traditional hierarchy largely prevails – in which the publisher is all-powerful. The humble agent,' (he gestures emotively to his breast with both hands) 'and the even more humble would-be author, is at the mercy of the publisher. No publishing contract, no food on the table.'

Skelgill nods sympathetically.

'So where do the others fit in, in that regard?'

Dickie Lampray momentarily takes hold of the tips of his shirt collar, as if he is straightening an invisible bow tie.

'Well, of course, Angela is something of a law unto herself.' He glances at DS Jones and says by way of explanation, 'She is a Literary Critic – syndicated to all the leading media outlets. With a stroke of her pen she can make or break a book – or a heart, come to that.'

'So she's top of the pecking order, really?'

'Rather soaring around above it, I should say, Inspector – since she is not really a link in the practical chain of origination and publication.'

'And what about Sarah Redmond?'

'Well, of course, once an author has 'made it', so to speak, they can call their own tune – and Sarah Redmond has certainly made it – there is a hardly a week goes by when she is not among the top ten bestsellers.'

Now Skelgill nods, as if the situation is becoming clearer.

'So at the retreat, sir – it was Mr Buckley that took charge?'

Dickie Lampray concurs.

'It was apparent after we had settled into our rooms and gathered for a discussion, that there was a requirement for a chairman of sorts. Rich quite naturally assumed that role and I was content to see him do so. Angela and Sarah strutted like smart peacocks amongst a flock of rather less brainy hens – they subtly complied only with the arrangements that suited them. The aspiring authors, of course, were desperate to impress – so I'm afraid to say they were somewhat taken advantage of when it came to communal chores and suchlike. When Rich died – only shortly before your own arrival, Inspector – as one of the more senior members of the group, in age if nothing else, I rather felt it behove me to take things in hand. But I had no formal role, and until then I took a back seat in what limited affairs there were.'

Skelgill's countenance has perhaps unwittingly hardened as he listens to this explanation – and he suddenly seems to become conscious he should overtly demonstrate this is not the interrogation of a suspect.

'Well, sir – it's very good of you to fill us in with these details – obviously I had a bit of an insight myself into the situation.'

'Oh, it is no trouble whatsoever, Inspector – just ask away – it is a pleasure to do one's civic duty.'

Skelgill nods several times, and he becomes conspiratorial in his manner. He leans forward, his elbows resting upon his knees and his hands entwined.

'You'll understand, sir, that I'm constrained in what I can say about the deceased persons – but it appears that Mr Buckley's death may have been brought about by the side-effects of a medicine he had in his possession, and in Ms Mandrake's case we believe she took an overdose of sleeping pills.'

Dickie Lampray is nodding in confirmation, as though this much has already reached his ears – either at the time of the evacuation from Grisholm Hall, or by means of some social grapevine since. Skelgill continues.

'So I don't know, sir, if – in the light of that knowledge – there's anything that struck you as notable as far as either of them were concerned – the state of their health, or something about their behaviour, for instance?'

Dickie Lampray nods slowly and gazes reflectively in the direction of the lounge window. A courier's van has pulled up outside, although its manoeuvre is just to let another vehicle pass, and it draws away.

'Well, Inspector – you saw Bella Mandrake for yourself – she certainly wasn't the most stable of personalities, so I am unsurprised by what you say regarding sleeping pills. However, from a point of view of external vigour she seemed entirely robust – quite a formidable presence, indeed, as you experienced, Inspector.'

Skelgill does not comment, but Dickie Lampray continues with barely a pause.

'As for Rich – well, he seemed in rude health, too. Certainly he was burning the candle at the midnight end, if you get my gist.' He blinks apologetically. 'You see, I'm a bit of a night owl myself, and I don't believe there was an evening when Rich turned in before me – but then again he was correspondingly late in rising.'

'What was he doing – in staying up late?'

'Oh, just generally socialising, Inspector – there was no shortage of alcohol,' (at this Dickie Lampray coughs rather discreetly, and DS Jones keeps her eyes fixed firmly upon her notebook), 'and always someone willing to keep Rich company – though I don't think any of us could match his staying power.'

'What about on the night before he died, sir – you mentioned previously that yourself, Ms Mandrake and Ms Cutting were the last to be up with him – until about two a.m. I believe you said?'

Dickie Lampray nods.

'That is correct, Inspector – although I was first to succumb to the lure of my bed – so I am afraid Angela is your best bet to provide any last minute details. When I left the drawing room the three of them were huddled on a sofa, ostensibly poring over a piece of writing Bella had produced and insisted they should critique – though I rather think they were humouring her.'

Skelgill nods.

'This work – that you were all supposed to do as part of your contracts – how was that organised?'

Dickie Lampray now looks a touch shamefaced.

'Well I must be honest, Inspector, it was hardly challenging. I was expected to give a short talk before dinner on a couple of evenings, and then to be loosely available for any of the authors who wanted to chat about things – how to find an agent, what to expect from them, how to treat them – ha-ha.'

'And how much were you called upon?

'Frankly, Inspector, the authors were jolly diligent – of course the primary idea of a retreat is to get one's head down and write away furiously in perfect peace – and that is what they seemed to do most of the time – so I think you'll get a similar answer from Angela and Sarah – which is that their services were not strenuously tested.'

'Was it not a bit boring, sir?'

Dickie Lampray shakes his head decisively. 'Oh, I always have plenty of work to do, Inspector.' He gestures to a neat stack of papers that sits beside the hearth. 'These days agents are exploited as free readers by publishers. I had a whole suitcase of manuscripts to work my way through. I almost sank that rowing boat single handed.' He sighs. 'Perhaps one day I shall discover my own Sarah Redmond.'

Skelgill gazes at the nearest set of bookshelves, although there is no flicker of recognition in his eyes.

'Were there no future best-selling authors on the course?'

Dickie Lampray, perhaps rather surprisingly, does not appear to dismiss this notion out of hand.

'Well, Inspector, Linda Gray's cooking was certainly fit for *haute cuisine*, especially in light of the limitations of the kitchen – but her writing was rather more *cafeteria*, if I may put it that way – nonetheless she certainly succeeded in showcasing her talents.' Then he shakes his head, perhaps reluctantly. 'But there are so many cookery writers these days – and of course fiction is my bag, in any event.'

'How about the others?'

'Well – I probably don't need to tell you about poor Bella Mandrake – may she rest in peace – her writing was of a juvenile standard, unfortunately. Dr Bond wrote stodgily and was such a terrible pedant about the Lake District – until you arrived to put him in his place – and the ex-solider chap, a little too facile – although there's probably more of a market in what he has to say.' He pauses, as if he is trying to remember whom he has omitted from his appraisal. 'Oh, yes – young Lucy Hecate – now she was a bit of a dark horse, somewhat retiring, her writing rather complex and deep – but an intelligent and knowledgeable girl – I sense she is destined to be an author, if that is what she wants – but of course you made rather an impression on her yourself, Inspector.'

Skelgill appears not to notice DS Jones's inquiring glance. He tips his head to one side in a casual gesture.

'I think that was just the coincidence of her being the person that summoned my help, sir – it could have been any of you.'

'Ah, but there you go, Inspector – just another example of her quiet determination – she had resolved to venture out and brave the storm, when all the rest of us had given it up for the night – and she was proved right – she found you!'

Skelgill opens his palms, as if to say 'these things happen', and takes the cue for his next question.

'When I appeared, sir – obviously you'd had the shock of Mr Buckley's death – but I got the impression you were all getting along very well as a group – considering, as you say, that you'd been thrown together largely as a bunch of strangers.'

Dickie Lampray considers for a moment, as if perhaps this generalisation is not entirely the case. His reply however strikes a conciliatory chord.

'Well, of course, it was a slightly artificial situation, to the extent that the professionals among us represented channels to publication – Rich, and myself to a lesser degree – but even rubbing shoulders with Angela and Sarah perhaps seemed like a harbinger of good fortune – so it was natural for the novice authors to want to impress us in whatever ways they could. I suppose that helped to create a harmonious and cooperative atmosphere.'

'You didn't sense any rivalries?'

Again there is some hesitation from Dickie Lampray; perhaps even the faintest twinge of discomfort, as if Skelgill's question has prodded a raw nerve. But quickly he gathers himself.

'Well, Inspector – as you witnessed – Bella Mandrake was no shrinking violet, she had few qualms about insinuating herself into whatever conversation was in progress. The others were less pushy as such, though Dr Bond was somewhat presumptuous – I shouldn't like to have been one of his patients

– and Burt Boston, frankly a bit of a show-off. Linda Gray was rather dowdy – but then she was able to let her food do her talking – and Lucy Hecate altogether more reticent.'

Skelgill's attention seems to waver during this answer – perhaps because these superficial impressions he had already assimilated during his time at Grisholm Hall. But he gathers his wits and develops his line of enquiry.

'How about among the professionals?'

Dickie Lampray shakes his head.

'Perhaps if instead of a publisher, an agent and a critic there had been three publishers all wooing Sarah Redmond, then it might have been a different matter – as it was, our sub-group was strictly non-competitive – apart from when it came to *Scrabble* – at which you of course gave us all a bit of a lesson in ruthlessness.'

Skelgill affects modesty; though it is plain he is pleased by this assessment.

'Put it down to beginner's luck, sir.'

'Oh, I think it was more than that, Inspector – do you do crosswords, by any chance?'

Skelgill appears guarded – until he remembers he has reinforcements at his side. He gestures casually at DS Jones.

'Actually, my sergeant here is more of a dab hand than me.'

Dickie Lampray regards DS Jones with interest.

'I rather imagined all modern detectives do crosswords – I suppose it comes from watching too much *Inspector Morse* – these repeats are never off daytime television.'

DS Jones nods politely. The course of the conversation has taken a diversion – of Dickie Lampray's making – but Skelgill seems content with this state of affairs. He slaps his hands on his knees and rises.

'Would you mind, sir – if I just nipped to your bathroom before we go?' He gestures to the cafetière, as if to pass some of the responsibility for his predicament to Dickie Lampray. 'I'm not a regular coffee drinker.'

Dickie Lampray looks momentarily discomfited, but he realises he has little alternative than to accommodate Skelgill accordingly.

'Of course, Inspector – be my guest – it is directly ahead at the top of the stairs.'

Skelgill nods politely and leaves the room. When he reappears a couple of minutes later, Dickie Lampray has moved to sit beside DS Jones on the leather settee, and they are both leaning over a folded copy of *The Times*.

'Ah, Inspector – your sergeant certainly *is* a dab hand.' He lifts the journal and wafts it triumphantly above his head. 'She has solved my final two clues: tanager and pelican – both of them birds – amazing how obvious they are once one knows the answer!'

Skelgill looks quizzically at DS Jones, who returns his glance with a slightly helpless expression, as though the exercise was thrust upon her in his absence.

'Well, sir – I'm glad we've been of some use to you.' Skelgill offers a hand, which Dickie Lampray reciprocates. 'We might have some luck tracking down the retreats company – but in the meantime if you hear from them please do let us know.'

'Certainly, Inspector.'

They shuffle out into the hallway. Dickie Lampray moves to head off the Cavalier, but the small canine seems content to remain nestled in its blanket – perhaps the run-in with the Morkie and Schnoodle gang has proved a little overwhelming.

'Well, thank you for your help, sir – and your hospitality.' Skelgill bows, rather ostentatiously. 'We shouldn't need to be troubling you again, sir.'

They take their leave, and exit from the diminutive front garden, which is mainly filled with shrubs such as *Buddleia* and *Cotoneaster*. As DS Jones turns to fasten the gate, she glances up to see Dickie Lampray watching from the bay window of the lounge. He is cradling his dog and, rather comically, manipulates one of its paws in a puppet-like farewell. DS Jones giggles and acknowledges the gesture.

'What is it?'

'They were just waving us off, Guv.'

'They?' Skelgill suddenly sounds alarmed.

'Him and the dog, Guv.'

'Ah.' Skelgill relaxes.

'What did you think I meant, Guv?'

Skelgill purses his lips before replying.

'Oh – just that there was someone snoring in one of the bedrooms.'

DS Jones's eyes widen.

'You didn't look in, Guv?'

Skelgill grins.

'You must be joking – it sounded like a bloke.' Then he pulls his mobile phone from his hip pocket. 'I did get this, though.' He fiddles with the screen and then holds the display so she can see it.

'It's one of the photographs he had on the wall, Guv.'

'Correct – but who's in it?'

DS Jones takes the handset and looks more closely.

'Well – it's Dickie Lampray – and several others – I don't recognise them.'

Skelgill's expression hardens.

'See the tall one, on Lampray's left?'

'Aha?'

'Pound to a penny that's Rich Buckley.'

8. RBP LIMITED

Tuesday 11am

'Yes – that is Mr Buckley.'

The woman nods, her jaw pushed forward with some determination. She is wiry and angular, and of medium height and late middle age. Her dark eyes are watchful, blinking evenly behind horn-rimmed spectacles that perch upon a beaked nose. Her sleek auburn hair is coiffed in a chignon style and her clothes – a grey twinset and toning tweed skirt – add to the impression of a PA from the old school. (Indeed she has a refined accent to match.) She is called Miss Constance Belgrave, and she is – unexpectedly – the sole employee of Rich Buckley Publishing Limited. The detectives have travelled back across town by London Underground, passing more or less beneath their night's lodgings, first to emerge blinking in the bright sunshine at Holborn (DS Jones schooling Skelgill in the pronunciation *"Hoe-bern"* and pointing out Staple Inn, an old Holborn landmark made famous by the eponymous tobacco), thence to continue on foot into the fringe of the up-and-coming Clerkenwell district. Here the firm has its offices on the third floor of what was once a lithographic printer's. The superficially renovated premises retain an industrial character, having exposed pipes, ducts, and vents, large steel-framed windows, and high ceilings with fluorescent lighting. The publisher's quarters appear to comprise a single large room at the corner of the building, divided into a series of semi-open-plan spaces by tubular shelving units of about six feet in height. They are now seated in what is an improvised reception area, where two minimalistic Bauhaus-style settees face one another across a chrome and glass coffee table. In scheduling their appointment, a detective constable reporting to DS Jones has outlined the purpose of their visit – primarily to acquire some background details on Rich Buckley – and Skelgill has begun by showing Miss Belgrave the awards ceremony photograph he clandestinely obtained en route to Dickie Lampray's loo.

'Naturally, madam, we appreciate this must be an upsetting time for you.'

The woman redirects her birdlike stare from the photograph to Skelgill.

'Why, Inspector – I am not upset in the least – Mr Buckley was a thoroughly unpleasant man.'

Skelgill is not easily knocked off his stride, though he is more accustomed to dealing with rough-and-ready country-folk than polished metropolitan sorts. He perhaps plays for time by taking a bite of the chocolate digestive with which he has been furnished. The opportunity, however, is too good to be passed over, and after a moment he has composed a response that ought to serve his purpose.

'I did rather get that impression from some of the ladies I met at the writers' retreat.'

This appears to be an astute tactic – despite lacking substance – for it allies the woman with notional kindred spirits, and there is a distinct release of strain in her taut frame.

'I am not surprised to hear that, Inspector.'

Skelgill tilts his head to one side.

'You're – you were – his secretary, madam?'

The woman appears to flinch at this suggestion.

'I was ostensibly recruited as *PA to the Managing Director*.' She emphasises the job title in a contemptuous tone. 'At exactly this time last year – but it has turned out that my role is almost entirely devoted to selling.'

'How does that work, madam?' Again the woman shows a flicker of disapproval – or at least some impatience, as if Skelgill's question is improbably naïve – and he quickly adds a caveat. 'You'll have to bear with me, I'm afraid – I'm a complete duffer when it comes to the book world – but ask me anything you like about sheepdog trials.'

The woman seems to soften a little at this admission, and – having cleared the hurdle of her admission to labouring in what she evidently considers a menial capacity – she elaborates with good grace.

'You could euphemistically call it publicity, Inspector – or marketing, come to that. For each book that we publish we need to gain trade support and media exposure. If it is not prominent upon the booksellers' shelves and display tables, and there is no public awareness of its merits, a book will simply wither and die. And then it is returned to us for a fate known as pulping.' She inhales, and for a second appears perturbed – but then she reaches into the handbag that rests beside her and brings out an electronic cigarette. 'Do you mind, Inspector... Sergeant?' Skelgill shakes his head. DS Jones looks a little alarmed, but does not comment. They might wonder if this is the mouse beginning to let down its hair now that the cat has perished. They watch with some interest as she 'vapes' – Skelgill seems fascinated by the little puff of steam that disappears into the ether. There is a brief flutter of her eyelids – a glimpse of pleasure – and then she resumes her explanation. 'A publisher has only a short window of time for each book to establish itself. These days, unless the author is famous – or infamous – it can be nigh-on impossible to achieve the level of coverage that will deliver profitability.'

'A bit of a thankless task, then, madam?'

'And a thankless taskmaster to boot, Inspector.'

Skelgill again resists any temptation he might feel to home in on the unpopularity of the late Rich Buckley. Instead, he picks up on the theme she has outlined.

'In terms of publicity, madam, there was a woman on the retreat – quite a well-known book critic, I'm led to believe – Angela Cutting.' He pauses to watch another puff of steam. 'Would she be someone you dealt with?'

For a moment Constance Belgrave looks distinctly peeved.

'Inspector, there were certain associates – perhaps those considered to be of a more senior level, or perhaps of a longer standing – that Mr Buckley kept to himself. I believe Angela Cutting fell into that category.'

'So they did know one another?'

'I am sure they did, yes.'

'Do you know the extent to which they were in contact?'

She shakes her head and sucks in another shot of vaporised nicotine.

'I was not privy to Mr Buckley's diary – if indeed he kept one.' She frowns censoriously. 'But certainly he was no stranger to the extended lunch hour – several times some weeks.'

Skelgill raises his eyebrows, mirroring her disapproval.

'There was some mention that Mr Buckley was interested in signing up the author Sarah Redmond?'

Skelgill leaves the question hanging.

'*Xara* Redmond, Inspector.'

'Aye – of course – the pen name.'

Now Constance Belgrave folds her arms, holding the cigarette against her left shoulder.

'I should have thought that was very unlikely, Inspector.'

'Why is that, madam?'

'The scale of advances an author such as Xara Redmond could command would be beyond the resources of Rich Buckley Publishing – especially under the current circumstances.'

Skelgill plays dumb.

'The current circumstances, madam?'

The woman now seems to ride a little roller coaster of emotions – perhaps a surge of glee, followed by a braking realisation of disappointment.

'Mr Buckley was in the midst of some very taxing divorce negotiations, Inspector – the financial implications, I understand, were putting considerable strains on the resources of the business.'

'Did Mr Buckley tell you this?'

For a moment she seems a little ashamed – as though she has betrayed a confidence that she ought not even to know. But then she is perhaps reminded that one can neither slander nor be rebuked by the dead, and she casts a hand in the general direction of what must have been Rich Buckley's workstation.

'When one person is talking loudly on the telephone, Inspector, the rest of us can overhear everything that passes.'

Skelgill nods – but rather than explore her revelation about finances, he picks up on what appears to be a little idiosyncrasy in her reasoning.

'Madam, when you say "the rest of us" – I thought it was just yourself that worked here?'

'Presently, that is correct, Inspector.' Constance Belgrave creases her lips as if there is a bitter taste in her mouth. 'But we chew up and spit out a constant stream of attractive young female interns.'

She rounds off this statement with a disapproving glance at DS Jones, who is diligently taking notes, and does not see that she has been unjustly targeted, simply for the crime of being an attractive young female – an impression perhaps compounded by her short skirt and low sitting position. Skelgill watches as Constance Belgrave draws rather more urgently upon the cigarette, and he reaches for his tea as if to create a lull in which the dust may settle.

'If I understand you correctly, madam – are you saying that Mr Buckley was the cause of the, shall we say, high staff turnover?'

The woman regards him sharply, as if trying to discern whether he harbours predatory tendencies of a similar nature.

'Certainly, Inspector.'

'Do you have staff records of these, er... young ladies?'

'We do not, Inspector.' There is an angry edge now to her voice. 'Since they were unpaid, there was little formal recruitment – just an ad placed on a local student jobs website – and a brief audition with Mr Buckley on the casting couch.' She indicates the settee upon which Skelgill and DS Jones sit. 'I think three months is the longest any individual has lasted during my tenure.'

Skelgill nods, and then frowns inquiringly.

'Just to be specific, madam – what would you say were their main reasons for leaving?'

The woman is quick to reply, as if she has had the words stacked ready to topple from her tongue.

'Primarily sexual harassment, Inspector.' She stares indignantly at Skelgill, but then she looks away rather fretfully, as if – paradoxically – there is an element of her outrage that she herself never suffered such a fate. But the distraction is short lived, and she gathers her wits. 'To that you can add Mr Buckley's traits of arrogance, intolerance, miserliness, rudeness and a wholesale lack of empathy as far as other human beings were concerned.'

'It must have been difficult for yourself, madam – were you not tempted to do something about it?'

She chooses to interpret the question in pragmatic terms.

'It is not easy for a woman of my age to gain employment in a prestigious sector of the economy, Inspector.' And with these words she seems to shrink, her shoulders to droop and the defiant façade to show cracks of vulnerability. She even allows a small sigh to escape from her compressed lips. 'And I do love books.'

Skelgill nods several times, furrowing his brow in an intelligent way, as if he empathises in particular with her latter point.

'I realise it's early days, madam – but what do you anticipate will happen to the company?'

But now a flicker of surprise crosses her features.

'Oh, I should imagine we shall be sold as a going concern – if nothing else the RBP brand has a strong identity.' She indicates beyond the settee on which the detectives sit. Behind them, against the window, stands a cardboard unit that holds a stack of new paperbacks, all identical – there is a backboard with an enlarged photograph of the book, and it appears to be a prototype for a store display. 'As well as our popular non-fiction list, we are outright market leaders in gay and lesbian fiction – and erotica.'

Skelgill cranes his neck, and squints into the bright sunny backdrop as though he is struggling to read the title – although it might be the somewhat lurid cover image that clamours for his attention. Just when it could be considered rather indecent to gaze any longer, he swivels back to face Constance Belgrave. He affects a vacant shake of the head.

'I thought that kind of thing was all online these days, madam.'

She flashes him an old fashioned look – as though she suspects his naivety to be disingenuous.

'The rehabilitation of the call girl and the social acceptability of sexual fantasies has led over the past decade to something of a mini boom in explicit belle lettres and bondage adventures, Inspector. We receive approximately three submissions per week in which a carnally repressed college student cavorts with an over-sexed American billionaire. The agents have given up on it, but hopeful authors keep them coming.' Now she gestures to a stack of unopened foolscap envelopes and A4-sized packages that rests with other items of mail and magazines upon a small table near the entrance. 'There you see this week's unsolicited manuscripts, and it is only Tuesday.'

Skelgill gazes at the pile for a moment.

'What do you do with them?'

'Mr Buckley would glance through them. If there is return postage we send them back with a standard rejection letter.'

'All of them?'

She shakes her head.

'He would pick out half a dozen every week. It would be the job of the intern to review them and present a critique of each to him. Of course – how could a raw undergraduate possibly know his mind? So then he would slap them down. Tear apart their reviews. Interrogate them on what they thought of the explicit passages. A thoroughly humiliating ritual. It clearly served some perverse purpose of his – although we never took on a new author that way.'

Skelgill nods pensively.

'You mentioned the agents – there was one on the retreat with Mr Buckley – called Dickie Lampray – are you familiar with him?'

The woman nods, although she exhibits no sign that his name holds particular significance.

'Yes – we published an anthology by one of his authors earlier in the year – a summer read supposedly – *Bondage Shorts* it was called.' She glances at the nearest unit of shelves, peering through her polished lenses, as if she expects the book to be in that section, but after a moment she gives up. 'Why we took it on, I don't know – the writing was of an abominably poor standard and the BDSM scenes positively toe-curling.'

It must seem contradictory to the two detectives, to hear these words uttered so matter of-factly by the severe-looking, prim and proper middle-aged woman. They might be forgiven for wondering if she perhaps leads a double life, and – once in the privacy of her own home – casts off her staid outer garments, dons the outfit of a dominatrix, and descends into a concealed dungeon equipped accordingly. Whether such thoughts tumble across the plains of Skelgill's mind it is impossible to know, though he spends a few moments wandering in reverie before he returns to the matter in hand.

'And, er... Mr Lampray – was his relationship with Mr Buckley – or the firm – any different to those other agents you dealt with?'

The woman considers for a moment, but then she shakes her head.

'Not that I am aware of, Inspector – as I mentioned, Mr Buckley tended to keep his business relationships to himself – I had no involvement with the contracts that were drawn up – and we publish around one hundred books per year – so each one of those could theoretically be represented by a different agent.'

DS Jones has placed some papers between herself and Skelgill, on the surface of the coffee table. The top sheet lists the names and occupations of the members of the retreat (the would-be authors simply classified as 'writers', along with Sarah

Redmond). Skelgill picks it up and hands it to Constance Belgrave.

'Apart from those we've mentioned, are any of these people familiar to you?'

The woman's spectacles are bifocals, and she stares down past the aquiline nose like a hawk surveying potential prey. But she shakes her head and returns the page.

'Sarah Redmond is the only author of whom I have heard, Inspector.'

Skelgill fans the page in the air between them.

'The others are all hopefuls, I understand, madam.' He replaces the paper on the table and takes the opportunity to scoop a chocolate digestive from the communal plate. 'So far we've been unable to trace the company that organised the retreat – we were hoping there may be some correspondence here among Mr Buckley's admin.'

'Unfortunately his email is password protected, Inspector.' Her sallow complexion appears to colour a little at this admission, and she quickly adds an explanation. 'I have already had cause to check – in an effort to resolve an inquiry yesterday from one of our book trade customers.'

Skelgill looks as though he understands entirely the need to investigate someone else's private email account.

'How about his desk – maybe there's a letter or something?'

'His desk is also locked.' But now she glances furtively between the two detectives. 'There is a spare key.'

'You know where it's kept?'

She nods; the blush around her cheeks diminishes, perhaps as she realises that in police work ends justify means.

'He made it rather obvious on a number of occasions – he was rather careless with leaving his own keys lying randomly about the office and had a spare set to take out when he couldn't find them.'

'Perhaps we could have a quick look before we go?'

'Certainly, Inspector.'

'What did he say about the retreat – about being away?'

'Very little, Inspector – but that was the norm.' Once more, she looks a little piqued. 'He could be going to a conference in Shanghai and would only inform me on the evening before – or perhaps even call in from the airport.'

'So you didn't make his travel arrangements, book hotels – that sort of thing?'

She shakes her head.

'As I mentioned, Inspector, Mr Buckley was miserly in the extreme – I don't believe he would have trusted anyone else to obtain the lowest possible prices.'

'Did you know he was attending the retreat?'

She shakes her head.

'It was just some parting comment about the frozen north and that he may be some time – I think he was humorously paraphrasing Captain Oates.'

Skelgill raises his eyebrows – perhaps disapproving of the slight upon his part of England – or maybe even at the ironically analogous outcome.

'How had he seemed prior to leaving – health-wise, state of mind – his behaviour?'

The woman ponders for a moment before she replies.

'I can't say I noticed anything out of the ordinary – but then again there was no 'ordinary' as far as Mr Buckley was concerned – he was prone to mood swings and flashes of temper and hyperactivity, and then there were periods of apparent depression – these could all occur within the same afternoon.'

Skelgill looks at DS Jones, who writes furiously to keep up, despite her shorthand skills. She glances briefly at him mid-flow. Skelgill puts down his cup and saucer and leans back casually against the sofa.

'Did he drink much at lunchtimes?'

'I should not say excessively, Inspector, despite the length of his engagements – he commuted most days by car, and I believe he was conscious of the risks – to his licence, at least.'

'How about drugs?'

Constance Belgrave appears puzzled.

'You mean medicines, Inspector?'

Skelgill slides the back of a forefinger beneath his nose in an ambiguous gesture.

'Including medicines.'

'Well... I shouldn't have thought a man of his generation would use *illegal* drugs, Inspector...'

This notion seems to have caught her by surprise; it appears her worldliness is restricted to the sphere of soft-pornographic literature.

'How about legal ones?' Skelgill holds out a palm in an inquiring manner. 'For instance, were you aware of him taking medication for what might have been irritable bowel syndrome?'

Constance Belgrave looks almost as disturbed by this as the idea of her former boss having a clandestine cocaine habit – although it could simply be the nature of the ailment itself. She shakes her head vehemently.

'As far as I am aware, Inspector – despite Mr Buckley's many failings – I am fairly certain that his physical health did not number among them.'

*

'So what do you make of the tablets, Guv?'

'I think they're the same, aren't they?'

'It looks like the identical packaging as those we found on the island.'

Skelgill shrugs.

'See what the boffins make of them when we get back, eh?'

'Sure, Guv.'

DS Jones pats her attaché case. Within is an evidence bag containing two packets of capsules discovered in Rich Buckley's desk. Miss Constance Belgrave, having retrieved the spare keys from their hidey hole inside a fake English dictionary, had appeared familiar with the general layout and contents of the drawers, and was patently surprised when the medicine was uncovered beneath a sheaf of overdue invoices and unsigned authors' royalty cheques. As regards the retreat, there was no documentary evidence to be found – in fact the publisher clearly operated on a very minimalistic system of paperwork altogether.

'Sounds like he was a nasty piece of work, Guv.'

Skelgill nods, his features grim.

'Usually people just avoid folk like that – killing them's a bit extreme.'

DS Jones looks expectantly at her superior – but he appears to have concluded his judgment and says no more. They walk on a little in silence – they are heading for Farringdon tube station – there has been a small change in their plans, in that they have concluded they will not fit all three remaining interviews into the time available, and are about to divide and conquer as far as Angela Cutting and Burt Boston are concerned. The former lives in Regent's Park, while the latter has an address near Paddington – the Circle Line will serve them both, Skelgill alighting first at Great Portland Street, while DS Jones must continue for four more stops to the west. Roughly contemporaneously, DS Leyton – supplied by digital means with the information that Rich Buckley was embroiled in divorce proceedings – ought to be en route (by taxi) to the exclusive village of Bray on Thames, to meet with the late publisher's spouse.

'Those books they publish, Guv – I noticed there's a distinctive *RBP* logo on the spine.'

'Aye?'

'Dickie Lampray had quite a few of them on his shelves.'

Skelgill scoffs.

'Probably for personal use.'

DS Jones chuckles.

'He's certainly a bit of an oddball, Guv – but I got the impression he's quite harmless.'

'They thought that about Crippen. He's probably got his last partner buried under the back patio. I'm surprised the dog didn't wander in with a human tibia in its jaws.'

She shakes her head in affected wonderment at Skelgill's little fancy.

'How did his manner compare to when you'd met him before, Guv?'

'Definitely a bit edgy – but they'd already broken out the gin and tonic by the time I turned up.'

'There's more of a connection with Rich Buckley than he was willing to admit.'

Skelgill nods but remains silent.

'I suppose it's only natural, Guv – for people to distance themselves – when there's some degree of suspicion – he must realise we have to investigate for foul play.'

'Aye – he might be odd, but he's canny with it.'

'Constance Belgrave, too, Guv.'

Skelgill grins and shakes his head.

'What is it, Guv?'

'She reminded me of a maths teacher we had – she would have been retired by the time you went up to the High School. Everyone thought she was a right frigid old battle-axe – until one evening a couple of girls dropped into the classroom after hockey practice and caught her cavorting in the store cupboard with the caretaker.' He beams broadly at the memory. 'Her name was Miss Trimble – Annie – you can imagine what she got called after that.'

DS Jones looks puzzled.

'This sounds like a cryptic crossword clue, Guv.'

'I'll leave you to work it out – but it's a lot easier than that, Jones.'

9. ANGELA CUTTING

Tuesday 1pm

As Skelgill strides purposefully northwards along Regent's Park's magnificent Outer Circle, the weather seems to be living up to its unseasonal billing, for he carries his jacket slung over his shoulder, one finger hooked through the coat loop. The sun, however, is already dipping past its zenith, and slanting golden rays tint the whitewashed neo-classical façade of Nash's Cumberland Terrace (the name a coincidence that has not escaped his attention). Here, property prices comfortably exceed their telephone numbers, and Skelgill would be excused for feeling a little daunted as he seeks out his destination.

About fifty yards ahead two stout ladies approach him, led by a pair of majestic Dalmatians, ears pricked and a spring in their step, though they trot with no sign of strain upon the leash. As they near a long black limousine with smoked glass windows, there is a blast of what surely must be the loudest motor horn in England. Though the noble carriage dogs are unperturbed, the women start in unison and frown their disapproval. Skelgill, too, seems cross, and his left hand strays to his hip pocket where his warrant card is stowed for safety. Perhaps he is tempted to remind the driver that it is an offence to honk whilst stationary, and also to idle – but any such ideas are dispelled when Angela Cutting emerges elegantly from a smartly painted front door and coolly raises a hand in his direction. Since he is precisely on time, it would appear she has been waiting inside the porch for his arrival.

Her slender form is draped in an ankle-length white fur – mink it would appear, with a contrasting trim of striped black and grey – and her heels are even more precipitous than those she wore at Grisholm, bringing her within an inch or two of Skelgill's height. Her raven hair is parted and pulled tightly over her skull, and the angled sunshine creates a two-tone effect of highlight and shadow. Her dark eyes are made up as if in readiness for Halloween – just a few days hence – and combine with her aquiline features to amplify her vampish mien. She seems pleased to see Skelgill and her scarlet lips part slowly in a sensuous smile that reveals her even white teeth with their gently pointed canines. Still on the step, she glances down as the distressed dog walkers bustle between them, her gaze drawn by the Dalmatians as though she might covet their striking coats. They pass and she extends a gloved hand to Skelgill.

'Inspector, how delightful to see you again – I am afraid, however, that something has come up – I have an interview – perhaps I can take you for lunch in order that I may keep my appointment?' She gestures casually towards the standing limousine. 'They have sent their car.'

Skelgill seems a little put out. His theory about the disarming quality of home turf has been turned on its head: this is Angela Cutting in her element – demonstrating an assertiveness that is not easily resisted. Any hopes he might harbour for a swift debriefing and a nice little stop-off at a café he has spotted near Great Portland Street station now have to be abandoned.

'Well – if it's okay by you, madam.' He still has his jacket slung over his shoulder, and makes a sign with his free hand to indicate his general attire. 'But I'm not exactly dressed for it.'

She surveys him with an appraising glance.

'Oh, no – it is very casual – and this *is* London, Inspector – it's not what you wear, it's *how* you wear it.'

Skelgill – never one likely to win any awards for sartorial elegance – appears uncertain of how to interpret this potentially ambiguous statement, but before he can fashion a reply Angela Cutting interjects.

'I would have one condition, Inspector?'

'Madam?'

'I thought we had agreed you would call me *Ange* in private?' She smiles archly. 'I shouldn't think our conversation is going to be overheard.'

Their journey is not a long one. From Regent's Park they are chauffeured briefly east on Euston Road, then south the full length of Gower Street to High Holborn. She points out features of interest en route, such as the nineteenth century properties formerly inhabited by Charles Darwin and – for twenty-first century television purposes only – Sherlock Holmes. Skelgill nods appreciatively; though in the soporific cocoon of the luxury car he spends much of the trip sunk deep in the comfortable leather upholstery, rather like a dental patient under conscious sedation – though perhaps it is the invisible tentacles of his companion's *No.5* that bind him in a cloud of bemused torpor. Soon they pick up Shaftesbury Avenue as it slices between Soho and Covent Garden. A final left turn takes them into the fringe of the latter district, where they draw up just short of Upper St Martin's Lane in a little confluence of narrow streets, outside what resembles – from ground level, at least – a diminutive Art Deco version of New York's Flatiron Building. There is a theatre opposite advertising *The Mousetrap* – and Skelgill might be excused for wondering if he has nodded off and become part of some murder mystery in his dreams.

He is shaken from any such musings by a blast of cool air and traffic noise as the soundproofed door is carefully opened by the muscular figure of a commissionaire, the man complete with top hat and frock coat, and polished black brogues that click to attention. Skelgill, having been last to get in, is first to clamber out and – unused to such protocols – he hovers uncertainly beside the vehicle, neither assisting Angela Cutting nor enabling the doorman to lend a supportive hand. However, she rises elegantly and they are swiftly ushered inside a narrow wood-panelled lobby where a standing crowd of would-be diners blocks their passage. Leading Skelgill unobtrusively by the cuff, Angela Cutting pushes through the overcoated throng to a doorway where they are held at bay by a dinner-jacketed *maître d'* – he looks stern, but his countenance changes as he recognises her and produces a honeyed, 'Ah, Madame – of course – come this way, please'. The main interior, dictated by the flatiron, is roughly triangular and they are led to a two-seater bench table facing back into the room from the middle of what is the triangle's hypotenuse, giving them, seated side-by-side, a panoramic view of the entire restaurant. While Skelgill dutifully holds her handbag, a waiting minion assists Angela Cutting in slipping from her mink to reveal a striking black silk mini dress that clings to her lithe figure and seems to leave little scope for underwear beneath. Plain gold jewellery is strategically placed about her person.

Skelgill watches with apparent alarm as a napkin is spread over his partner's lap, and then seems surprised when the same service is performed for him. He might reflect on how they have walked into such a prime table – with a queue of hopefuls waiting, the place packed to the gunwales, and no indication of a prior reservation. There is a cacophony of chatter and the clinking bustle of serving as white-shirted staff, impeccable in bow ties and waistcoats, heave to and fro. He looks about – perhaps in wonderment that this is a mere Wednesday lunchtime in late October – and becomes conscious that eyes flick in their direction, dropping away as his own gaze falls upon them. But Angela Cutting seems completely at ease; she watches him for a moment with an amused smile teasing the corners of her mouth.

As if by magic a wine waiter has materialised before them proffering a chilled bottle. He hovers in a manner suggestive that Skelgill should taste its contents. Angela Cutting touches him lightly on the forearm.

'I have a preferred Chablis, Inspector.' Skelgill inhales as if he might protest, but she anticipates his objection. 'I appreciate you may not wish to drink since you are on duty – but a bottle allows for at least a sip or two.'

Skelgill shrugs. 'When in Rome.' He holds out his glass. Frowning, and taking half a pace backward, the sommelier decants a little, which Skelgill promptly swallows. 'Perfect.'

The waiter nods, rather superciliously, it must be said – and then rounds to pour for Angela Cutting before returning to

Skelgill. He does not demur, although he leaves the glass untouched and waits for a moment while a lesser-ranking second server darts forward to charge their crystal tumblers with sparkling mineral water – and drinks half down. He places the glass carefully upon its coaster and, with his head lowered in a rather confiding manner, leans a little towards his dining partner.

'I get the feeling you have some admirers.'

Angela Cutting, who has mirrored his movement, brings her wine goblet to her lips and gazes at him conspiratorially over its rim.

'Oh – I rather think it is *you* they are looking at, Inspector.'

Skelgill perhaps does not grasp the nuance in her words – that curious onlookers, if indeed there are such, are likely speculating about *who* it is *with her*, rather than who it is for his own sake. However, this line of inquiry is interrupted by the return of the *maître d'*, who exchanges pleasantries and confirms that their table is satisfactory and offers to take their food order. Angela Cutting turns to Skelgill.

'Since we are short on time, may I recommend to you the steak pie and chips?'

Skelgill grins, as though he thinks she must be joking. She detects his hesitation, and elaborates accordingly.

'It is one of their most popular productions – almost a signature dish.'

Skelgill glances at the *maître d'*, who nods in confirmation.

'Can't argue with that – saves me choosing something in French and hoping it's a mammal.'

Angela Cutting smiles.

'Birds are okay, are they not? Even in French?'

'Not if they're an Ortolan.'

'Good point, Inspector.'

'Then there's the matter of foie gras.'

Angela Cutting shakes her head in apparent sympathy with his view.

'Sadly, *très délicieux*.'

Skelgill nods and evidently decides to call it quits – perhaps before the language gets any further beyond his limits.

'What are you going to have?'

She pouts an indecisive kiss, but only for a brief moment.

'I never can resist the lobster – though it is to the garlic butter in which it swims that I rather suspect I am addicted.'

She looks at the *maître d'*, and dismisses him with a flutter of her eyelids. He backs rather obsequiously from the table.

Skelgill frowns.

'Won't that be a bit – you, know – inappropriate for your job interview?'

She tilts back her head and laughs – though her manner is generous, and she takes a gulp of wine as though to demonstrate a point.

'I ought to have explained, Inspector – it is not *that* kind of interview – it is for the *Book Programme*.'

Skelgill looks suddenly embarrassed, and a little flush of colour rushes to highlight his prominent cheekbones. It has obviously not occurred to him that it could be an interview in which she calls the shots.

'Aye – well, you'll look very good – I shall keep an eye out for you on the telly.'

Again she rests a palm upon his sleeve.

'I appreciate your chivalry, Inspector – though I rather suspect from what you said at Grisholm Hall that it is not your regular viewing – and do not fret – why should it be – I prefer you the way you are – an unpretentious man of action.'

Skelgill folds his hands together on the white tablecloth and glances about nervously, as if he is concerned about eavesdroppers. However, her earlier assertion is accurate; the ambient cacophony creates a little bubble of privacy around their table. But he might wonder what purpose her compliment serves – and also he must be conscious they have limited time and he has questions to ask. Indeed, he shakes his head modestly and contrives to engineer a link from one to the other.

'The last you saw of me – *Ange*,' (he stresses the name to please her) 'I was being shepherded off to bed – not exactly action man.'

'I was sad to see you go, Inspector – we were quite a team.'

Skelgill raises an eyebrow, and his manner becomes more serious.

'Now one player down.'

'Ah, very unfortunate – poor Bella.'

'I must ask you, Ange – what transpired after I went to bed?'

Angela Cutting takes a drink of wine and – the amount consumed having passed halfway – someone in uniform is there to top it up.

'Little of note, if I recall, Inspector. *Scrabble* was won, our lead was unassailable – we packed that away and after a while, at that preposterous imposter Burt Boston's insistence, tried a game of charades – but it never really got off the ground. It descended into general chit-chat around the fire, with some people drifting in and out of slumber on the spot.'

'How about Bella Mandrake – can you remember how she was?'

'She had been rather disturbed all evening – in fact ever since Rich's body was found – though she was prone to drama at the least excuse – she was also well oiled, as no doubt you could tell, Inspector.'

Skelgill nods. There is nothing here he does not already know.

'When did she go to bed?'

Angela Cutting picks up her glass and swills the pale golden liquid around. The restaurant has extensive windows, leaded in a fine diamond pattern with a harlequin-like mixture of coloured and opaque glass. The sun, which from its low autumn meridian cannot be shining directly into the room, is finding a way by means of successive reflections to radiate gently upon their table.

'I can't actually recall – no wait, Sarah and I went upstairs together – Bella had insinuated herself between Burt and Dickie – I wasn't paying too much attention, since I was discussing Frankfurt with Sarah.'

'Frankfurt?'

Angela Cutting smiles patiently.

'The world's largest book fair, Inspector – it was earlier in the month.'

Skelgill nods. However, he spurns any temptation to digress.

'Despite your conversation – can you remember who else was left in the drawing room as you left?'

'I think only little Lucy had gone to bed.' She closes her eyes momentarily, revealing lids artfully smeared with peacock blue translucence. 'But maybe the elderly doctor chap – Gerald Bond – as well.' I am afraid you might have to ask the others if you wish to piece together the situation.'

Skelgill shrugs as if it is not of too much importance.

'But Bella Mandrake – apart from her behaviour as you described – there was nothing to suggest she might be liable to take an overdose of sleeping pills?'

Angela Cutting flashes him a suddenly stern glance.

'I truly hope it was an accident, Inspector?'

Skelgill is silent.

'You don't think otherwise, surely?'

Skelgill tilts his head from one side to the other.

'There's going to be a Coroner's inquest – we just have to keep an open mind while we gather all the available facts. There are strict rules governing the certification of deaths.'

Angela Cutting regards him pensively.

'And this applies to Rich, as well?'

Skelgill nods.

'I spoke with Mr Lampray this morning – he suggested you might be able to cast some light on Mr Buckley's state of health – that you were one of the last to be with him on the night before he died?'

For the first time a hint of discomfort disrupts Angela Cutting's measured demeanour. Her eyes narrow and there is a just-discernable tensing of the fingers that caress the contours of her glass. She takes a drink and rolls the wine around her mouth like a connoisseur performing a tasting exercise.

'Dickie is right – although, I am afraid to say, I left Rich in Bella's clutches – he seemed not unhappy with that. As for his health – I should say he was as vigorous as ever.'

Her intonation, though flat, has a brooding quality, as though she is reassessing the virtues of her actions. There is also a suggestion that Skelgill might have trespassed upon her hospitality, via a question that points to uncomfortable territory. But, for him, foraging beyond the pale is his bread and butter, and he takes another speculative step.

'His secretary complained that he could be a bit forward with the ladies.'

The statement is an invitation for Angela Cutting to confirm or deny, but she is evidently too wily a vixen to allow herself to be cornered.

'Oh – one man's *forward* is another man's missed opportunity, Inspector.'

The reply – accompanied by a beguiling smile – is cryptic, to say the least, but Skelgill grins back as if he gets her drift, and she seems satisfied.

'Rich talked a good game, Inspector – I shouldn't go too much by what you hear.'

Skelgill nods.

'How well did you know him?'

Now Angela Cutting enfolds the base of her wine glass with the fingers of both hands, her long, perfectly manicured nails meeting like a gathering of red soldier beetles.

'At a personal level – only superficially – in publishing circles there are continual events – launches, ceremonies, conferences – we float about afterwards with cheese and wine and make pleasantries as if we are all old friends. RBP has been on an upward trajectory for some years – Rich was the driving force, so he was widely known to many in the book trade.'

Skelgill nods.

'Were you surprised to find he was at the writers' retreat?'

'Not at all, Inspector.'

Her reply is quite matter-of-fact and suggests she feels no need to elucidate. Skelgill probes further.

'I just wondered what would take a busy man away from his work for a week or more.'

Angela Cutting chooses to interpret the question as if it is obliquely aimed at her.

'Why not a few days away from it all – no digital interference, an idyllic location, a blind date or two?' She bats her eyelashes mischievously. 'And an attractive fee.'

'Which may not be paid.'

Now she shrugs indifferently.

'So I understand from one of your constables, Inspector.'

If the loss of her fee is an issue, she does not show it. Skelgill reverts to her allusion to romantic liaisons.

'Do you think Mr Buckley was availing himself of – as you put it – blind dates?'

Now her demeanour becomes distinctly coy. She leans back against the settle and folds her hands demurely on the edge of the table.

'Though I was in the next room to Rich, the thick walls in that old place definitely do not have ears, Inspector. Of course, one senses movement in adjoining chambers, and footsteps crossing the landing – but there is nothing I could put my finger on.'

'You mean you heard something?'

'Oh, I'm sure there was the odd bump in the night – but I was safely tucked up in bed – I hadn't bargained for the cold and it would have taken wild horses to drag me out to investigate – even had I been so inclined. And unlike yourself, Inspector, I am a very deep sleeper.'

Purposefully, she regards him as if she anticipates a challenge – but after a second or two, since he does not react, she relents and stretches languidly. She lifts her napkin casually from her lap and begins to rise from the table.

'If you will excuse me, Inspector, I shall just powder my nose before our food arrives.'

Skelgill has no alternative but to acquiesce with good grace. When Angela Cutting returns, their order immediately follows – as if their table has been under sympathetic observation –beneath glinting silver cloches borne shoulder high and delivered to their place settings with a practised flourish. At this juncture Skelgill's baser instincts kick in, and his attention gains a new focus. He is easy meat, therefore, for an enlivened Angela Cutting. Their conversation – thus far a game of subtle but intense fencing – becomes relaxed, and ranges widely. Playing to his ego, she leads him across hill and dale – and lake – by quizzing him about his Cumbrian homeland and his exploits on and off duty. When the region's gourmet reputation comes up, she asks to try a small taste of his pie, and reciprocates by feeding him a bite of precious lobster from her fork. If this is a ploy to eat up their available time, it succeeds – for Angela Cutting seems suddenly to realise she may be late and signals to the staff that she wishes to depart.

The *maître d'* seems to take excessive pleasure in handing the bill to Skelgill. Heroically he reaches for his battered wallet – his eyebrows unable to conceal his reaction at setting a Beamonesque personal best for the price of a pie supper – but his attempt to pay is thwarted by Angela Cutting, who reaches across and pins down his hands with her own.

'Oh no, Inspector – you are my guest – it is I that brought us here.' Skelgill begins to protest, but she continues. 'Not only do I have an account – but in any event I can claim this back.' She slides the black leather presenter from his grasp and returns it to the waiting *maître d'*, who clicks his heels and – without a glance at Skelgill – bows briefly at Angela Cutting and turns away.

Skelgill holds up his wallet.

'Perhaps I can leave the tip?'

She shakes her head.

'It is already included, Inspector – London practice.'

'Well – thanks very much – I wasn't expecting this... Ange.'

His addition of her name sounds rather dutiful, but she smiles appreciatively and again reaches to press his nearest hand.

'I am only sorry I was unable to entertain you at my home, Inspector – but perhaps there will be another occasion.'

Her intonation makes this more of a statement than a question, but as Skelgill follows her towards the exit he again seems distracted by the trailing glances of other diners, and his response is rather vague.

'We have a six o'clock train for Penrith.'

127

Angela Cutting is reunited with her five-figure mink coat and Skelgill watches respectfully as she wriggles into the garment and then tips the young female cloakroom assistant. As the street door is opened for them, Skelgill allows her to go ahead of him. The limousine is drawn up directly outside, but as she moves towards it the figure of a man blocks her path, with another close beside him.

'Oh, not now, please – I'm already late.'

Angela Cutting's response suggests she is accustomed to such unsolicited approaches – but her subsequent sharp intake of breath winds back this notion; the man is brandishing a knife.

'Oh, my word.'

Automatically Skelgill steps between them. In this stand-off neither party speaks, but as Skelgill holds up his right palm in a placatory gesture the assailant with a lupine snarl raises the glinting blade to shoulder level as though he is about to strike.

And now, in one of those curious blink-of-an-eye and yet slow-motion moments, a flashing left hook sinks into the man's jaw and transforms his expression of hostile aggression through a sequence of surprise, shock, fear and pain, and his face becomes a distorted mask of anguish – all in the split second before his lights go out and the force of Skelgill's punch slams him against the car, thence to collapse limp upon the sidewalk. The knife clatters onto the ground and slides harmlessly beneath the vehicle.

Angela Cutting screams and staggers back in horror. She is prompted not by the sudden explosion of violence, but because the knifeman's accomplice – with remarkable opportunism and an impressive disregard for his partner in crime – snatches her designer handbag, vaults his stupefied ex-ally and hot-foots it in the direction of Soho. In response, Skelgill tears off his jacket, thrusts it into the hands of the thus-far immobilised doorman (so much for his imposing presence), and sprints away in pursuit.

When he returns grim-faced just over two minutes later there is a trickle of blood dripping from his brow. One of his trouser legs seems to have a rip at the knee. His hair is dishevelled and flopping down over his forehead. But his left hand has the arm of the mugger firmly – in fact *very* firmly – twisted and rammed hard up between his shoulder blades, as he is marched squealing to face justice. In Skelgill's right hand is Angela Cutting's handbag, still fastened and apparently none the worse for its little adventure.

Already three uniformed beat bobbies are on the scene. They have the recovering, if clinically concussed, knifeman in handcuffs, and are delighted to relieve Skelgill of his new charge and subdue him likewise (with the handcuffs, rather than the concussion). Skelgill shows his warrant card to the more senior officer – a few words suffice to explain his presence, and role in the incident; indeed the police have already gleaned from Angela Cutting and the doorman what has transpired. And now official vehicles, sirens blaring and ignoring the local one-way system, arrive from all directions to block off the narrow streets. A crowd gathers, rather as though this is another one of those impromptu Covent Garden street performances.

10. LUCY HECATE

Tuesday 3pm

When Skelgill rings the bell to Lucy Hecate's apartment the blood has long ceased to drip from the nick on his forehead caused by the crook's heel as he brought him crashing down to earth in Greek Street. A hand in one pocket, absently he fingers the silk scarf Angela Cutting pressed upon him – literally so, as she tended to his wound with a concern worthy of a more serious injury. She had purred throatily, a fire in her eyes and a heat in her touch that saw him acquiesce when ordinarily he would have shrugged off such a minor inconvenience. But her intimate on-street ministrations were short lived. Effusive in her thanks and profound in her apologies, she was obliged to yield to the combined exhortations of her mobile phone, the driver, and the advancing hour – the television studio could wait only so long. She had insisted that Skelgill retain the flimsy garment – and that he must soon allow her to thank him properly – before she had planted a full-bodied kiss upon his unsuspecting lips and retreated into the car like a reluctant hermit crab that knows the ebb tide is about to claim her shell.

For his part Skelgill had melted into the watching throng – in good part Australian tourists mesmerised by the sight of the sulking criminals awaiting deportation – and for the past forty-five minutes he has wandered the streets of Soho, stopping once for a sandwich in a small café, and later purchasing a chocolate bar from a minimarket. His amblings have brought him full circle, since his next destination is barely two hundred yards from the restaurant, a short way down a narrow street that forms one of the spokes of Seven Dials. He checks his watch – he is on time, but DS Jones has not made their rendezvous. A text message has informed him that she is en route on foot from Paddington, where sudden industrial action has closed the London Underground and trapped all available taxis in the ensuing gridlock.

While Skelgill waits he pulls out the white scarf and stares at it pensively. A passer by – not knowing him – might reasonably speculate that he is wondering which washing cycle will remove bloodstains from so delicate an item. However, this would not be a successful wager. Indeed, there are probably no odds long enough to represent such a possibility. More likely he revisits the memory of the moment he restored the handbag to its owner. Despite the confused aftermath of the stramash and his need for first aid, Angela Cutting had keenly checked an internal zip pocket, before producing the scarf as an improvised dressing. And maybe he rues a failure to explore certain lines of enquiry that – clear to him as he walked about afterwards – at the time were subsumed in the blur and bustle of the restaurant, such as rumours there might be concerning Rich Buckley's financial status, marriage, or recreational habits; and about what liaisons or rivalries may have surfaced on the island – either among the professionals or the amateurs, or between members of both camps. Certainly Angela Cutting – hovering above them all, as Dickie Lampray put it – is well placed to possess knowledge and opinions on these matters. But has she contrived, by orchestrating a highly ritualised luncheon, to keep Skelgill's questioning to its most superficial level? Has her siren call, having drawn him out of his depth, had him treading water while the minutes ticked by? Or should he just remind himself that, after all, these are witnesses not suspects he is interviewing, and anything other than gentle probing is wholly inappropriate? And yet, if his gut instinct is to be trusted – that the haunting sense of suspicion regarding events at Grisholm Hall has some substance – then they are neither witnesses nor suspects, but grey ghosts that drift in between.

'Please come up – it's the only door on the first floor.'

Even through the metallic intercom Lucy Hecate's voice has a girlish quality – simple, plain enunciation, well spoken without being affected; a clipped soprano to Angela Cutting's husky contralto. Skelgill, wrapping up his thoughts, is too slow to reply. There is the rattle of the handset being replaced on its cradle, and the microphone is cut off. An electric buzz sounds from within the jamb as the lock is released from above. The stair is entered not directly from the street, but from a triangular piazza, reached through lockable gates, that provides similar access to several such sets of apartments. On the ground floor are boutiques and a design business – the sunken courtyard affords partial tiptoe views into their rear windows, and glimpses through to the streets beyond. Skelgill has already recced this area, and has determined which first-floor windows must pertain to Lucy Hecate's accommodation – each of these covered by plain roller blinds drawn down to sill level.

'Hello, Inspector.'

'Lucy.'

Skelgill bows his head and smiles inoffensively. He has evidently decided to employ first-name terms.

'Please come in.'

Lucy Hecate steps aside and holds open the sprung front door. She waits for a moment after he has entered, and glances back into the empty landing.

'My sergeant has been delayed – she's caught up in the tube strike.'

'Oh, I see.'

She fastens the latch and holds out an arm to indicate that Skelgill should turn left. He goes ahead of her into a small sitting room. The windows give on to the narrow street below, and face similar apartments opposite, thus requiring heavy net curtains for daytime privacy. A pair of navy blue cubist sofas makes a right angle either side of the entrance, though where there might be a television set instead a wall-mounted electric fire provides the focal point. A large arty print adorns each of the three walls, but otherwise there is little biographical detail to describe the flat's occupant. On the coffee table lie a slim aluminium laptop and a black e-reader, illuminated at a page of text. Since these appear to reserve Lucy Hecate's place on the right-hand settee, Skelgill lowers himself down on that to the left of the door. She, however, remains standing.

'Tea, Inspector – although I only have Earl Grey, I'm afraid?'

Skelgill, who has been known to express colourful non-PC opinions about men who drink Earl Grey tea, nods vigorously.

'Very kind of you, Lucy – milk and three sugars, please.'

The cramped galley kitchen is immediately across the little hallway, although Skelgill would have to peer around the door to see his hostess, so despite her proximity he opts to check his messages while she readies the tea-things against the background rumble of a kettle. The apartment has just two other rooms – their white panelled doors matching those of the lounge and kitchen – and, by a process of elimination, these must be a bathroom that overlooks the internal courtyard and a small bedroom facing the street side. It would appear, therefore, that the petite property is only suitable for single occupancy – or for a couple who get on well together and own very few possessions.

Skelgill watches as Lucy Hecate carries in two mugs of tea and a plate of mini Swiss rolls – his antennae have detected the crackle of cellophane, and here is the explanation. The china mugs are decorated with rather clumsy illustrations of freshwater fish, and Skelgill might wonder if they have been selected as a conversation piece – he gets a too-pink salmon, while she has an overenthusiastically mottled trout. However, he chooses not to remark, and instead dips his nose into the tea and watches as she settles down gracefully across from him. She is dressed rather in the manner of a ballet dancer in training gear, a faded grey-and-pink ensemble of pumps, rucked legwarmers, calf-length leggings, and a wrap-top over what might be a leotard. The effect is to emphasise her dainty frame and careful movements, and she perches on the edge of the sofa with a curve in her spine that contrasts with Skelgill's somewhat more relaxed slouch. He swallows a mouthful of the hot tea and smacks his lips.

'Very good – I'm parched – it's thirsty work getting around London.'

Lucy Hecate regards him quizzically.

'I would have thought for a fell-runner it would be easy, since it is so flat.'

Skelgill grins modestly.

'Maybe it's age catching up with me.'

She gazes at him, unblinking.

'Wasn't Bob Graham forty-two when he achieved his landmark round?'

Skelgill affects a little jerk of surprise.

'Actually, Lucy – he was forty-three – but I'm impressed you've even heard of him.'

She permits herself an abridged smile.

'There was a book on the history of fell running in the library at Grisholm Hall.' Her long blonde hair is drawn back into a ponytail, but a few strands have escaped, and she pauses to brush these from her face. 'It's hard to imagine how anyone can run for twenty-four hours in that rugged terrain.'

This is something of a gift horse for Skelgill, an invitation to expound upon his own exploits, and he pulls back his shoulders as though he is about to do so. Then it appears some thought must strike him – or at least an underlying sense that any such showing-off will not in fact win bouquets from this young woman. Her tone is flat and reserved, and her cool façade suggests impregnability to endearing advances. Accordingly, Skelgill's considered response – albeit a little out of character – endeavours to turn the spotlight back upon her.

'Are you writing about the Lakes – is that why you were reading the book?'

Lucy Hecate is cradling the mug between her two hands, like a hiker on a cold day – indeed the flat is far from warm – and she takes a small sip before she replies.

'I read as widely as I can, Inspector. Though the Lake District would make a good backdrop for a mystery – but I think Sarah Redmond will beat us all to it.'

Skelgill's expression is politely inquisitive.

'In what way?'

'She hinted that she intends to kill off her Edinburgh detective – Frances Furlough.'

'And start again with a new one based in Cumbria?'

'I got that impression, Inspector.'

Skelgill shakes his head.

'No one would believe it – like I said the other night, nothing ever happens.'

A pair of little furrows forms between Lucy Hecate's fair eyebrows.

'Except at Grisholm Hall.'

Now Skelgill folds his arms.

'Aye – but two natural – or at worst accidental – deaths are not going to make a great whodunit, Lucy.'

In employing the words *natural* and *accidental* Skelgill may simply be toeing the official line. However, another interpretation could be that it is a subtle test of her reaction – for he does indeed elicit one; the creases between her brows deepen, and her expression becomes openly puzzled.

'But why are you investigating?'

Skelgill unfolds his arms and leans forward in an avuncular manner. 'It's out of our hands. When the Coroner's involved – which can be for a minor technicality – we have to go through the motions. You did the right thing, Lucy – in trying to attract assistance.' He scratches his head absently. 'Not that I was much help.'

'I felt we ought to do something – we might not have sat idly by if we had been at a retreat on the shore.'

Skelgill nods sympathetically.

'If you'd have been on the shore Mr Buckley might have phoned a doctor and had treatment in time. Ms Mandrake might not have got herself in a confused state. I might have caught my record pike.'

Skelgill falls silent, no doubt recalling his outstanding bet. Lucy Hecate watches calmly. She does not react to his ironic reference to his curtailed fishing trip, but instead – in her characteristic fashion – she points out the obvious facts.

'We did have a doctor, Inspector. Dr Bond has been retired for only two years. He stated at the welcome meeting that since we were rather isolated anyone should feel free to consult with him.'

'But Mr Buckley didn't call upon his services?'

'He may have done, Inspector – I don't know. Though I saw them talking on several occasions.'

Again Skelgill thinks for a moment before proceeding.

'How did everyone react when Mr Buckley was found to have died?'

She looks at him as if this is a rather superfluous question.

'There was initial shock, as you would expect – although Dr Bond and Mr Lampray announced it to the rest of us, so it was handled in a professional manner. Apart from Bella, I was a little surprised by how quickly the others took it in their stride.'

'You're quite a lot younger than the rest.' Skelgill seems to be implying that her elders were more phlegmatic in the face of bereavement.

'I'm twenty-six.'

He regards her searchingly. She does not look twenty-six – after all, that is the same age as DS Jones; and it is unimaginable that this waiflike creature could command the authority among hard-bitten adults that his colleague demonstrates daily. Yet, he ought not be surprised – he has this information already. Among the details collected before the members of the retreat departed were their ages: Lucy Hecate the youngest at 26, Sarah Redmond 34, Angela Cutting 37, Bella Mandrake 39, Burt Boston 42, Rich Buckley 45, Linda Gray 46, Dickie Lampray 59 and the retired Dr Gerald Bond 62.

'Did anyone try to put you off – from going outdoors?'

Lucy Hecate is nodding even before Skelgill has finished the question, as if she has been expecting it.

'I got the impression they all thought it was futile.' She twists a strand of hair around a finger. 'Burt Boston said the same things as you did – that it would be pretty impossible to get a signal through the storm – although he was wrong in assuming there would be nobody brave enough to be out on the lake.'

Skelgill winces theatrically at what he takes to be a compliment.

'I think *crackers* is the word you're looking for.'

She stares evenly at him, as though flattery were not on her mind in making the statement.

'Only Dr Bond made any effort to stop me – he said there was a danger of a falling tree – or that I could be washed off the rocks.'

Skelgill grimaces, perhaps in part to conceal his frustration, since she declines to acknowledge his wit.

'It was blowing a bit – but Derwentwater's not exactly Cape Wrath. I'll give him the tree, though – there's always that risk.'

'I felt safer in those woods than in the house.'

Skelgill's eyes narrow – but perhaps he identifies with her sentiment, for he opts not to interrogate her meaning.

'It was bad luck – just when you have no communications, a healthy person goes and has a heart attack.'

'I searched about to see if there were some other means we could use – like an abandoned rowing boat – but Grisholm is rocky all around.'

Skelgill nods; an old beached dinghy, hull uppermost, is not an uncommon sight about the Lakes – but whether such a craft would be watertight is another matter.

'I wondered, Inspector – if your men have searched the island – I lost a knitted scarf somewhere.' Skelgill looks a little surprised, and she backpedals, as if she realises this is asking too much. 'Its only value was sentimental.'

'I'm afraid not, Lucy – at the moment we've no plans to commit that level of resources – this is just a routine matter.' However he appears sorry to disappoint her. 'But you could contact the owners of Grisholm Hall – or at least their agents – I'll get one of my sergeants to send you the details.'

She nods thoughtfully.

'Thank you, Inspector. Actually, I can probably find the number myself.'

Skelgill follows her gaze towards her laptop.

'How was the technology ban received?'

'I think most people felt it was a good idea. It was a retreat, after all.'

Skelgill is silent for a moment.

'You're aware we still haven't managed to trace the organisers?'

Lucy Hecate nods.

'I have forwarded the emails to your officers, Inspector.'

Skelgill runs the fingers of one hand through his hair, avoiding the side of his head that bears the wound.

'Unfortunately – I'm informed by my HQ – emails to that address are being returned as undeliverable.'

'Oh, I see.'

Skelgill looks pensive.

'I mean no disrespect, Lucy – I can understand how it would be easy to identify the likes of Sarah Redmond, she's famous – but how would they know to email you – and the other unpublished authors?'

Lucy Hecate appears to take no offence. Her features remain calm and composed. Then she suddenly seems to remember the untouched plate of Swiss rolls, and leans forward to slide it closer to Skelgill.

'Inspector?'

'Don't mind if I do, thanks.'

'Help yourself – I bought them for you.'

'Very kind.'

She makes a small nod of the head – perhaps in lieu of a "You're welcome" – and watches rather expressionlessly as he takes one of the cakes and bites it in half. Just when it seems she might be intending to skirt around the question, she returns to the point.

'Of course, it could have been random spam – I receive plenty of emails for products and services I never use – but I think that is unlikely. Most probably they are obtaining lists of people who have shown interest in writing courses, that kind of thing.'

'Have you – shown an interest?'

She nods.

'I subscribe to several e-newsletters – for instance, from writers' centres that I have registered with, and online book groups – and second-hand booksellers probably rent out their lists.'

Skelgill nods pensively, as though he has not considered this possibility.

'Was it costly?'

Lucy Hecate seems perplexed, as if she understands what he means but wonders why he is asking her something he already knows.

'The retreat – at Grisholm Hall?'

'Aye. It can't have been cheap.'

'It was free, Inspector.'

Now it is Skelgill's turn to look confused. Plainly, this is news to him.

'But how does that stack up? Someone must have paid for the whole shebang.'

Lucy Hecate looks like she doesn't entirely agree.

'It is not unprecedented, Inspector.'

She leans over and wakes her laptop with a tap upon the touchpad. Her fingers are slender and her nails short, unbitten and unvarnished. Deftly she types in a search term, and clicks upon the first result.

'Look – here is one in Scotland.'

Skelgill cranes to see, but the reflected light from the windows and the acute angle makes it difficult for him to discern the display. Before he can move, Lucy Hecate scoops up the laptop and steps nimbly over his outstretched feet. She drops lightly beside him. The matching sofas, in keeping with the restricted proportions of the apartment, are small, and their hips and elbows touch. She points her toes and balances the machine on her knees. Skelgill seems rather discomfited by her closeness, and sits rigidly, with his hands folded upon his lap.

'This entire castle is given over year-round to writers. If your application is successful you stay for a whole month. All board and lodging is free of charge. It holds six people at a time. There is a full live-in staff who cook and clean.'

'Where is it?'

'Near... *Peebles*?'

Skelgill nods, though he does not turn his head to look at her. 'It's on the upper Tweed.' Much of his knowledge of Scottish geography is based upon his experience of depriving its waters of their fish. 'But if the writers don't pay, who does?'

Lucy Hecate clicks on the 'About Us' tab. Details appear of a long-dead billionaire philanthropist of popular food brand fame.

'This one is supported by a private trust. Some of them are funded by quangos. For those that charge, there are often grants and bursaries.'

'So what about Grisholm Hall – what was the process there?'

'You just had to respond to the email and state how you would benefit from being on the retreat and why you would be a good contributing member of the group.'

'What did you say?'

Lucy Hecate pauses for a moment, as though she is considering whether this is a confidential matter.

'That I was no more deserving than a thousand other aspiring writers.'

Now Skelgill glances at her – but as he does so an alarm sounds in the street outside and he rises purposefully, as if duty bound to investigate any such disturbance. He steps between the coffee table and the other sofa, and parts the net curtains for a better view. Below, there is a traffic warden investigating an illegally parked car, a newly registered sports convertible with its hood down and hazards flashing. An expensively dressed young woman emerges nonchalantly from a boutique and swings a large carrier bag into the passenger seat and drives away, apparently without a word. Skelgill turns to face Lucy Hecate.

'Maybe that's what did the trick – not blowing your own trumpet.'

She does not react and he moves back over, though now he sits in her former place on the empty sofa. He picks up a second Swiss roll and, perhaps prompted by the little slice of London life he has just witnessed, he employs the cake as a baton and makes a sweeping gesture about the apartment.

'Must be pricey living here – how do you manage – we have you down as a student?'

She looks at him evenly.

'That is correct – I am enrolled on a creative writing course – but it is only evening classes.' Now for perhaps the first time she lowers her eyes, as if she is slightly embarrassed. 'I work in retail – nothing permanent – but there are plenty of part-time jobs.'

Skelgill shrugs casually. He has no reason to decry her efforts as a shop girl. Instead he contrives an expression of minor wonderment.

'Whenever I come to London, I always think *what* recession?'

Lucy Hecate nods slowly.

'There is a recession of sorts in the literary world, Inspector. Bookshops are closing every week. Publishers are going out of business or being taken over. Agents are becoming irrelevant.' She indicates her e-reader on the table. 'There is the future of the book – if it is not already the present.'

Skelgill frowns at the small device, as though he disapproves of its presence.

'I can't imagine my *Wainwrights* on one of those. What happens when you're a day's hike into the fells and your battery goes flat?'

'But you use your mobile for navigation, Inspector.'

She phrases this as a statement rather than a question, even though she cannot be certain of the answer. Skelgill shrugs a little sheepishly, to confirm she is correct.

'How about on the retreat – were they all of the old school?'

'Actually, no.' She shakes her head. 'We had a number of discussions about e-books, and I would say just about everyone has embraced them. Mr Buckley gave a talk about how certain, more sensitive, genres are especially compatible with an electronic format.'

Skelgill scowls, as if there is too much jargon for his comfort in this sentence.

'What did you make of him?'

Lucy Hecate looks a little startled, as though it would be above her station to offer an opinion on a leading industry figure.

'I understand he was a very successful publisher.'

'How about on a personal level?'

There is a discernable tightening of her features, rather like a sea anemone that retracts its tentacles in response to the clumsy poke of a child's finger. Skelgill polishes off the remainder of the Swiss roll, and then reaches over to retrieve his mug. He drinks some tea, though the silent hiatus caused by this little procedure does not encourage Lucy Hecate to bloom. Skelgill widens the scope of the question.

'What I mean is, how did he... *interact* with the other members of the group?'

This seems to be a more acceptable form of words.

'I think perhaps the females found him a little intimidating.'

'Verging on predatory?'

'I could not really comment, Inspector. Some people welcome advances that others would find uncomfortable – but I tended to keep to myself in order to optimise my writing time.' Again she coils invisible locks around a crooked index finger. 'Dr Bond argued with him on a couple of occasions – but I imagine you noticed that he was rather opinionated.'

Skelgill raises his eyebrows, as if to indicate his impatience with the good doctor.

'I suppose he's had a lifetime of being listened to.'

Lucy Hecate does not reply. Skelgill continues with the theme.

'How did you get on with the others?'

'Very well.'

For a budding writer, Lucy Hecate is singularly economical with words – but perhaps there is a skill in that. Skelgill is again obliged to supply a prompt.

'Ms Mandrake seemed to ruffle a few feathers.'

Lucy Hecate considers this statement for a moment.

'She was rather self-obsessed. It perhaps does not help a group dynamic when one person seeks all the attention.'

Skelgill nods. Clearly, he witnessed for himself this aspect of Bella Mandrake's character.

'Lucy, you mentioned each person had to outline their contribution – what was hers?'

'She said she was an actress, and that she had a unique insight into written dialogue.'

Skelgill affects a ducking motion, as if to suggest this notion goes over his head.

'I suppose that's quite unusual.'

Again Lucy Hecate offers no comment.

'And the others?'

'Dr Bond... is a doctor. Linda Gray, a chef.'

'Very practical – it's not exactly writing, though.'

'The same could be said of Burt Boston, Inspector.'

'Aye?'

'He said his survival skills would ensure we were kept warm and fed.'

Skelgill scowls disapprovingly.

'The larder seemed well enough stocked – I reckon the red squirrels were safe for a week or two.'

Lucy Hecate stares at Skelgill, as if the idea troubles her.

'And what about you, Lucy – what's your special talent?'

'I can speed read.'

Skelgill grins and raises his mug in a 'cheers' gesture.

'You and me both.' However, this claim is only valid if the definition of speed reading includes it being done by a subordinate, after a cursory scan from Skelgill. 'So, how would that be useful?'

'I offered to proof read other people's work – to review their manuscripts. Bella Mandrake brought a three-hundred-thousand-word romantic novel.'

Skelgill raises his eyebrows.

'And who said romance is dead?'

Lucy Hecate looks rather startled – and Skelgill must suddenly realise that in glibly unfurling this cliché he has sailed into choppy waters. He heaves to and changes tack.

'Are you planning to go on more retreats?'

'I should like to. Though it is easier to gain acceptance once you become published.'

Skelgill looks at her sympathetically.

'I believe that's not easy.'

'Publishers are very blinkered towards untried authors. Unless, perhaps, you are a former *Page 3* model.'

Skelgill shifts uncomfortably in his seat, as if by previous association with any such spectacle he shares some of the blame for the frivolous state of the books business.

'From what I'm hearing, it sounds like you have potential as a writer.'

Lucy Hecate flashes him a wary glance, and then rather glowers at the screen on her lap. Her countenance is stern, and perhaps she has difficulty in receiving the compliment. She makes a little ungracious shrug of her shoulders. Skelgill, however, continues to encourage.

'So don't give up your night job, eh, lass?'

She inhales as though she is about to answer, but there is a sudden sharp buzz of the apartment's intercom. He checks his watch.

'That'll be my sergeant – but I think we've just about finished, Lucy. I'll catch her on my way out.'

11. NEWS OF BURT BOSTON

Tuesday 5pm

'Don't tell me – he's not in the SAS and never has been.'
'You were right from the start, Guv.'
'Apparently he didn't fool Angela Cutting, either.'
'Really? He thinks he carried it off the whole time they were on the island.'

Skelgill shrugs.

'Well, at least one of them was humouring him.'

DS Jones nods ruefully.

'So, would you like to hear the real story?'

'Fire away, sergeant.'

She grins.

'Burt Boston *is* his real name – other than Burt being short for Engelbert.'

Skelgill flashes her a sceptical glance.

'His mother was an opera singer from Cologne – apparently the original Engelbert Humperdinck was a German composer.'

Skelgill shrugs reluctantly.

'And he's gay, Guv.'

'Right.'

'He was quite open about the deception – he told me immediately. He's a masseur. He works from home.'

'Is that an official job?'

'He made a point of telling me he pays all his tax.'

Skelgill shakes his head doubtfully.

'Sounds dodgy to me.'

DS Jones considers Skelgill's assertion.

'Thing is, Guv – there's a probably a market there – for females – who wouldn't generally feel comfortable with a male masseur.'

Skelgill makes a scoffing sound.

'I hope he didn't make you feel too comfortable – else I'll be wondering why you were late.'

'Guv...'

DS Jones makes a disapproving face. However, her determination not to be sidetracked suggests she is convinced by what she has discovered.

'I think he was being pretty straight, Guv – I reckon I'd know. The apartment is set up professionally – there's a plaque downstairs and certificates in the hall – and a treatment room immediately as you enter – a proper massage table and all the fittings.' She grins and adds a postscript. 'And he's got a Chihuahua called Butch.'

'I'm relieved to hear it.'

'He admitted the macho act was to impress the judges, so to speak – he sounds desperate to become an author.'

Skelgill nibbles with uncharacteristic decorum on a piece of shortbread. Having collected his colleague outside Lucy Hecate's apartment, they have walked up through the university district to Euston, where – foot-weary and rather subdued by the stifling air of a chain coffee shop – they await the arrival of DS Leyton, and subsequently their train north. They sit beside one another on a spacious though rather lumpy leather sofa, with a low table for their drinks and Skelgill's snack.

'So, what's the SAS thing all about?'

'It's from one of his clients, who's serving in the army. Apparently he's full of these fantastic adventures – but the Official Secrets Act gags him – so Burt Boston wants to fictionalise them. He figures he'll stand a better chance of getting published if he poses as the soldier.'

'I think he'd find his cover would soon be blown.'

DS Jones nods thoughtfully.

'Though he looks the part, Guv – he might pull it off.'

Skelgill seems a little irked by this observation.

'So long as he doesn't take his Chihuahua to the interview.'

DS Jones smirks agreeably. Skelgill dips the remainder of his biscuit experimentally into the foam on top of his coffee, then quickly withdraws and swallows it.

'So what did he have to say about his comrades at Grisholm Hall?'

DS Jones has her notebook on the table, and flips it open at the page retained by a rubber band. Skelgill squints briefly at the neat lines of shorthand, and then settles back cradling his mug.

'I started off with our inquiry into Wordsworth Writers' Retreats. His experience seems to be identical to the others – an email inviting him to apply, followed by a confirmation. He assumed it was some kind of promotional trick – that he'd be told he hadn't quite satisfied the criteria but he could still participate if he wished to pay – so he was pretty shocked when he received the offer to go free of charge.'

'And no other contact details?'

DS Jones shakes her head.

'He says he thought it was too good to be true – but once he'd been selected he just kept his head down and turned up at the meeting point as instructed.'

Skelgill nods. Lucy Hecate's elucidation of the funding of retreats, and perhaps, too, the details of the fees offered to the experts, has taken some of the mystery out of the otherwise rather unquestioning compliance of those who attended the gathering.

'And then?'

'He says they all settled in quickly – it was a bonus to discover they had a chef in their midst – the place was comfortable enough – the writers got down to work and the specialists contributed when asked. There was a certain amount of late-night drinking – less so among the writers – but generally speaking it was quite orderly and everyone got along.'

'What did he have to say about Rich Buckley?'

'That he liked to be the centre of attention – and to think of himself as a ladies' man – which was a bit awkward at times.'

'In what way?'

DS Jones contrives an old-fashioned look. She refers to her notebook

'To quote, Guv, *"Bet you'd give her one, eh, Burt?"* – which I guess put him in a quandary.'

'In relation to which female?'

'He says it was indiscriminate, Guv – whoever was within ogling range at the time.'

Skelgill seems to be staring aimlessly into space, though perhaps he is picturing the comings and goings about the grand rooms of Grisholm Hall.

'And did anything come of this bravado?'

'Not that he knows of.' She taps her notebook. 'There is one thing, though, Guv. On the night before Rich Buckley died, Burt Boston says he went to fetch a drink of water – he thinks it was about two a.m. – and he found Bella Mandrake on the main landing. She claimed she was doing the same thing, and asked him to go down to the kitchen with her because she was afraid of the dark.'

'Any indication of where she'd come from – or where she was really going?'

DS Jones shakes her head.

'He says he only noticed her when he got within a couple of paces. She was standing still in the middle of the landing.'

'So much for being afraid of the dark.'

'I know, Guv.'

'And do you believe Burt Boston?'

'In what respect, Guv?'

'Remember – the bedrooms are all en suite. If you needed a drink of water, why trail downstairs?'

DS Jones nods reflectively. Skelgill's practical experience on the island has provided him with little insights that otherwise might easily be overlooked.

'Good point, Guv.'

Skelgill shrugs nonchalantly.

'What else?'

'He says he was relieved when you appeared, Guv.'

'How come?'

'They were all expecting him to solve the problem of summoning help – he says he was on the verge of owning up – but once you took over he was able to keep up the pretence.'

Skelgill tuts.

'Like I say, he didn't fool me.'

DS Jones nods respectfully.

'He was generally complimentary about the other members of the retreat. He did ask me if Dickie Lampray had said anything about him.'

'Meaning what?'

'He was a bit cagey, actually, Guv. But then he claimed that Dickie Lampray had remarked that his work had some potential and there might be a possibility of taking him on as a client. It does kind of correspond to what Dickie Lampray told us.'

Skelgill leans his head back on the sofa and gazes at the woodworm-effect tiles of the suspended ceiling.

'Maybe there was an ulterior motive, Jones.'

DS Jones flashes Skelgill a sideways glance, and then briefly makes a face of mock shock- horror. Skelgill rocks forward and puts down his empty mug. He gazes speculatively at the queue at the counter, as if he is contemplating what to have next. He combs back his hair with the fingers of both hands, and DS Jones suddenly notices the blackened smear of dried blood on his temple.

'Guv – what happened? That's quite a bad cut you've got.'

Skelgill glances at her uneasily, and then looks away, as if he is deciding whether or not to relate what took place.

'Bit of a fracas – couple of hoodlums tried to mug Angela Cutting.'

DS Jones looks concerned.

'When was this, Guv?'

'It turned out she had a television interview – so she offered to buy us lunch, to save time – some posh restaurant not far from Lucy Hecate's flat.'

'What was it called?'

Skelgill frowns.

'I can't remember – I mean I didn't really notice – it was opposite a theatre showing *The Mousetrap*.'

Now DS Jones's eyes bulge.

'That's *The Vine*, Guv! It's where all the celebrities go.'

'I didn't see any.'

'There's a permanent six-month waiting list for tables.'

Skelgill shrugs indifferently.

'Well, she just breezed in – they seemed to know her.'

DS Jones squints as though she is trying to recall something.

'So, what happened, Guv?'

'Not a lot. They snatched her bag as we walked out. Between me and the local plod we put a stop to it.'

DS Jones shakes her head, and her expression softens to one of mild wonderment.

'I'm surprised you weren't papped, Guv.'

'Come again?'

'Photographed – the paparazzi are always hanging around there – and *Stringfellows*. It's just around the corner.'

'Why would anyone want to photograph me?'

'I think *I* can answer that one, Guv.'

The two detectives swivel round in surprise – for this voice, complete with its Cockney brogue, belongs to DS Leyton. Rather red in the face, and looking a little dishevelled from his journeying, he has appeared behind them, wheezing lightly, lopsidedly weighed down by his overnight bag, and eagerly brandishing a copy of the afternoon edition of the *Evening Standard*. He rounds their sofa and settles down with some relief in an armchair opposite.

'You certainly made an impact, Guv.'

'What are you talking about, Leyton?'

DS Leyton opens the newspaper and, turning it around, spreads it out over the coffee table for his colleagues to see. He points to a quarter-page photograph and the headline, 'The Bodyguard'.

Skelgill and DS Jones lean forward, Skelgill scowling his disapproval and DS Jones once more wide-eyed. The picture shows Skelgill in the split-second that his fist made contact with the knifeman's jaw. In the background is a shocked-looking Angela Cutting, and the tall figure of a somewhat cowering commissionaire. The sub-heading states: 'Undercover policeman comes to the rescue of well-known literary critic.'

DS Jones pores over the article, and reads aloud.

"'At lunchtime today literary critic and London socialite Angela Cutting was the victim of an attempted mugging by knife-wielding assailants outside *The Vine* restaurant in Covent Garden. Fortunately a mystery detective was on the scene to intervene. Ms Cutting is currently estranged from her boyfriend, former European cruiserweight boxing champion turned Hollywood tough-guy, Vinnie Nails, who is on police bail following a charge for the possession of a Class-A drug.'" She glances up at her colleagues. 'I remember reading about this – I just hadn't made the connection to Angela Cutting.' She returns to the article. "'Restaurant staff would not elaborate upon whether Ms Cutting and the detective had dined together – but if she seeks an able replacement for Mr Nails, it appears she need look no further. The Metropolitan Police reported that two Caucasian males have been detained in custody, but declined to comment upon the circumstances of the arrest.'"

The two sergeants gape at Skelgill, who is clearly experiencing a conflict of emotions: the opposing ends of this spectrum being swagger and shame. He sets his jaw determinedly and returns their stares.

'What?'

DS Jones bites her lip and glances at DS Leyton. For a moment he looks disconcerted, as though – in the role of messenger – he is about to pay the time-honoured price. But he shrugs his bulky frame inside his jacket, returns Skelgill's stare and then breaks into a broad grin.

'What a beauty, Guv!'

Skelgill is still glowering.

'What do you mean?'

DS Leyton jabs a stubby index finger at the photograph.

'You've half caved his face in, Guv.'

Skelgill sits back and folds his arms.

151

'He was pointing a knife at me, Leyton – he's lucky I had to chase his hoppo – else that's not all I'd have caved in.'

12. DS LEYTON'S FINDINGS

Tuesday 6pm

Skelgill's strategy for the three-hour return journey to Penrith is to occupy a table in the dining car, ostensibly on the grounds that this will guarantee a degree of privacy. His subordinates will no doubt suspect, however, that this stone is cast at two birds, the second of which to be served upon a plate in the form of a handy chicken dinner. It being late October – indeed Halloween falls on the forthcoming Friday, and British Summer Time ended whilst Skelgill was deep in slumber on Grisholm – sundown is presently occurring around the four-thirty p.m. mark, and thus the train sets off to the neon-streaked but otherwise invisible backdrop of London's dense northern suburbs and over-populated home counties. Soon it will pass into the darker realms of the East and West Midlands' borderlands, before slicing through the Cheshire-Lancashire urban plain, and finally slipping into the velvety blackness of Cumbria's fellsides. Lacking external distractions, and despite the obvious fatigue that can be a function solely of travelling – never mind the sustained concentration required for interviewing – all three detectives appear keen to deal with work matters. Thus, Skelgill and DS Jones attend to DS Leyton as he begins to recount his visits to Grisholm Hall's property agents, Rich Buckley's general practitioner and – firstly – the recently widowed Mrs Myra Buckley.

'Worth a bob or two, that's for sure, Guv – my old man always used to say, if there's a cedar in the garden, there's a monkey in the bank.'

'A monkey?' DS Jones produces a bemused grin.

'Five hundred nicker, girl – in those days that was a lot of bread and honey.'

Skelgill scowls.

'A day in London and you're regressing into a Cockney, Leyton.'

'You know what they say, Guv – you can take the boy out of the East End.'

'Aye – well let's have it in plain English now we're north of Watford.'

DS Leyton makes an acquiescent shrug of the shoulders, although it is doubtful this rebuke will censor his vocabulary.

'Right, Guv – anyway – big old detached house, Elizabethan style – must have a couple of acres of garden – new *BM Dub* in the drive.'

Skelgill glances at DS Jones. She nods to confirm her understanding that this means *BMW*.

'What about the wife?'

'I'd say business as usual, Guv.' DS Leyton glances phlegmatically at his notebook. 'I started by explaining about the Coroner and offering our condolences – and she told me straight out about the divorce – I didn't even have to raise it.'

'What did she say?'

'That she assumed we knew – she didn't ask how. I said we did. She said she obviously felt a bit shocked when she heard about his sudden death, but that she couldn't honestly say she was devastated – "Not a nice man", she said.'

'Did she elaborate?'

DS Leyton tilts his head from one side to the other.

'Nah, Guv – I asked her what she meant and she kind of switched it over to the business side. She said he was ruthless and the gentlemen in the book trade weren't a match for him – that's why he was successful – plus he had no scruples peddling soft porn.'

'Her words?'

'Give or take, Guv.'

'What about family?'

DS Leyton shakes his head decisively, and his fleshy jowls tremble.

'None to speak of, Guv – at least, *they* don't have kids. Married seven years – she's quite a bit younger than him. He's got no previous family – she's got a grown-up child from a former relationship, that she had young and was brought up by the father. Buckley was an only child and his parents have passed away. She said he'd been married twice before, though – but had no contact with either of his exes as far as she knows.'

'Did she ask about the funeral?'

'I had to prompt her, Guv. I explained the Coroner has to release the body – but it didn't seem like it was top of her action list – she was togged up as if she was about to go horse riding.'

Skelgill purses his lips.

'This corresponds to what we've been hearing about Buckley.' He glances at DS Jones who nods in agreement. 'Especially from his secretary.'

'Right, Guv – well, I asked her about the financial situation, and she claimed she had no idea how the business was doing – she said she had no involvement, and he didn't speak about it.' DS Leyton runs a finger around inside his shirt collar, as though the heat of the carriage is bothering him. 'She didn't seem too fussed, Guv – she says it's a Limited Company and Buckley was the sole Director – seems like she's insulated from any debts.'

Skelgill is absently feeling the cut on his temple.

'She knows enough, then.'

DS Jones is nodding.

'I bet they had the house in her name, Guv – just as a precaution. It's a popular arrangement to protect against negligence claims. Except that would have put her in the box seat in any negotiations between lawyers. And now she'll presumably inherit the shareholding – it could be valuable – if Constance Belgrave is right and the business is making a trading profit.'

Skelgill and DS Leyton appear surprised by her succinct analysis. Skelgill raises an eyebrow, while DS Leyton bows in her direction before he continues.

'I asked her if she thought he was the suicidal type – she said he was moody, but that he was far too self important ever to admit anything was his fault. She reckoned he'd be the last person to kill himself.'

'How about the medication?'

DS Leyton shakes his head.

'Nothing that she knows of. She said since we'd been in touch she's checked all his cupboards and drawers and there's no trace of anything. She thought hangovers were his only ailment.'

Skelgill glances at DS Jones. She reaches into her attaché case and brings out the evidence bag containing the packet of tablets.

'We found these in his office.'

DS Leyton leans forward with interest.

'Maybe that's the answer, keep it at work – if he didn't want her indoors to know – perhaps he was embarrassed.' Now he contrives a rather helpless expression. 'You know how the missus always finds out about everything?'

Skelgill and DS Jones look like they don't, but humour him with weak smiles. DS Jones returns the medication to her bag. Skelgill casts a hand vaguely into space.

'What was she like?'

'Pretty fit, Guv – small, slim, young-looking for forties – blonde – though you never know at first with blondes, do you?'

DS Jones lets out an involuntary giggle and subconsciously reaches for her own hair, which is shoulder length and a naturally streaked amalgam of fair and light brown. DS Leyton appears suddenly ill at ease.

'Sorry, Emma – I didn't mean...'

But Skelgill intervenes.

'Leyton – neither did I – not what she *looks* like – what she's like – her personality?'

'Oh – sorry, Guv.' He shakes his head in self reprimand. 'I'd say pretty cold, actually, Guv. Has a kind of way of looking at you as though she can't be bothered with you – got her own little agenda going on.' He shrugs. 'She never offered me a drink or nothing – at least, not until I was about to go – and then she said she'd only got Earl Grey, and I remembered what you'd said about it, Guv – so I gave it a miss.'

'Good for you, Leyton.' Skelgill's features remain implacable, in the way of someone fighting back a pressing twitch. 'What does she do – has she got a job?'

'She works part-time in a kindergarten in –' (DS Leyton consults his notes) ' – in *Eton Wick*, Guv. Three mornings a week, she says. Not doing it for the money, I don't reckon.'

Skelgill nods.

'What's your gut feel?'

DS Leyton shakes his head.

'If she was holding out on us, Guv – I'd say it wasn't about Rich Buckley's death. I kind of touched on why they were getting divorced, and she definitely didn't want to talk about that – just said it was by mutual consent. I did notice a guy pull up outside in a Range Rover while I was waiting for the taxi. He sat in the car on his phone for as long as I was there. Pretended he hadn't noticed me.'

'Maybe the riding instructor, Leyton.'

DS Leyton glances at his superior and then furtively at DS Jones, as if he is trying to determine what is an acceptable level of innuendo at this juncture. But since they are both rather non-committal he continues.

'I was trying to work out, Guv – usually there's one party more to blame than the other – and she wasn't slow to slag off Buckley – I wondered if maybe she'd got something on him, was forcing his hand.'

Skelgill folds his arms and furrows his brow.

'Aye, well – according to his secretary, he wasn't too happy with the way things were panning out. Did you ask about his extra-curricular activities?'

'In a roundabout way, Guv – I tried – but she wasn't having any of it – I think she's twigged she's just won the lottery and ain't going to upset the applecart – all she'd say was that if he did have any vices he didn't bring them home – but that he wasn't home a great deal, anyway.'

Skelgill picks up the menu card and taps it several times on the formica of the table. Then he leans out into the aisle and glares impatiently down the train. As yet, there has been no sign of a waiter.

'This is not the service I'm accustomed to.'

DS Jones grins – she guesses he refers to his lunchtime assignation with Angela Cutting.

'Why don't I go and get us some teas from the buffet counter?'

Skelgill is quick to accept.

'Good thinking, Jones – see what snacks they've got while you're at it.'

He rises and steps away from their seat to let her out, and then occupies her position beside the window. For a few moments he presses his forehead against the glass – the dim lights of a rural station flash by, but it is impossible to read the signs at 125 mph and he returns his attention to DS Leyton.

'So what did Buckley's doctor have to say?'

'I couldn't get an appointment, Guv – three weeks was the first he could do.'

'What?'

Though Skelgill speaks quietly he sounds mildly enraged. DS Leyton chuckles.

'Only joking, Guv – you know what it's like.'

'Very funny, Leyton.'

'Nothing to add, really, Guv – I think our boys got all there was when they phoned him in the first place. He said the last time he'd prescribed any medication for Buckley was three years ago, and that was for a fungal toenail infection. He'd had one of those private medicals last January and the GP had been sent a copy of the report – he said he'd double checked that and there was nothing significant – a minor blood problem,' (here DS Leyton refers to his notes) 'slightly high uric acid level, probably from drinking too much red wine – causes gout, apparently, Guv.'

Skelgill shrugs and appears only vaguely interested. Then he is distracted altogether as DS Jones reappears, empty-handed.

'It's closed at the moment, Guv – they've got some sort of electrical problem – they've shut the buffet counter and the kitchen – they're hoping to get an engineer on board at Crewe.'

Skelgill glowers irritably.

'Might have to make a dash for a kiosk when we stop.'

DS Leyton frowns.

'It's a bit risky, Guv – what if you didn't get back on board in time?'

Skelgill smiles candidly.

'I wasn't thinking of being the one fetching the scran, Leyton.'

DS Leyton pulls his head into his broad shoulders, rather like an old tortoise that is accustomed to taking regular self-preservation measures.

'Right, Guv.' He swallows and then suddenly perks up. 'I suppose, looking on the bright side, if you were stranded at least you'd have three burgers for company.'

Skelgill frowns his disapproval, as though he has not considered this eventuality. He points to DS Leyton's notebook.

'Anyway – carry on Leyton. You've not missed anything, Jones.'

'That's it for the doctor, Guv – then I went back into town to the property agents. Eventually I found this tiny little place down an alley just off Piccadilly. It was like walking into a Dickens novel – what with a decrepit old geezer in the darkest corner and hardly any lights on – I tripped over a Labrador lying in the middle of the floor.'

'That'd be the dog you mentioned – does the admin.'

DS Leyton laughs, as he recalls his original assessment.

'So it would, Guv – wish I'd thought of that – reckon I'd have got more sense out of it than old Ebenezer himself behind the counter.'

'This doesn't sound promising, Leyton.'

'Like drawing teeth, Guv.' DS Leyton puffs out his cheeks in recollection of the ordeal. 'And top line is we're no further forward. They rent out Grisholm Hall for house-party weekends and corporate junkets. They've got a little crew of locals that stock it up and do the cleaning and maintenance – according to what's needed. They took a booking from Wordsworth Writers' Retreats about two months ago – he thinks by email but he couldn't find it – the computer looks like something out of a black-and-white episode of *Doctor Who*. They received a down payment by cheque seven days in advance of the entry date.'

'How much for?'

'Three grand, Guv – to cover the food and drink, mainly.'

'Have they got the cheque?'

DS Leyton shakes his head dejectedly.

'Nor a copy of it, Guv. With it being near the end of the month they've posted a whole batch off to the bank – so they don't even know if it's going to clear – never mind whether it's bona fide.'

'Was it an account in the company name?'

'He can't recall, Guv – he'd actually forgotten I was coming, and he was struggling to remember where Grisholm Hall is – they've got hundreds of properties on their books – cowsheds and cottages and castles on country estates from John's End to Land O'Groats.'

DS Jones once more giggles involuntarily, and DS Leyton looks puzzled – until he mouths the phrase again and hears his transposition error.

'It might as well be that, for all the use they were.' He picks up his notebook and then lets it drop back down upon the table. 'I've put one of the lads onto contacting the bank, but they're saying three to five days before the cheque comes out in the wash.'

Skelgill folds his arms and looks decidedly frustrated. DS Jones makes an effort to rally their spirits.

'We've still got three interviews to do, Guv.'

Skelgill stares out into the black void beyond the window and slowly shakes his head.

'I'm concerned by how little we've found out.'

His subordinates sit uneasily for a moment, perhaps trying to read his mood. After a few seconds DS Leyton speaks in a consoling tone.

'Maybe there is nothing, Guv?'

Skelgill gives no visible indication of whether he agrees or disagrees with this idea.

'It's like the bloody Loch Ness monster – how do you prove a negative? You can't. Until we bottom this business of the retreats company, we're in limbo. The economics of it don't stack up – but that doesn't mean it's not genuine. If we knew it was bogus – and had some inkling of who was behind it – we'd know what we're looking for. In the meantime, we're guddling around in the dark.' He turns back and looks first at DS Leyton and then at DS Jones. 'Has one of these people got something to hide – or are they perfectly normal innocent human beings? Aye – a couple of them have been a bit cagey – but there's not one obvious lie – and we all know what folk can be like when the Old Bill turns up.'

DS Leyton is nodding sympathetically.

'I know what you mean, Guv – only takes the missus to start on me and I confess to things I've not even dreamt of.'

Skelgill looks coldly at his sergeant and DS Jones is obliged to disguise a snigger as a sudden cough. Skelgill continues unprompted.

'And if there were some bedtime shenanigans – why would you admit it? Especially if the other party is dead.'

DS Leyton appears still to be out of step with the rhetorical nature of his superior officer's monologue.

'Who's not got a skeleton in their closet, Guv?'

Skelgill is evidently not listening. He gazes down the carriage and speaks in the manner of someone talking into the clip-on microphone of a mobile telephone.

'Logic says the start point must be Rich Buckley. His secretary tells us he was a sexist boor, he harassed and humiliated female interns, he was miserly, and he was in the middle of an acrimonious divorce. "A thoroughly unpleasant man," she said. "Not a nice man" – from his wife. To some extent, that's what we've heard from Lucy Hecate and Burt Boston. But... he already knew Dickie Lampray and Angela Cutting – and the pair of them have played down these bad reports. So why is that?'

DS Jones coughs again – although this time she clears her throat in a way that signals an intervention.

'He obviously had a direct business relationship with Dickie Lampray, Guv – and perhaps there was something similar with Angela Cutting?'

Skelgill stares at her, an expression of doubt clouding his features.

'So what?'

DS Jones hesitates – as though she hasn't really got a clear answer to this.

'Maybe if they had something to protect, or that they didn't want made public – they would try to deflect things away from an investigation into the publishing firm?'

Skelgill shrugs listlessly.

'Aye – it's possible – that's all very well – but take things on a step or two – why would they want to see him disappear from the scene? He's the kingpin that keeps the likes of them in a job.'

Of course, this is something of a sweeping statement – RBP is just one of many fish in the publishing ocean, and a minnow at that – at least by international standards. It seems that Skelgill – to paraphrase his own angling metaphor of a few moments earlier – is for the time being casting aimlessly. However, this may be no bad thing; as DS Jones alluded to with regard to the solving of crossword puzzles, the hopeful charge down a blind alley is the first sign that the subconscious has detected an as-yet indefinable pattern. Indeed, while the little group ponders, it falls to DS Leyton to iterate this conundrum.

'What we need are connections, Guv.' He throws his hands apart and then clasps them together in mid air, shaking them symbolically. 'Like Harry Cobble finding your boat.'

Skelgill looks irked.

'That's not a connection, Leyton – that's a coincidence – life's full of them – I've had a hatful today.'

DSL looks surprised. 'Really, Guv?'

Skelgill begins ostentatiously to count on his fingers.

'For one, I woke up and saw a pelican – how often do you do that, Leyton?'

'Er, not very often, Guv – never really, I suppose.'

'Couple of hours later and Jones here solves a clue in Dickie Lampray's crossword.'

He stares at DS Jones. She understands she is to answer.

'Pelican, Guv.'

Skelgill glares at DS Leyton.

'Now, Leyton – that doesn't make Dickie Lampray one iota more suspicious, does it?'

'True enough, Guv.' He screws up his features rather grudgingly. 'Though there's some would say it was a sign.'

Skelgill scoffs.

'Next I call upon Angela Cutting. Where do I work?'

'You, Guv?'

Skelgill stares defiantly at his sergeant. He is clearly determined to play out this game. DS Leyton relents.

'Cumbria, Guv – we all do.'

'Excellent, Leyton. Cumbria – and the part of Cumbria that Penrith is in, in old money was known as?'

DS Leyton shrugs and shakes his head.

'Search me, Guv – I dunno, Scotland?'

Skelgill's stare becomes a glare.

'Leyton – I take it you failed geography and history.'

'And all the ologies, Guv.'

Despite his uncompromising manner, Skelgill is forced to laugh. He looks to DS Jones to provide the solution.

'Cumberland.'

'Correct – and where does Angela Cutting live – but Cumberland Terrace. Does that make her any more suspicious? No. And it's not a sign, Leyton. And finally, Angela Cutting takes me for lunch – she can't possibly know where I'm going next – but what does she do – in the biggest city in the European Union she picks a restaurant that's less than a minute's walk from my next destination – Lucy Hecate's flat. Does that make either of them any more suspicious?'

By now DS Leyton is obediently shaking his head. But DS Jones seems tense and – in spite of Skelgill's mini-tirade – readies herself to speak.'

'Guv – Dickie Lampray had that photograph with him and Rich Buckley in it.'

Skelgill flips the palms of his hands towards her.

'And that – ladies and gentleman – *is* a connection, although – as I said a few moments ago – if it's the best we've got we're up the creek. We could pick a bunch of randomers and find they've got more in common than this lot.'

For a minute or two the trio sits in dissatisfied silence, until DS Leyton rather glumly offers a suggestion.

'So, do you think we should just wrap things up first knockings tomorrow, Guv? I can easy enough cancel the interviews.'

However, despite Skelgill's pessimistic assessment of their progress, DS Leyton's proposition seems to find some objection within him. He leans his elbows on the table and lowers his chin broodingly upon the heels of his hands. He closes his eyes. Perhaps he rekindles the memories of his own experience on Grisholm, the mainstay of his determination thus far. After a few seconds he sits upright and shakes his head.

'Ask me again after we've had a burger.'

The other two laugh in a relieved manner, and relax into their seats. Skelgill does likewise, and runs his fingers through his hair and stretches his arms above his head, as though he is preparing to settle down for a nap.

'I do have one *un*connected question, Jones.'

'Guv?'

'What was the clue if the answer was pelican?'

DS Jones's full lips stretch into a satisfied grin.

'I'll trade you, Guv – if you tell me what you called Miss Trimble.'

13. Ms J SMITH

Wednesday 8.00am

In order efficiently to mop up the three outstanding interviews with members of the Grisholm retreat Skelgill has decreed that DS Jones will meet Dr Gerald Bond and DS Leyton Linda Gray – both of these relatively local affairs in Cumbria – while he shall undertake the two hundred mile round-trip to Edinburgh to visit Sarah Redmond. The cynic might speculate that this allocation has something to do with the fact that Skelgill has got to know each of the candidates, and is expressing some personal preference – although an equally robust hypothesis might identify the opportunity such a trip provides to inspect various fishing haunts, the route intersecting as it does the Esk and the Eden in England, before picking up the source of the Tweed in the Scottish Borders and following its course for some twenty miles, and subsequently crossing smaller but no less interesting waters such as the Tarth and the North Esk. Certainly, Skelgill has planned to delay his departure until around eight a.m., when it will be fully light, and angling reconnaissance optimised. His appointment with Sarah Redmond is scheduled for eleven a.m. at her apartment in the Scottish capital.

However, a salient item of news reached the weary detectives during the latter half of their train journey yesterday evening, and this has impacted upon Skelgill's itinerary. The credit card in the name 'Ms J Smith' found among the late Bella Mandrake's personal possessions has been traced to an address in Leith, the ancient port town on the Firth of Forth, where a teenage Mary Queen of Scots landed to reclaim her throne in 1561, and which today is contiguous with greater Edinburgh. The local Scottish police have identified a rented property, and access arrangements have been made through the factor. Thus Skelgill sets off in darkness at six a.m., for a rendezvous with his regular contact for such cross-border affairs, DS Cameron Findlay.

Some two hours later they meet near DS Findlay's home in the western Edinburgh suburb of Corstorphine (one of Scotland's many unpronounceable place-names – Kus-*tor*-fin being a near-enough rendition, with the stress on the middle syllable), where Skelgill leaves his car at a large chain hotel near the zoological gardens. DS Findlay has thoughtfully furnished them with takeaway coffees, and the pair catches up on various matters as they cross the city. Edinburgh's rush hour is a peculiar affair, and mainly takes place between 08:20 and 08:40 during term-times only, when thousands of affluent parents in oversized vehicles deliver their small (and not so small) charges to the illustrious private schools that serve their particular dynasties. DS Findlay's suggestion of meeting at eight a.m. has served to position them ahead of this unruly tsunami of traffic, and they move steadily as they set out to cover the remaining five miles of Skelgill's journey.

Their route from the zoo in Corstorphine passes the great rugby stadium in the adjoining Murrayfield district, where understated Edwardian terraces house much of Scotland's legal profession, to Roseburn (crossing the Water of Leith) where DS Findlay makes a dog-leg through a semi-industrial area of delivery depots and working men's clubs and blackened stone railway bridges. They skirt past Tynecastle, home of the *'Jam Tarts'* (Heart of Midlothian FC), and pick up the old Caledonian Railway line, now a motorised highway that cuts into the city centre. Lothian Road, the Grassmarket, Cowgate and Canongate bring them to Holyrood, where the palace and the parliament glower at one another across centuries of antipathy. Here, too, there is the sudden shock of the park, with its mini-mountains and thrusting volcanic escarpments that make Edinburgh the 'Rio of Europe', and St Margaret's Loch where wintering wild ducks patiently await the arrival of mums and toddlers, and unsuitable food in the form of artificially coloured extruded snacks. Exiting Holyrood Park they dip down into an area less familiar to Skelgill – though between the blocks of drab post-war tenements he gains glimpses of Meadowbank stadium and the green-and-white painted Hibernian FC ground at Easter Road. There is a *haar* sliding in off the North Sea, and the very tops of the pylons that bear the floodlights for these gladiatorial arenas are dissolved in the brackish mist. Skelgill might be a little disoriented, but DS Findlay's superior local knowledge has served them well and, just fifteen minutes after their departure, they slide into the southern fringe of Leith, by one of its lesser-known access roads.

'Glad to see the old radar's still in working order.'

'This is Roadworks City, Danny – use the satnav and you never get anywhere on time, if ever.'

Skelgill grunts his agreement, and again more vocally as DS Findlay without warning swings the car beneath an archway that separates two five-storey stone buildings. He conducts them along a narrow cobbled thoroughfare that opens on the right into a yard some eighty feet by forty. Their surroundings give the impression of a bonded warehouse – and, indeed, that was its original purpose. Today, like almost all that survive of Leith's hundred-odd nineteenth century whisky repositories, it is converted into flats. And here, in Constitution Street, they hope to unravel the mystery of 'Ms J Smith'. DS Findlay nudges the marked police car into an empty resident's parking bay and applies the handbrake with a flourish.

'Welcome to Leith – did ye ken, the first penguins for Edinburgh Zoo were brought ashore here by the whalers over a century ago?'

Skelgill shakes his head and chuckles.

'That's what it is – remember last time I saw you – I told you there's a career waiting for you as a tour guide.'

'Och, aye – but they'd never let me loose with the double-decker bus, Danny.'

Skelgill ducks out of the vehicle and together they saunter across to the entrance of the stair. Though the building is Victorian, it has been renovated from a gutted shell, and its main door, sash windows and communal post-box unit are fashioned of modern materials and uniformly painted in an agreeable olive green. The cobbled yard is tidy and litter-free, and the stone edifice itself has been pressure-washed and belies its age. Skelgill looks about appreciatively, and is only distracted when the laughing cry of a Herring Gull causes him to glance skywards. The large grey scavenger bends like an iron bar against the irresistible easterly, and wheels away out of sight.

'Sounds like we're beside the seaside.'

'A good stone's throw would do it, Danny.'

Skelgill nods.

'Nice job they've made of these flats.'

'Aye – and, according to the records they were converted above ten years ago.'

'They look as good as new.'

'That's the benefit of having a factor – they collect in the money and make sure all the repairs are done.'

Skelgill has moved across to inspect the mailboxes. The gabled unit is fixed to the pale sandstone wall of the property. There are twenty-four numbered doors, each with an aluminium letterbox and an individual lock.

'Do you have a key for these, Cam?'

DS Findlay fishes out a jangling bunch from his jacket pocket. With his thick fingers he separates them into a little fan and squints determinedly.'

'Aye – maybe this long thin yin.' He approaches the unit. 'Flat eleven, now.'

The key turns the lock but the plywood door is recalcitrant, perhaps a shade warped, and requires a sharp tug to open. He stands back and gestures to Skelgill that he should go ahead.

'Be my guest.'

The interior of the box – measuring about eight inches tall by eighteen wide and the same in depth – is jammed full of envelopes and flyers. The first impression is that it has not been emptied for some time, but as Skelgill pulls out an armful and begins to sift through, it becomes clear that one or more enterprising leaflet-distributors have taken the opportunity to divest themselves of their stocks, for there are multiple repeats advertising unmissable pizza deals, takeaway restaurants, window and rhone cleaning, and superfast broadband.

'It's all junk mail, Cam – no wait – look at this.'

He swivels at the waist to show DS Findlay a large manila envelope that he has uncovered about halfway down the pile. DS Findlay appears perplexed.

'Bella Mandrake? I thought we were looking for a Jane Smith?'

'Bella Mandrake's her pseudonym – pen name, stage name, or whatever. It means you've brought me to the right place, Cam.'

DS Findlay contrives a severe expression.

'You're dealing with Police Scotland, now, laddie – none of your Sassenach amateurs.'

Skelgill pretends to be offended.

'I take it you don't include Cumbria in that definition?'

'Och, no – you Geordies are just like us... gie or tak a sense o' humour.'

DS Findlay has a glint in his eye – this is not the first time he has, perhaps mischievously, misplaced Skelgill's provenance – and his strait-laced joshing is sufficiently endearing to pass muster. Skelgill stuffs the bundle of mail under his arm and closes the door of the box with a firm shove.

'Come on, let's have a gander inside – I'll sort this lot later.'

They approach the entrance and DS Findlay successfully matches one of the keys on his loaned bunch to the brand name on the lock at the first attempt. Unlike a typical Edinburgh tenement there is a modern feel; the stair is light and airy, with brushed steel handrails, freshly emulsioned white walls, grey marble-effect linoleum and the smell of recently applied lemon-scented floor-cleaner. However, it is not this pleasing combination of features that causes the detectives to pause on entry, but a large tabby cat that eyes them from the head of the first flight of stairs. Skelgill makes a kissing sound by sucking air between his lips, upon which the animal turns and disappears from sight. He shrugs and they begin to climb, Skelgill holding back so as not to outpace the older, bulkier man. Two flights separate each landing, and DS Findlay is panting heavily by the time they reach the third floor, where they spy the number eleven on a door at the end of a short corridor to their right.

'It's a wee while since I climbed my last Munro, Danny.'

Skelgill grins affably.

'You should get the missus down to the Lakes for a weekend – I'll point you in the direction of a couple of decent walks.'

'A couple of decent pubs might be more the ticket.'

'Aye, we've plenty of them, too.'

Skelgill moves aside to allow DS Findlay to tackle the front door. There are two separate mortise locks, and he has to try both of these – one is for the landlord's use between lets and has not been engaged – but the brass keys are almost identical. The door opens into a narrow hallway about twenty feet long, and the immediate impression is of a householder who has decamped from a larger, older-style property. A mahogany sideboard blocks half the width of the passage, and oversized landscape paintings and an ornately framed mirror are too big for the walls and the low ceiling. The air is stale and cloying, hanging with an invisible mist of lavender-scented talcum powder. They pass an internal bathroom on the right, gaining glimpses of a sizeable collection of toiletries, and ahead of them a small bedroom: lacking a bed but crowded with wardrobes, a dresser – itself stacked with an array of cosmetics – and a writing bureau with an upright chair set before the window. The corridor turns sharp right and passes a second bedroom adjacent to the first (this one housing a double bed, an elaborate affair with a carved oak headboard and footboard, that dominates the cramped space), before opening into a larger room that is an all-in-one kitchen, diner and lounge. It is situated at the corner of the building, overlooking the cobbled lane and yard, and has good natural light from windows on two sides, and a set of French doors that open onto the tiniest of balconies, really nothing more than a broad sill enclosed by a safety rail. The fitted kitchen is entirely modern, and clashes rather with a teak Jacobean-style dining table and chairs. The lounge section into which it merges is, like the other rooms, fussily cluttered with elaborate ornaments and over-sized furniture, in particular a purple velvet upholstered chesterfield. Upon its nearest arm, resting in the heraldic pose known as *couchant*, is the tabby cat. Winking, it watches them warily.

'Struth – how the deil did that get in here?'

Skelgill shakes his head.

'Maybe it's a cat burglar?'

DS Findlay lumbers back out into the corridor – he returns nodding his head.

'There's a cat-flap, Danny – it's painted the same shade as the door – I didnae notice it.'

'Me neither.'

Skelgill meanwhile is making a second attempt to endear himself to the feline. It is a large, striking specimen, beautifully marked, and it seems well fed and quite at ease in these surroundings. He makes more pishing sounds, and this time the animal permits him to stroke it across the top of its head.

'Looks like it's home alone, Danny.'

Skelgill nods. He leaves the animal – which rises into a sitting position – and checks about the room.

'There's no food or water – or litter tray.'

'Maybe it belongs to someone else in the block – it could be just visiting. Or maybe a neighbour's feeding it. When did the woman leave here?'

Skelgill purses his lips.

'It would be about a week ago, Cam. I think you must be right.'

'Well it seems happy enough.'

'Aye.' Skelgill shrugs and moves across to the French doors, from where he can just glimpse DS Findlay's car in the yard below.

'So what are we looking for, Danny?'

Skelgill turns to face his colleague. He puts his hands on his hips in a purposeful fashion.

'Identity's the main thing – Ms Jane Smith, if that's who she is – next of kin, first and foremost. Relatives, friends – details of her GP would be handy. Also any medicine that's kicking about.'

'The report I received from your boys suggested the case wasn't suspicious.'

'Aye, well – *I'm* suspicious, Cam.'

DS Findlay nods, his features assuming an even more grim set than is his natural demeanour.

'What about that mail? It's usually a good bet.'

Skelgill has left the contents of the mailbox on the dining table. They move across together. DS Findlay begins sorting through the main heap, extracting bills and suchlike. Skelgill, however, examines the brown foolscap envelope marked for the attention of Bella Mandrake. The name and address is written in a flowery, feminine hand, and the contents weigh heavily in his hands.

'Cam – these are Scottish stamps aren't they?'

Without his reading glasses DS Findlay has to lean away, but he nods in the affirmative.

'Aye, they are that.'

'It's postmarked London. I think I know what this is.'

'Exciting?'

'Not exactly – but it's just given me an idea.'

Skelgill crosses to the kitchen units and pulls open a drawer. His first guess is correct and he finds a small vegetable knife. Watched by DS Findlay he slits the package and extracts its contents, a uniform sheaf of A4 papers with a compliments slip clipped to the front. He reads the typed message and then hands the bundle to DS Findlay, who this time reaches inside his jacket for his spectacles case. Thus armed, he reads aloud.

'It's from *Romance Publishing*. "Dear Ms Mandrake, thank you for your submission of the synopsis and opening three chapters of your romantic thriller, *Head over Heart in Love*. While it features distinctive characters and an imaginative plot, unfortunately this is not quite right for our list at this time. We wish you good luck in placing it elsewhere. We are returning your materials in the SAE you provided." It's a Dear John letter, Danny.'

'Aye – Dear Jane in this case.'

DS Findlay returns the papers to Skelgill.

'So what's your big idea?'

Skelgill holds up a palm, evidently wishing to play down DS Findlay's hyperbole.

'Not exactly big – but let's have a look at that box room.'

They file out into the hallway and squeeze between the oppressive furniture of the smaller of the two bedrooms. The talc-scented ambience grows more oppressive. Skelgill opens one of the wardrobes to reveal a rail crammed with ballgown-like dresses, beneath which are new-looking shoes with stiletto heels arranged upon little stacks of paperback novels. There is Daphne du Maurier, Catherine Cookson and Barbara Cartland, and heaps of Mills & Boon. He closes the door and steps over to the bureau – and then with a start he recoils: the cat has installed itself upon the chair.

'Think it's trying to tell us something, Cam?'

DS Findlay has opened a drawer of the dresser, but the contents – elaborate underwear – seem uninteresting and he slides it shut, although only with some difficulty and the loud screech of wood on wood vexes the cat, which leaps from the chair and darts out of the room.

'Maybe it's just taken a shine to you, Danny – I've heard cats can spot a fisherman a mile off.'

'Smell 'em more like.' Skelgill is nothing if not pragmatic. He raises an arm and sniffs the sleeve of his jacket. 'I accidentally had this lying on a landing net in the back of my motor.'

DS Findlay chuckles and gestures to the bottles and potions that crowd the dresser.

'There's plenty of perfume if you want something to mask it.'

Skelgill raises an ironic eyebrow.

'No sleeping pills, though?'

DS Findlay inclines his head towards the door.

'I'll have a look and see if there's a cabinet in the bathroom.'

Skelgill nods, then turns and squats down on his haunches and begins to investigate the drawers of the writing desk. The lower one contains unused papers and envelopes. The second, however, is packed with what appear to be the draft manuscripts of novels; on top of these on one side is a pink document folder. It bears the words *'Bouquets & Brickbats'* written in the same extravagant hand as the self-addressed envelope, and is illustrated with little cartoon drawings of flowers and what might be the occasional piece of flying masonry. Skelgill stands up and places it upon the lowered flap of the bureau. The file contains some fifty or sixty typewritten letterheads and compliments slips, all from different senders. He reads the first, and then begins to flick through them with just a cursory glance at each, until he stops abruptly at what is perhaps the tenth document in the pile. The stiffening of his demeanour must be plain to the eye, for DS Findlay, who has stuck his head back around the door to convey some observation or other, remarks instead upon Skelgill's reaction.

'Found your big idea, Danny?'

Skelgill is still staring at the page, though his mind's eye seems focused far away. After a moment's silence he replies.

'It could be what I'm looking for.'

'What would that be?'

'In a word – a *connection*.'

14. SARAH REDMOND

Wednesday 11am

Coincidences may not be connections in Skelgill's book, but he must be cognisant of DS Leyton's remark that some folk would consider them an omen, as he stands shivering on the steps beneath Sarah Redmond's flat: in *Cumberland* Street. Located on the north side of Edinburgh's New Town (the latter something of a misnomer, being, according to DS Findlay with his tour guide hat on, "The largest intact area of Georgian architecture in the world"), the east-west thoroughfare is perfectly aligned to channel the icy air that streams unhindered from the Skagerrak. Indeed, on reflection, given the prevailing conditions, simply getting *off* Cumberland Street is probably foremost in his mind at this moment.

The Leith address has yielded no further clues of significance – for instance no medicines beyond over-the-counter cold remedies, corn treatments, antiemetics, laxatives, and various homeopathic concoctions. Thus Skelgill has been dropped off by DS Findlay in order to conduct his scheduled eleven o'clock interview. The Scots sergeant, meanwhile, has continued on to police headquarters at 'Letsby' Avenue (Fettes, actually, but it is Skelgill's little ongoing joke), to organise the tracing of Bella Mandrake's next of kin and medical practitioner, procure a constable to knock-up the residents of the apartment block, and locate a suitable means for containing a cat in his office. Ah, the cat. Upon leaving the flats and returning to DS Findlay's car, the two detectives discovered the creature once more demonstrating its elusive Pimpernel-like qualities as it apparently awaited them, resting upon the bonnet and perhaps enjoying what residual heat radiated from the engine beneath. Urged on by Skelgill, and despite protests that his 'dug' (a grizzled and pugnacious Border Terrier that rather resembles its master) "fair hates the wee deils", DS Findlay has agreed – "temporarily, mind" – to take the feline into protective custody until background checks can be conducted. They parted with the plan that he would return at one p.m. and ferry Skelgill back to his car.

*

'I didn't realise you knew Ms Mandrake.'

Sarah Redmond's electric-blue irises seem to enlarge, but this effect is in fact an illusion caused by the slight contraction of her pupils. It is an involuntary reflex that betrays an otherwise phlegmatic countenance.

'Inspector, there is knowing and there is *knowing*.'

Skelgill tips his head to one side, inviting her to elaborate. He, too, perhaps is putting on a front, since his assertion is a shot in the dark.

They do not face one another, but sit just a little apart upon a large and accommodating sofa, of the kind that would be referred to as a *Davenport* stateside. Sarah Redmond's New Town flat – its sought-after location reflecting her writing success – is tastefully furnished, with magnificent Turkish rugs spread about the stripped and varnished floorboards, original artworks – a superb *Bellany*, for instance, a buoyant and bruising puce fishing boat that momentarily halted Skelgill's progress – and original oak shutters folded back beside each of the long sash windows. Flames lick eagerly amidst a recently set fire of smokeless briquettes, drawn by the brisk easterly that skims the rooftops – but the centrally heated apartment is already comfortably warm. Indeed Sarah Redmond wears only a pair of faded blue figure-hugging stretch denim jeggings and a flimsy white vest top; her copious fiery locks cascade onto her bare nape and shoulders as she tosses her head with a degree of indifference.

'I usually run one of the writers' workshops at the festival,' (she refers to the Edinburgh International Book Festival, which occupies Charlotte Square each August) 'she was a regular – and prominent – attendee.'

'Were you aware she lived in Edinburgh?'

'Not until we met at the retreat – there are hundreds of bibliophiles who come back to the festival every year – it's the largest literary event in the world, you know?'

'Seems like you have more than your fair share of world number ones – my Scottish colleague was instructing me on the history of your New Town.'

'I'm not an Edinburgher myself, Inspector – and the New Town is rather austere, don't you feel?'

'A good setting for your crime stories, then?'

She shrugs languidly.

'I suspect they have run their course – I'm searching for something a little more original.'

She stares at him, unblinking, the glint of a challenge in her eye. Skelgill, at the age of thirty-seven, is three years her senior, but inside him lurks the spirit of *Peter Pan*, that will be forever seventeen. Perhaps Sarah Redmond's novelist's intuition detects this chink in his regulation policeman's armour, for she seems ready to confront him with the same blend of confidence and mischief that she was quick to employ at their previous encounter. Skelgill, however, responds to her probing thrust with a somewhat oblique parry.

'So Dickie Lampray was correct – when he accused you of researching your next novel?'

She glances away, for a moment giving the impression that this question bores her.

'I shouldn't say that exactly, Inspector – the scenario was rather like *Lord of the Flies*, don't you think?'

Skelgill creases his brow.

'Wasn't that something to do with pigs?'

Now she smiles benevolently.

'I understand where you are coming from, Inspector.'

Skelgill shakes his head.

'It's just – coincidences and all – Grisholm means *Isle of Pigs*. It's an Old Norse name.'

'Ah – now you are teaching me, Inspector.'

She settles back and crosses her legs; the tip of a blue-and-white plimsoll hovers within touching distance of Skelgill's nearest knee. He adjusts his position, so that he can look at her more easily.

'It's *questions* I need to ask you.'

She opens her palms and surveys him coyly.

'Ask away – I am at your service.'

It is noticeable that Skelgill has thus far avoided his habitual use of the stock title 'madam' – normally a safe fall-back, albeit rather formal – but neither has he trespassed upon the intimacy of her first name.

'You'll be aware from contacts with my colleagues – we've not managed to get in touch with the retreat organisers – but, that aside, what made you decide to attend?'

'Overwhelmingly the change of scene, Inspector – I'm between novels – at a loose end, even – and, you know, I'd never been to the Lake District until last week.'

'What did you think of it?'

Skelgill's tone suggests he anticipates a glowing review. There is an impressionistic watercolour above the hearth, suggestive of a windswept Hebridean seascape. Sarah Redmond gazes searchingly at what might be glaucous swathes of swaying marram, foreground to a turbulent oceanic sky.

'There isn't the sense of wilderness one finds in Scotland,' (she glances at Skelgill, and it must be evident he is a little crestfallen, for she elaborates with additional emphasis) 'but there is a special kind of – how can I put it – handsome cragginess. Let's call it designer stubble to Scotland's unkempt full beard.'

Skelgill looks suitably mollified. Subconsciously his hand wanders to his chin, with its two-day-old growth of the non-designer kind.

'Can't say I've ever heard it described like that – I know what you're getting at – but don't be fooled – it can be as dangerous a place as anywhere when the weather decides to take a turn – you saw the storm on Sunday.'

She nods, and – as if she realises how easily she has led him to digress – grins contritely and steers the dialogue back around to his own question.

'So it felt rather like going off on a singles holiday – not knowing whom I should meet or how it would all work out. Rather exciting, really.'

She bats her eyelashes in an exaggeratedly naïve manner.

'You didn't know Rich Buckley would be there?'

She is quick to shake her head. It is a denial that appears convincing.

'I had no idea, Inspector.'

Skelgill considers her reply for a moment or two, and then, intoning rather mechanically, reveals a snippet of information gleaned during his inquiries.

'It has been mentioned that you're thinking of changing publisher.'

She raises her palms in affected shock.

'I really don't imagine my readers would feel comfortable to find my books in the Buckley stable.' Then she breaks out into an improvised and lascivious smile. 'Unless, of course, there was my racy new Cumbrian detective.'

Skelgill's cheekbones colour, and for a moment he appears to flounder about in search of a response. Sarah Redmond, still grinning, fills the little silence.

'I take it that was from Dickie Lampray?'

'I think it was – aye.'

'Don't worry, Inspector – nothing gets past old Dickie, fact or fiction – he's the gossip queen of the literary court.'

Skelgill nods sheepishly, evidently relieved that his indiscretion is excused.

'He seems to have quite a reputation.'

Now she flashes him an old-fashioned look.

'That depends what you mean, Inspector – but, certainly, if you're struggling to become published, he's your man.'

'So why wouldn't everyone flock to him? He sounded hard pressed for work.'

'Because, Inspector, a contract arranged by Dickie is known in the trade as the next nearest thing to vanity publishing.'

Skelgill looks somewhat blank.

'You'll have to explain that one to me.'

'In short, the author pays. The agent gets his cut. The publisher is quids in.'

'I see.' Skelgill ponders for a moment. 'That seems to defeat the object of writing a book.'

Sarah Redmond considers his response. Then she shrugs in a resigned manner.

'I know this from my workshops, Inspector – there are so many people out there who are just desperate to get their book published – I should say finance is a secondary consideration.'

Skelgill nods, his eyes thoughtful.

'So how does this all work then? Agents and publishers – who would I go to if I'd written a novel?'

'You could approach either, Inspector. An agent is more likely to look at your work – and a publisher will generally listen to an agent – they both know not to waste one another's time. Many publishers these days don't accept unsolicited manuscripts – and those that do oblige the author to wait months for the rejection letter.'

'You make that sound like it's a foregone conclusion – being rejected.' Skelgill's tone suggests this apparent inevitability offends his sense of fairness. 'Surely if you keep trying, eventually you'll get accepted.'

She regards him with some sympathy, as though she admires his spirit but pities his naivety.

'Not if you can't write, Inspector.'

For the first time, there is just the hint of self-importance in her choice of words, though not in her tone. Skelgill looks as though he identifies with those who can't write.

'What about Bella Mandrake?'

Sarah Redmond seems to detect his inner discord. Her features soften, and she shakes her head gently.

'Sadly, Inspector, no.'

Now Skelgill looks perplexed.

'Shouldn't someone have told her that?' He folds his arms purposefully. 'I mean – if I've got a junior officer who's obviously not up to scratch – I don't keep stringing them along – they get the boot. It's only fair to everyone – them included.'

She smiles again, more broadly, as though his practical ruthlessness appeals to her.

'The publishing business, though cut-throat in its own way, is nothing if not polite – even the most incomprehensible of manuscripts will receive a positive-sounding rejection letter.'

Skelgill responds to this with a blank stare. It is perhaps evident to Sarah Redmond that he is distracted in thought, and so she provides a postscript.

'And you never know, Inspector – why cause offence when you can't see into the future?'

Skelgill breaks from his reverie and nods as if he knows what she means. His next question perhaps confirms his understanding of this insight.

'Have you had books rejected, yourself?'

'Inspector – my first three novels are still gathering dust.' She flicks up her hair with the fingers of both hands, and rolls her eyes to the ceiling. 'And they are probably exactly where they deserve to be.'

'I'm sure they're very good.'

She looks back at Skelgill and smiles sweetly, perhaps she edges nearer; indeed it seems she gently pounces upon his throwaway compliment and magnifies its import. She lays her hands one on top of the other on her thigh, her slender fingers pointing towards him. She bows her head a little so that tresses of hair fall to frame her eyes, and emphasise her coquettish demeanour as she gazes up at him.

'So, Inspector – is it a *murder* investigation yet?'

Skelgill is clearly unprepared for this question; too fast to conceal, a flicker of alarm creases his features.

'No, no – it's just routine – it's a requirement for the Coroner – it's –'

However, Sarah Redmond interrupts.

'But shouldn't you be asking me about Rich Buckley and Bella Mandrake – what was their state of health and mind – since there is no suspicion of foul play?'

Now Skelgill looks a little sheepish.

'These are on my list of questions.' He points to his temples with the index finger of each hand – as if to indicate, in the absence of a notebook, the location of his substitute paperwork. 'I just like to rotate the order – it gets monotonous asking the same thing over and over again.' Now he holds up both palms in a confessional gesture. 'And what with you being a – detective writer.'

Sarah Redmond leans back against the settee; her body language easing the pressure of her subtle interrogation. She smiles again, now demurely.

'Oh, you have me bang to rights, Inspector.' She shakes her head, and takes hold of a lock of hair, and begins weaving it between her fingers. 'But a girl can't help wondering – such a delicious set-up – and, hey presto, two deaths occur.'

'It was just a coincidence.'

Skelgill's hasty negation carries little ring of conviction, and she continues unchecked.

'Wouldn't it be neat, Inspector – if Bella somehow bumped off Rich and then took her own life once the gravity of her offence had sunk in?'

Skelgill seems ready to object – but then perhaps his instincts overrun the defences erected by his training – and he abandons his post and signs up to her cause.

'Why would it be neat?'

'Neat for the *real* murderer, Inspector.'

As Skelgill stares at her, she springs up to her feet.

'A glass of wine, Inspector – or are you driving?'

He takes a second to answer, as if his mind is still wrestling with the writhing hypothesis she has just thrown at him.

'I'm driving, later – but you go ahead.'

'Just one moment, please.'

Sarah Redmond glides lightly across the blood oranges and vibrant purples of the geometrically patterned carpet, watched by

Skelgill from his half-turned position on the settee. She is slightly above average height for a woman, long-legged; she throws her feet gracefully, the curves of her calves, thighs and buttocks accentuated by the clinging hipsters. Her mane of hair is elegantly shaped, and its longest tresses reach down to the small of her back, brushing the curve of exposed pale flesh at the base of her spine. As she leaves the room Skelgill rises and removes his jacket. He folds it into quarters – and then sniffs it suspiciously a couple of times – before crossing to the windows and placing it upon the seat of a Shaker rocking chair. He tries to check his appearance in the pane, brushing his fingers through his hair, but there cannot be sufficient reflection – in any event he hears the clink of glassware as Sarah Redmond re-enters the drawing room, and he moves his hand into a salute, as though he is shading his eyes while observing the street below.

Sarah Redmond glances at him and smiles; she carries two goblets casually in one hand, inverted with their stems between her fingers, and in the other a bottle of chilled white wine that is already attracting condensation. Its foil and cork have been removed and it does not appear entirely full, as though a glassful has already been consumed. Skelgill follows her and they resume their former positions on the settee. She pours a generous measure for herself and about half the amount for Skelgill.

'I don't normally drink before lunch, Inspector – unless I'm seeking inspiration, that is.'

She smiles again, more coyly this time and raises the goblet. Skelgill stares at his glass – he has a curious expression on his face, perhaps he is reflecting that this could become a pleasant habit – and after a moment's hesitation he reaches for it and reciprocates her gesture. He appears careful, however, to sip rather than to gulp.

'You are left-handed, Inspector.'

Skelgill appears a little surprised by her remark; he glances rather stupidly at the glass in his left hand, and then at how she holds hers in the same fashion. She nods as if to confirm his assumption.

'I noticed at dinner – how you switched over your cutlery.'

'Aye, well – I've never got the hang of it – feels like driving on the right.' He lifts his glass and takes another small sip. 'Bit of a handicap, really.'

She shakes her head, quite vehemently.

'Oh, no Inspector – we are the lucky ten per cent. Although in the creative professions the statistic is less skewed. Witness at Grisholm Hall: as well as you and me, there were Linda and Lucy – and Rich. What are the odds of that – five out of ten?'

'Life's full of coincidences.'

'And clichés, Inspector.'

Skelgill hesitates.

'So what does it mean?'

'I understand we can call upon a part of our brain that is off limits to mere mortals, Inspector – a skill to be celebrated.'

Skelgill grins sardonically.

'I'll try that one with my boss.'

Sarah Redmond, with studied care, kicks off her plimsolls to reveal manicured toenails coloured to match her hair, and – exhibiting an enviable flexibility of the joints – tucks one bare foot beneath the opposite thigh, enabling her to sit side-on in a kind of half-lotus position, facing Skelgill directly.

'Where were we, Inspector?'

Skelgill appears to edge slightly away from her, although this movement enables him to swing a casual arm over the back of the settee, and to rest the opposite elbow on the furniture's arm behind him. Now he, too, is largely facing her.

'You were solving my crime – not, I stress, that there is any evidence of a crime having been committed.'

Sarah Redmond takes a slow drink of wine, scrutinising him over the rim of her glass.

'Nonetheless, Inspector, it is fascinating to speculate – there must have been previous occasions when things were not all that they seemed.'

Skelgill produces a non-committal shrug of the shoulders.

'I'd say that's par for the course – criminals don't generally leave us a note of their MO.'

'Unlike in the whodunit, Inspector.'

Now Skelgill frowns.

'I'm no expert on crime fiction – but I thought these stories were all about red herrings.'

His remark is more of a statement, but Sarah Redmond shakes her head. Locks of hair fall across her eyes, and she blinks rather alluringly through the Titian veil.

'I should say, Inspector, that the ideal whodunit allows for each of the possible suspects to have a motive – even if it is not explicitly outlined by the narrator – call them red herrings, but I believe they are more sophisticated than that.'

If Skelgill is harbouring doubts about this line of discussion he does not show it. Yet it must strike him that the woman is intent upon some course of her own. And there is the police protocol of not discussing an investigation with a member of the public – one who, after all, is a possible suspect (if there are such persons in this case). But, perhaps swayed by the comfortable privacy of their surroundings, and the first reckless flush of the alcohol, he is willing to be led by her subtle manoeuvres. His fluctuating attitude is perhaps reflected in his use, for the first time, of her name.

'So what would *your* motive be, Sarah?'

Sarah Redmond appears delighted by his question. She smiles contentedly and takes another languorous drink of her wine, and then swirls the contents of her glass and considers the glistening maelstrom, as if for inspiration.

'To kill Rich Buckley – I think... revenge.' She throws Skelgill an experimental glance. 'To kill Bella Mandrake – to silence her.'

Skelgill looks distinctly shocked.

'And why is that?' This is all the reply he seems able to muster.

'I don't need to approach the problem from your perspective, Inspector. You have incomplete knowledge. There is much about me you don't know. Rich Buckley took me as a lover – then spurned me just as I was emerging as a novice author – he destroyed my confidence and set back my career – it took me years to recover. Bella Mandrake ran a local drama group – she took me under her wing – she helped me rebuild my self-assurance – and my reputation as a writer – we had a torrid lesbian affair – I ended it against her wishes – and so she threatened to expose both relationships – unless I complied with her demands.'

Skelgill sits in silence, slightly open-mouthed, a little wide-eyed, and breathing audibly.

Sarah Redmond is deadpan; then suddenly she bursts into a peal of laughter and reaches forward to press a hand on Skelgill's thigh.

'I'm *joking*, Inspector!'

'Aye – well – aye, I presumed you were.' Skelgill is blushing and looking stiffly down at her hand. 'Clever story though – I can see why you're good at your job.'

Sarah Redmond smiles with satisfaction. Slowly she withdraws and helps herself to more wine. Skelgill takes a rather large gulp from his own glass, and does not object when she offers him a top up.

'So you see, Inspector – it would be convenient for me – the murderess – if you were to believe that Bella disposed of Rich and then killed herself.'

Skelgill produces what is clearly a somewhat forced and uncomfortable grin. But he opts to hear more.

'So, the others – what would be their motives?'

She drinks and then eases herself into the corner of the sofa, leaning back and stretching out her legs, so that her bare toes make the lightest of contact with Skelgill's thigh. As he glances down, she closes her eyes meditatively.

'Dickie Lampray, Angela Cutting – well they both go back some years with Rich Buckley – I have seen them in their coven, late at night, conspiring – perhaps they acted together – some old rivalry?'

'Wouldn't money be a more likely motive, given their business connections?'

She opens first one eye and then the other, and concedes with a toss of her head.

'Perhaps Rich double-crossed them – and they decided an alternative fate would be most suitable.'

'Alternative to what?'

'Dickie's connections run very deep – compared to him Rich was just a new kid on the block – I imagine Dickie could call in a few favours if he wanted to damage Rich.'

'And what about Angela?'

'As the saying goes, the pen is mightier than the sword. We all tread carefully in the presence of a renowned critic.'

Skelgill ponders for a moment, perhaps reflecting upon his own experiences to date.

'And Bella – why would they kill her?'

'I think – I think – that Bella was the architect of her own destruction.'

'In what way?'

'You saw how she was, Inspector. She sought the limelight, in her own peculiar way. When you arrived she redoubled her efforts – she made the killer – or killers if it were Dickie *and* Angela – think that she knew something of what they had done. So she had to be eliminated.'

Skelgill frowns; he does not appear convinced.

'But she was going on about ghosts and whatnot.'

'Forces of evil, as I recall, Inspector – sufficiently ambiguous to suggest she meant in human rather than supernatural form.'

Skelgill nods in acceptance, though he might recall that Sarah Redmond had played her part in rather mercilessly winding up an already disturbed Bella Mandrake.

'Okay – if it weren't them – what about the writers?'

She furrows her brow and turns out her bottom lip in a petulant manner.

'I should have to drink and think a little more – to explore what might be their motives.' She does indeed drink. 'To kill Rich Buckley would appear to be a spontaneous act, since these are unknown and as-yet unpublished authors. Would he have provoked some anger that prompted such a drastic response? Knowing what little I did of him – certainly he was capable of causing offence, without remorse – but could something so damaging have occurred in those few days?'

'There's been talk that he was something of a ladies' man.'

Now – perhaps for illustrative purposes – she makes a blatantly flirtatious gesture, turning a naked shoulder to Skelgill and fluttering her lashes suggestively.

'Oh, I believe we *ladies* could handle Rich, Inspector – although perhaps he would have considered the aspiring authors to be easier pickings.'

Skelgill inhales as though he is about to comment upon this observation, but Sarah Redmond holds up a palm, like a medium suddenly hearing a voice from the other side.

'I think – I think – perhaps instead we should consider *insanity*. That's it.'

She raises her glass and takes another mouthful of wine; she holds it for a moment, before, in a rather melodramatic fashion, tipping back her head and swallowing. Skelgill watches her, intrigued.

'Insanity.'

His response consists of a simple restatement of the noun, but Sarah Redmond seems to understand it is a question.

'Were not the deaths caused by – in effect – *poisoning*?'

Now Skelgill looks like he might wish to back-track.

'My scientific colleagues believe that Rich Buckley died from heart failure, caused by an adverse reaction to some medication he was using – he'd probably obtained it privately and therefore had no proper guidance on how much to take.'

Sarah Redmond glares with mock censure.

'Inspector – so formal – you are spoiling our little game.'

'It's just a medical fact.' He shrugs apologetically. 'If it's any consolation it doesn't completely rule out some interference. Same with Bella Mandrake – took too many sleeping pills, on top of the alcohol – but it's impossible to say she acted alone.'

Sarah Redmond seems content with these caveats. There is the glimmer of excitement in her eyes.

'There you are, then, Inspector – a psychopathic doctor – that is your murderer.'

Skelgill stares at her with some alarm.

'Or a deranged cook.' She holds up a long slim finger with its chiselled nail, and then runs it around the rim of her glass. 'A fly in the soup? A killer in the kitchen. Or, of course, any one of us could have tampered with the drinks. I recall that Burt and little Lucy were most eager to wait upon us.'

'That makes seven suspects.' Skelgill shakes his head in a cartoon manner. 'Now you see why I don't go in for brainstorming.'

'So how shall you solve the crime, Inspector? Do you follow the methods of Poirot, or Holmes, or perhaps our local Inspector Rebus?'

'I prefer not to think about it.'

'But you must grasp the nettle sooner or later.'

'No, I mean it literally – that's what I do – I *don't* think about it – and at some point...'

'*Eureka?*'

'Aye, if I'm lucky.'

Sarah Redmond has gradually been inching forwards, a cold blue fire of icy anticipation burning in her eyes. Then suddenly she snaps them shut, and freezes, as if possessed by a moment of powerful introspection – as though she is committing something to memory, forming a connection that will serve her in future.

'Perfect.'

She opens her eyes. They seem to have an unnatural light that comes from within, a sapphire beam that she fixes upon Skelgill. Maintaining eye contact, she puts down her glass and claws at her hair with both hands, pulling it tight across her scalp and away from her face. Her ears are small and neat and from their delicate lobes dangle pendants of gleaming lapis lazuli. She tilts back her head to expose her slender neck and the milky skin of her throat; Skelgill stares entranced, vampiric.

'Inspector – you look half-starved. Perhaps there is something you want before you go?'

15. POLICE HQ

Wednesday 4pm

'Alright, Guvnor – how'd you get on up north?'
Skelgill gives a non-committal shrug.
'Aye, well – they let me back into England without a passport.'

DS Leyton makes a disapproving grunt.

'That'd be all we need, Guv – criminals would have a field day if there was an international border thirty miles up the road.'

Skelgill and DS Leyton have crossed paths just inside the rear entrance of Penrith HQ. Skelgill, arriving shortly ahead of his sergeant, has paused to read a staff noticeboard, there being a small ad for a vintage split-cane spinning rod that has caught his eye. DS Leyton, hurriedly returning after some errand or other, bears a small though bulging brown paper bag. The team has a scheduled catch-up meeting for which they are both already overdue.

'Er, Guv...'

'Aye?'

'I just walked past your motor.' DS Leyton scratches his head in an obvious acting-dumb fashion. 'Not meaning to be nosey, or nothing, Guv – but I could have sworn there was a cat in there, asleep on the passenger seat.'

Skelgill swings around and stares at his colleague. DS Leyton looks suddenly anxious – perhaps his superior's trip has not gone well and now he will be on the end of an undeserved admonishment. But Skelgill's severe demeanour can be misleading – sometimes it is slow to catch up with his fickle sentiments. He sighs in a bored manner – rather like a schoolboy returning home to his overbearing mother, and the tiresome and inevitable question about what kind of day he has had. Why, after all those skirmishes, stresses and strains, would anyone want to relive them?

'Aye – well, you saw right.'

DS Leyton appears relieved.

'I thought it was, Guv.'

Skelgill sets off along the corridor. He glances over his shoulder at DS Leyton, who still seems hopeful of a more detailed explanation.

'It's a long story, Leyton.'

Skelgill's clipped intonation suggests the long story is not imminent. In short, it is that DS Findlay had returned to collect Skelgill as agreed, still accompanied by the cat, and with tears streaming down his cheeks and a handkerchief to his nose. "I didnae ken I'd be allergic tae the wee deil," had been his choked words. His plan had been to return the cat to the apartment block, on the assumption that it would resume where it had left off, freeloading a good living, as only cats can. Skelgill, however – likely influenced by the creature's leaping upon his lap as though he were its long lost owner, and his own rather carefree spirits at that moment – had petitioned otherwise, on the sworn promise that he would return it to its rightful owner, if any such claim were to be made. That Skelgill keeps at home a volatile Bullboxer incentivised by doggie treats to vanquish cats from his garden (they raid his breeding pond) is a variable in an equation yet to be resolved.

'Is Jones back in?'

'I said we'd meet her in the canteen, Guv – she's getting tea organised.' DS Leyton holds up his bag like a trophy. 'I've got the special ring doughnuts you like, Guv.'

Skelgill casts a contemptuous eye in his sergeant's direction.

'It'll take more than that, Leyton – I've not had any lunch.'

DS Leyton, still a couple of paces behind his superior, casts his eyes to the heavens and shakes his fists in frustration.

'Right, Guv.'

The cafeteria is close by, and Skelgill shoulders open the door like a gunslinger announcing his presence in the town's main saloon. This is perhaps rather fitting, for most of the twenty-odd faces that turn in his direction do so with a collective expression of reverent awe – until first one, then another and then most of them break out into a burst of clapping and raucous cheers. Skelgill is stopped in his tracks. Nonplussed, he turns round – as if they can't mean him – but only DS Leyton is behind. His trusty sidekick, quickly recovered from the routine snub, steps alongside and mutters under his breath.

'It's the street robbery you foiled yesterday, Guv – some of the other newspapers have picked it up.'

Skelgill glances about self-consciously, evidently doing his best to meet the mixed requirements of his audience by appearing at once humble and triumphant; conditions that are not easy bedfellows. The effort seems to disorientate him, and he is clearly relieved when he spots DS Jones signalling from a relatively isolated table across in the far corner of the dining area, partly screened by some portable display boards. As the commotion subsides, he acknowledges the congratulations of those colleagues whom he passes closely, but otherwise, with DS Leyton riding shotgun, he reaches DS Jones without major interruption and takes a seat with his back to the rest of the room.

'Beam me up, Scotty.'

DS Jones grins; perhaps she humours him, for – despite his protests – he shows no inclination to decamp to the privacy of his office.

'Tea, Guv – that's yours with the sugars in the blue mug.'

He reaches out and drinks thirstily.

'Right Leyton, break out those doughnuts for starters.'

DS Leyton glances at DS Jones.

'He means *starters* – he's had no lunch.'

DS Jones looks as though she is about to make some kind of mischievous observation, but she freezes, as the first word is about to form on her lips, and stares beyond her boss's head.

'Hear you've got a cruiserweight contest coming up, Skel.'

Skelgill does not look around. The voice, with its querulous Mancunian drawl, belongs unmistakeably to DI Alec Smart.

'Very funny, Smart.'

'Thought you were getting a bit old for fisticuffs, Skel.'

Now Skelgill does turn in his seat, his cheeks reddening. DI Smart loiters a little beyond reach. He wears a trendy suit with drainpipe trousers and winklepicker shoes that must be a good three inches longer than his feet, and a designer haircut slicked back with gel. He is grinning, though his leer is directed at DS Jones, as if he is pleased to imply that he is by a few years the younger of the two Detective Inspectors. Skelgill stares woodenly and does not reply (this can be a danger sign); DI Smart looks slightly wary and keeps his distance.

'Just thought I should warn you, Skel – in case you didn't know – you wouldn't want to rub her boyfriend up the wrong way.'

'I shan't be rubbing anyone up the wrong way.'

'Not counting the Chief.'

'What's that supposed to mean?'

DI Smart pretends to look hurt by Skelgill's impatient tone.

'Don't shoot the messenger, Skel – I just thought you'd want to see *The Gazette* – evening edition's just out.'

He reaches across the little invisible belt of no-man's land and proffers Skelgill a folded newspaper. Reluctantly Skelgill takes it, and grudgingly nods his thanks. But DI Smart is not looking at him; instead he ogles DS Jones, winks at DS Leyton, spins on his heel, and saunters away.

Skelgill turns back and places the newspaper disinterestedly on the table.

'Prat.'

His sergeants nod in concert, and DS Leyton shoots a disapproving scowl after their unwelcome visitor. But DS Jones is more interested in the local journal – she spreads and smoothes it flat – and promptly giggles as she absorbs the headline above the evidently syndicated and now familiar photograph of Skelgill punching out the lights of the mugger. She spins the paper round for her colleagues to see. Even the normally reserved *Westmorland Gazette* has gone to town on the story – a copy editor's dream – with the predictably alliterative and partisan headline *"Cumbria Cop KOs Cockney Knifeman"*.

Skelgill regards the article with a mixture of affected disdain and poorly disguised interest, and chews one side of his mouth as he reads the short paragraph that – given the dramatic picture – has no need to misrepresent the circumstances. He shakes his head and folds up the paper, although it is noticeable that he puts it to rest close by, as though he has now taken ownership of it.

'Bit harsh, that, Guv.'

'In what way, Leyton?'

'About him being a Cockney, Guv – how do they know? Just 'cause it happened down in London – don't mean to say it were one of the local villains.'

Skelgill shrugs.

'I can't help you with that one, Leyton – he seemed to lose the power of speech before I was able to inquire after his place of birth.'

DS Leyton shrugs phlegmatically. He resumes his task rudely interrupted by DI Smart, and tears open the bag of doughnuts.

'Dive in, everyone.'

Skelgill grunts his approval and does as invited; he chews thoughtfully for a minute or two, perhaps considering a point that may not have occurred to his colleagues – that, since the first article appeared in the London press, describing him as a 'mystery detective', he has been identified. He might reasonably wonder by what process this has occurred, and what ramifications it will have.

While he and DS Leyton continue to tuck into the doughnuts, DS Jones watches on calmly – neither of her colleagues expecting her to partake in such an unhealthy afternoon snack. After a minute or two she opens a file that lies on the table before her.

'Shall I update you on a couple of things, Guv – there's some interesting new forensics?'

Skelgill swallows and takes a gulp of tea.

'Interesting – or significant?'

DS Jones narrows her eyes.

'Significant – to the extent they can be trusted.'

Skelgill nods sharply for her to continue.

'Dr Herdwick has received the results of the more detailed blood and fluid tests that he sent away to the lab. I don't know if this is a coincidence, Guv–' (Skelgill twitches involuntarily) 'but the same point applies to both Rich Buckley and Bella Mandrake. The residual levels of the chemicals that may have caused each of their deaths – atropine in Buckley's case and benzodiazepine in Mandrake's – were approximately *ten times* greater than could have been achieved by swallowing the medicines found in their possession.'

She looks up from the page. Skelgill is staring at her intensely – it is hard to tell where his thoughts might lie: whether this news has struck a chord, or if he is simply just distracted by some appraisal of his attractive colleague.

DS Leyton is more transparently perplexed.

'Maybe we missed some empty packets?'

DS Jones shakes her head.

'That's exactly the point, though – apparently it's not a matter of quantity – it's to do with concentrations. Dr Herdwick said – well – his words were along the lines that you can't get drunk on shandy, Guv.'

Skelgill laughs ironically, knowing the cantankerous pathologist would not have used the expression *drunk*.

'So what's he telling us?'

DS Jones speaks with careful and deliberate enunciation.

'That if the substances that proved toxic came from medicines, the pills weren't what they said on the packets.'

DS Leyton offers a suggestion.

'Maybe they were counterfeit?'

But DS Jones is shaking her head.

'We've had a report back on the packaging – it's genuine – in both cases sold under strict licence in the UK.'

DS Leyton is still frowning.

'So, what did you mean about not trusting the results?'

DS Jones glances at the printed notes and turns a page. She taps a paragraph with a neatly sharpened nail and nods, as if she is reminded of what she needs to know.

'It's a statistical point. Remember at school, the null hypothesis?' She glances at each of her colleagues in turn; they look like they don't. 'This result is only accurate at the ninety-five per cent confidence level.'

DS Leyton grimaces.

'That sounds pretty confident, to me.'

DS Jones makes an ambivalent face.

'It means that if you did the test a hundred times, you'd get a false result five times because of sampling error.'

'One in twenty.' Skelgill makes this conversion.

'That's right, Guv – it's still a reasonably high probability – but as a standalone fact you might struggle to impress a jury.'

Skelgill sticks out his jaw and rubs his stubble with a knuckle.

'Look – I was rubbish at maths – at most things, come to that – and this week I'm getting sick of the word *coincidence* – but there must be some statistic in our favour – since *both* of them had inexplicably high concentrations of the drugs in their blood.'

DS Jones nods eagerly.

'And Dr Herdwick agrees with that, Guv.'

DS Leyton has taken out his mobile phone and begun to tap away at the keypad. He suddenly makes an involuntary start and emits a little *cor blimey* whistle.

'What is it, Leyton?'

'I was just doing the odds, Guv. See – one in twenty, that's nineteen-to-one against, in racing parlance. You put a pound on a double on two nags both at nineteens and you'd get four hundred nicker back, including your pound stake.'

DS Jones is grinning widely; her colleague may have struggled with the concept of statistical confidence levels – but by viewing the equation through the eyes of a bookie he has delivered a striking outcome. Skelgill is nodding slowly.

'One in four hundred sounds a lot more significant than one in twenty – chance of it being a mistake, that is.'

Now DS Jones turns another page of the report.

'There's more on times of death, as well, Guv. For Rich Buckley we think around two p.m. on Sunday, with a margin of a couple of hours either side. A bit more accurate for Bella Mandrake – quite close to two a.m. on Monday.

Skelgill folds his arms.

'Just remind me – neither of their bedroom doors were locked?'

The two sergeants shake their heads in unison: it was DS Jones who first entered Bella Mandrake's room; and DS Leyton is hotfoot from his interview with Linda Gray, who discovered Rich Buckley.

'What are you thinking, Guv?'

Skelgill raises his shoulders and rotates his head, as though his neck is stiff.

'If their doors were generally left open, then someone could have tampered with their medicines. Seems unlikely to have happened while they were in their rooms – though not impossible. Buckley, I wouldn't expect to lock his door – but if you'd have asked me to bet whose door *was* locked on Sunday night, I'd have said Bella Mandrake's.'

DS Jones holds out an upturned palm, offering a suggestion.

'Though she was prone to nocturnal wandering, Guv – remember what Burt Boston told us. She could have gone downstairs again on Sunday night, and then forgotten to lock her door when she came back?'

Skelgill dunks and eats the final bite of the last odd doughnut and then drains his tea. He licks his fingers and leans forward, resting his elbows on the table. For a moment he stares down at the soggy crumbs in the base of the mug. Perhaps in the absence of tea leaves they provide a satisfyingly distracting pattern, mirroring the irregular images that populate his mind, stirred up by Sarah Redmond's quick-fire improvised hypothesising – to which he can now add this afternoon's revelations. After a minute or two he sits back and stares at DS Leyton.

'Get us a top up, will you, Leyton?'

DS Leyton seems perplexed, as if he has been expecting something more profound than a request for more tea, and the command does not immediately register. Then he starts, and rises, and reaches for their three mugs as ordered.

'I'm fine, thanks.' DS Jones politely declines.

'Something to eat, as well, Guv?'

Now it is Skelgill who stares rather vacantly, as though this question baffles him. Evidently, competing thoughts bar the way to the basic processing function of his brain. After a short delay the question gets through, but – to DS Leyton's evident wonder – Skelgill waves him away.

'Not just now, Leyton.'

Frowning, Skelgill watches DS Leyton lumber across to the serving counter. Then he turns back to face DS Jones. He ducks his head, and speaks in a hushed voice.

'Bella Mandrake had a novel rejected by Rich Buckley Publishing. I found the letter in her flat. They gave her a scathing review.'

DS Jones's eyes widen.

'Are you thinking she killed him and then committed suicide?'

Skelgill grins, clearly surprised, and breaks out into an uncharacteristic chuckle.

'What is it, Guv?'

He shakes his head – but clearly her rapid deduction has prompted some comparison in his mind.

'You're not left-handed, are you?'

'No Guv – er, well...'

'Well, what?'

'I'm ambidextrous, actually – but you know how, when you're at school, they try to get you to do everything right-handed – to avoid smudging the ink – cutting-out with scissors – and hockey, you can only play right-handed.'

Skelgill makes an ironic face.

'Aye, well – hockey wasn't one of my strong suits.'

'That's darts ain't it, Guv? I thought you were fairly handy down the pub?'

This is DS Leyton chipping in, as he leans over to place replenished mugs on the table.

Skelgill glances at DS Jones. 'He means the *oche* – it's where you chuck from.'

DS Jones nods obediently; though it is likely she knows this fact, being a useful darts player herself.

'So, how did it go with Gerald Bond?' Skelgill pulls his mug towards him and, peering critically into the liquid, asks this question in an offhand manner.

DS Jones reaches to extract her notebook from the case at her feet. She is wearing a low-cut top and Skelgill and DS Leyton casually look away – but their simultaneous action finds them staring with surprise at one another, unprepared to speak. There is a moment of comic silence, until DS Leyton suddenly breaks into an exaggerated bout of coughing.

DS Jones glances up inquiringly, but seeing Skelgill nod that she should go ahead, she lays down her notebook and speaks first from memory.

'On a scale of one to ten, Guv – I'd say five in terms of being uncooperative.'

Skelgill nods once.

'Interesting.'

DS Leyton, too, nods in agreement, although his quizzical expression suggests he has less of an idea why this might be thus.

'I think he's blaming us for ruining his career as an author, Guv.'

'He didn't have a career as an author.'

'No, Guv – but he seems to believe he was on the verge of a breakthrough, and we spoiled it by calling off the retreat.'

Skelgill scoffs.

'What did he expect – two deaths and it's still *Carry On Camping*?'

'I get the impression he would have happily carried on, Guv.'

Skelgill gnaws at a recalcitrant finger nail.

'Aye – he probably would. While I was there – not long after he'd pronounced Buckley dead – he was trying to talk everyone into staying.'

'He claims he'd canvassed opinion – even after Bella Mandrake had died – and there was a majority in favour of seeing out the full week.'

Skelgill shakes his head.

'It's all very well – in his job he probably dealt with a death every few days. Ordinary members of the public just don't experience this kind of thing – even we don't.'

DS Jones nods.

'I don't think he's really accepted that he's retired, Guv – his study is still kitted out like a consulting room – with an examination table and all the equipment – he's even got a skeleton.'

Skelgill appears pensive, his features contracting into a scowl.

'Did he confirm what Lucy Hecate said – about having a special contribution to make?'

DS Jones nods.

'He did, Guv – more or less word for word as you told me. And he was able to reel off the reasons the others had given – though he didn't sound impressed – I think he considered himself a cut above the rest.'

'What did he have to say about Rich Buckley?'

DS Jones squints at her notes, and flicks over a couple of pages.

'His exact words were, "Congenitally rude" – he was quite matter of fact about it, though, Guv.'

Skelgill lets out an ironic hiss.

'That's a laugh, coming from a Yorkshireman.'

'Maybe that's why they had a couple of barneys – it's not all of us can bridge the north-south divide, eh, Guv?'

This contribution comes from DS Leyton, and Skelgill looks a bit nonplussed by the notion. However, DS Jones continues.

'He did become a little agitated when I suggested he hadn't got on well with Buckley. He wanted to know who had said that.'

'What did you tell him?'

'I wasn't in a position to relate confidential conversations.'

'And what did he say?'

'I don't think he was impressed, Guv.'

Skelgill tuts irascibly.

'And what about Buckley being ill – or asking his advice?'

She shakes her head.

'He said the only person to consult with him – as he put it – was Bella Mandrake – and she was basically begging paracetamol at every possible opportunity – he described it as attention seeking.'

'And did he give her anything?'

'He said all he'd taken to the island was a small supply for personal use, and she'd used that up in the first two days.'

'And nothing to Buckley?'

'No, Guv – and he says he had no idea that Buckley was taking any medication – he's heard of the drug, though – and he says there's no way that could have killed him.'

'Really?'

Skelgill sounds disappointed to hear this diagnosis.

'Aha. He reckons these commercial preparations are tested to extreme levels of safety – even an overdose ought to be completely safe.'

'Aye – we know that now.'

DS Jones is nodding.

'That was the one time I got a smile out of him, Guv – when I said the police surgeon had confirmed heart failure as the cause of death.'

'Because he was right.'

'Aha. And he said a similar thing as Dr Herdwick – that in a significant proportion of sudden cardiac deaths a clear cause is never identified – especially in ostensibly healthy victims.'

'What about Bella Mandrake's overdose?'

'He was quick to pontificate on that, too, Guv. I told him top-line what we know – to see how he reacted. He just said it's difficult to overdose on sleeping pills, because of the reduced strength that they make them nowadays.'

Skelgill scratches his head in a gesture of frustration.

'Did you ask him if he thought the deaths were suspicious?'

'Yes, Guv.'

'And?'

'He said not in the least, Guv. He said he'd seen many far more suspicious cases – and plenty worse than these that had

201

never been referred to the Coroner. He seemed quite indignant – almost as if he were taking it personally.'

Skelgill is again contemplative for a few moments.

'Did he ask any questions?'

'Just wanted to know why you weren't there, Guv. I got the feeling he expected someone more of his own rank.'

'What did you tell him?'

'That you were coordinating the investigation, Guv – I didn't give any specific details.'

Skelgill nods, seemingly content with this response.

'He did ask whether this would be all, Guv. He's due to go hiking for the month of November to finish the research for his hillwalking guidebook – so he won't be easily contactable.'

Skelgill sniffs rather disdainfully.

'Wouldn't you be bored out of your brains with all that time on your hands?'

His sergeants regard him wryly, as if they know exactly what he would be doing under such circumstances: the phrase "rod, perch and pole" perhaps springing to mind. This is one of Skelgill's little aphorisms, which he uses interchangeably with "hook, line and sinker", the former sounding curiously apposite, despite having no connection with angling (the three synonyms representing five-and-a-half yards, or one fortieth of a furlong). As if subconsciously making the connection to land measures, DS Jones attempts to get the conversation back on track.

'He's got a big house to look after, Guv – sits among fields and woodland just the other side of Bolton.'

Skelgill's ears prick up.

'Is it near the Eden?'

'As far as I could tell, Guv, the grounds run right down to the river.'

Skelgill now looks like he wishes he'd accompanied her. He shakes his head regretfully.

'There's some cracking Grayling along that stretch. Two pound and above. You have to trot a worm downstream, sometimes far as the eye can see.' Suddenly his left hand is up in front of his face, and he is gripping a rod, feeling for the fish.

'You get a knock-knock-knock and then it's *bang!* – into the fight – you always know a Grayling – feel it nodding as you bring it back.'

DS Leyton looks momentarily alarmed – for it seems that Skelgill is about to hand him the invisible rod in order to experience exactly what playing a Grayling is like. But, to his relief, his superior casts the equipment into the ether, slaps both hands on the table in a perfunctory manner and looks him in the face.

'So, what about you, Leyton – how was Linda Gray the galloping gourmet?'

'How d'you know that, Guv?'

'Know what?'

'She's got a stables.'

Skelgill grins rather inanely – it appears he has invented the phrase purely for limerick-like purposes.

'And why not?'

DS Leyton appears more confused.

'There's no horses any more, Guv – it's been converted into her restaurant, *The Stables*.'

Now Skelgill lifts an imaginary phone to his ear.

'A table for Mabel at *The Stables*.'

Quite what has possessed Skelgill it is impossible to know. Perhaps it is the sugar rush of five doughnuts. But bubbling beneath the surface of his typically enigmatic demeanour is a little well of euphoria that appears to be in danger of erupting in a display of unpredictable outpourings – indeed it would not be difficult to imagine him suddenly go gallivanting about the canteen and join in a waltz with a bemused member of the catering staff. Or maybe that would be going a bit far.

'Guv?'

'Aye?'

'Linda Gray, Guv.'

'Fire away, Leyton.'

Skelgill clasps his hands together and leans forward, regarding his sergeant with an expression of deep-set concentration.

'Righto, Guv.' DS Leyton composes himself. 'Seems a nice lady, Guv. When I explained about the Coroner and the probable causes of the deaths, and how we're obliged to investigate, she burst out in tears.'

'What?'

'That's right, Guv. The full waterworks. She said she's been worried stiff that it was something to do with her.'

Skelgill's abnormal burst of energy appears to be subsiding.

'Because of her cooking?'

'That's right, Guv – she said she'd done her best – but the kitchen was a bit antiquated and the food was all supplied in advance – mostly tinned and vacuum packed – she said it ought to have been alright – but she likes to source her own ingredients so she knows they're fresh and completely safe.'

'Her food tasted fine to me, Leyton – and as far as I could see everyone else was tucking in.'

DS Leyton nods.

'That's right, Guv – she said they all complimented her – but I suppose you never can know with food – the bugs are invisible.' He wipes a hand across his brow and shakes his head. 'After that last time we were at the *Taj*, Guv – I mean – I was never out of the khazi all the next day.'

DS Jones giggles at her colleague's bald admission, but Skelgill is back in serious mode and she curtails her mirth. He points a finger skywards to emphasise his response.

'Anyway – if she'd poisoned Bella Mandrake on Sunday night she'd have poisoned the lot of us – we all ate the same soup and hotpot.'

If a little seed has been sown by Sarah Redmond's scatterbrain ramblings – in this instance that a deranged chef would be well placed to administer poisons – Skelgill appears underwhelmed by the idea. Indeed, given that servers brought out the food from the kitchen where Linda Gray toiled, there would be no guarantee that a doctored plate would reach its intended target.

'I pointed that out, Guv – but she's been doubly worried because she was the one that found Rich Buckley – she said

Sarah Redmond told her that in half of all murder cases, the killer leads the police to the body of the victim.'

Skelgill grins ruefully and shakes his head. It seems Sarah Redmond's mischief making extended beyond the baiting of Bella Mandrake. Nevertheless, he would perhaps identify with her methods – there is something about provocation that lifts the veil of feigned naivety, and it is a technique he is not averse to employing when the opportunity arises.

'So what about Buckley – what's the story, there?'

'Pretty much as she told you, Guv.' DS Leyton refers to his notes. 'Went up to speak to him about dinner at just after four p.m. – that was their regular afternoon tea break – and found him spark out on the bed. She said she didn't touch anything in the room – rushed down and got hold of the doctor.'

'And we think time of death was mostly likely two o'clock.' Skelgill glances at DS Jones, who nods in confirmation. 'Though it could have been as late as four.'

He leaves this suggestion hanging in the air – and apparently has no corollary to offer. After a moment or two DS Leyton continues with his account.

'I did ask her what she thought of him, Guv.'

'Surprise me, Leyton.'

'Actually, Guv, she was quite civil. She said he was a very bright man and that he'd obviously got a lot on his mind. She said the first night before dinner he'd asked her what she was writing, and then on the second night he asked her exactly the same question.'

Skelgill raises his eyebrows.

'Sounds par for the course.'

'I think she's the accommodating type, Guv – I suppose you need to be in her line of work.'

'I thought that was hoteliers?'

'Very good, Guv.'

Skelgill grins abruptly.

'And what about musical bedrooms?'

'She was a bit shocked when I suggested that, Guv. She said she went to bed early every night – since she'd volunteered to be up to prepare breakfast. Plus the day was tiring, what with writing *and* doing the cooking.'

'Remind me, is she married?'

'Divorced, Guv.'

'Where's the restaurant?'

'Egremont, Guv – bit of a trek, actually. I didn't think there was civilisation past Whitehaven.'

'Some would say it stops long before there, Leyton.' Skelgill purses his lips thoughtfully. 'Still – might give it a give it a look in, next time I'm out that way.'

'The food's alright, Guv.'

Skelgill folds his arms and cocks his head on one side. DS Leyton has made a minor slip of the tongue.

'She insisted I had lunch, Guv – she's good as gold – I would have felt bad refusing.'

Skelgill nods grudgingly. While it is not ideal protocol to accept a meal under these circumstances – whether paid for or otherwise – it is unimaginable that he would have left such a gift horse in the stables, so to speak.

'Let's hope she's not poisoned you, Leyton.' He grins wryly. 'And talking of lunch.'

He casts an eye over towards the servery. It is still half an hour before high teas will be available, but such rules are made to be broken. He appears to be assessing which members of staff are on duty, and therefore whom to target with his charm, when he becomes aware of a person standing politely beside him, awaiting his attention. It is a young WPC from the Chief's office. Skelgill casually turns towards her, in the manner of a self-confident celebrity to an autograph-hunting admirer. Accordingly, almost curtseying, she reaches out and presents him with a folded sheet of paper.

'Message for you, sir.'

Skelgill opens the page. It is a handwritten note, the script penned in an angry, expressive style. However, its contents comprise a succinct one-sentence summons. Skelgill nods to the WPC, and turns to his sergeants.

'Chief wants to see me – I reckon we've got enough to keep her happy, eh?'

They nod eagerly. Skelgill resumes his perusal of the food counter, but then he realises that the WPC is still standing to attention. He looks at her inquiringly.

'I was to accompany you upstairs, sir.'

Skelgill, for a second, appears as if he will object – but, lunch or not – perhaps he has a pang of sympathy for the agitated constable, who looks like she ought still to be at school. Moreover, given his propensity to interpret orders from on high with whatever degree of latitude he can get away with at the time, it is perhaps no surprise to him that a chaperone has been despatched to ensure his attendance. He shrugs resignedly and rises to his feet.

'Leyton, do us a favour – get us a burger or something – whatever they'll rustle up.' He glances at DS Jones. 'She only wants to see me for five minutes – we'll carry on the meeting in my office – I'll give you the lowdown on Bonnie Scotland.'

He straightens his jacket and falls in with the WPC, who walks gingerly beside him, plainly afraid to make eye contact. As they reach the exit door he can be heard saying in a jocular tone, "What is it about redheads? It has to be *now*."

*

When an audience with his boss has gone badly, and he has been pulled up either for lack of progress or – as is more usually the case – his maverick approach to some aspect of an investigation, Skelgill is wont to return to his office with a face like thunder; a sign that warns his unfortunate subordinates to tread upon eggshells until his temper has subsided. On this occasion, however, there is something radically different about his entire demeanour. While such a berating usually comes as at least a partial surprise to Skelgill (although rarely to anyone else concerned in the matter) – which must add fuel to the flames of his indignation, having expected praise and received a rebuke – whatever has just passed has exceeded the norms in terms of its capacity to shock him back into line. Indeed, while under similar circumstances his waiting sergeants would do exactly that – *wait,* until he has something to say – such is his pallid and stunned countenance that they both look shocked themselves, and DS Jones is unable to contain her concern.

'Guv – what's wrong – are you okay?'

Skelgill, upon entering his office, has rounded his desk. There is a burger and chips in a polystyrene takeaway package, and – whereas his normal response would be to fall hungrily upon this meal before all else – now he ignores it and stands awkwardly behind his chair.

'I'm on leave.'

DS Leyton looks confused.

'What do you mean, Guv?'

'I'm off the case.'

'Guv – why?'

Skelgill swallows as if he has a mouthful of grit.

'Dr Gerald Bond has made a complaint.'

At this revelation, DS Jones's face falls; her lower lip starts to curl and her eyes glisten as though they begin to flood with tears.

'Guv – but – that must be my fault – I know I was a bit hard on him.'

Skelgill glares at her, penetratingly.

'You *were* hard on him.' He raises an index finger and jabs it at her. 'And you know what? You did a good job.' (There is an expletive deleted here, an Anglo-Saxon adjective.) 'And you know what else – that's exactly what I said to the Chief.' He lowers the finger and rests both hands on the back of his seat. 'Furthermore – she agreed with me.' He shakes his head. 'He did mention the interview – but that's not the substance of his complaint.'

'Well, what is it, Guv?' DS Leyton sounds incensed. 'We can't have punters deciding who runs an investigation. Especially when they're a suspect.'

Skelgill bares his teeth, in a somewhat manic grimace.

'That's the operative word, Leyton – *suspect*. Technically, I'm one, too. I was there when Bella Mandrake died. I socialised with the group while off duty. I formed "relationships" that might influence my judgement.' He makes inverted commas in the air with his fingers around the word relationships.

'But he must want you off the case, Guv – he must have a reason for that – something to hide?'

Skelgill shrugs.

'That'll be for Smart to discover.'

Now there is a descent into an enhanced state of despondency. DS Jones, ashen-faced, lowers her eyes under Skelgill's searching glance. DS Leyton leans across from where he is sitting and head-butts a metal filing cabinet, causing trophies on top to fall over. Skelgill ignores this and steps across to the window; he stares out, thoughtfully watching the dusky sky, as orange-tinted clouds drift above the burnt umber of the landscape. Perhaps he is already assessing the conditions for fishing.

What he has not told his team is the full story. It is correct that Dr Gerald Bond has telephoned the Chief to register a complaint. And he did mention the interview with a tenacious sergeant whom he referred to as having *Stasi*-like qualities; both Skelgill and his boss warmed to this description. He also exaggerated Skelgill's role during his evening on the island – to paraphrase, he claimed the inspector was drunk and had to be helped to bed. Skelgill couldn't deny there was a semblance of accuracy in this – although he had said in his (somewhat weak-sounding) defence that he felt ill rather than inebriated.

Ironically, it appears that this would not have been sufficient to see Skelgill despatched for gardening leave. Indeed, the Chief had already made allowances for Skelgill's involvement on the Sunday night, and had overruled potential objections on the grounds of his valuable insider's perspective. The killer blow, so to speak, evidently relates to events that took place yesterday in London's Covent Garden. Skelgill had defended his actions in knocking out the street thief as a split-second decision that concerned his own self-defence and the protection of the female being robbed. On the whole, the Chief had accepted this point of view. What she could not accept, however, nor could Skelgill so easily deny, was the photograph of Skelgill taken *inside* the restaurant, showing him being spoon-fed at close (indeed intimate) quarters by Angela Cutting – who, just like Dr Gerald Bond, is a potential suspect in the case. No matter how much Skelgill had protested, it is a fact that the camera never lies – it just doesn't tell the whole truth. As for how the Chief had become aware of this photograph, Skelgill was not to learn – although she showed it to him on her tablet, and he was able to discern its source as a notorious gossip website that masquerades as a purveyor of news that is in the public interest. (If there is any consolation in this for Skelgill, it is that the image was not *the* most compromising of yesterday's brief moments that might have been captured upon film.)

'But DI Smart, Guv – it won't wash – never mind we don't want to work with him.' DS Leyton despairingly breaks the silence that has cloaked the office like the enfolding darkness beyond the window. 'His whole system depends on snouts and grasses, Guv.'

DS Jones now joins in the fray.

'He'll never work this one out, Guv. He's not got the patience.'

Skelgill stares at her with surprise. On another occasion, this observation would clearly merit some further explanation – for even Skelgill would admit that, in his personal interactions, he is not renowned for this desirable human quality. But what DS Jones has perceived, of course, is that Skelgill *does* possess an immense inner patience, one that no fisherman (and perhaps detective) can succeed without. But now he shrugs off her oblique compliment and – in his typically sardonic fashion, makes a virtue out of necessity.

'Never mind, chaps, I might be buying you all drinks on Friday night.'

DS Leyton scowls.

'Not if DI Smart has anything to do with it, Guv.'

'I wasn't thinking of Smart.' Skelgill forces a somewhat crooked grin. 'I've got two full days to catch a twenty-five pound pike and save myself a grand.'

16. THE TOXICOLOGIST

Thursday 10am

Having rowed a good two miles from his temporary berth at the north end of Derwentwater, and despite there being half the distance again still to cover to reach his intended destination, Skelgill has been unable to pass Grisholm without coming ashore.

He ties his boat to the same mooring post as before: a clove hitch, a double half hitch, and an overhand knot. The conditions are considerably more benign than during his last visit, and indeed are forecast to improve further, as the ridge of high pressure that was responsible for yesterday's easterly in Scotland drifts north-west across the British Isles, drawing the benign bulk of the anticyclone from the continent. His boat rocks gently against the wooden pier, and he steps easily ashore onto the pontoon.

He can see at a glance that the planked boathouse is empty; although he enters and replaces on its brackets the boat hook he had employed to prod for his presumed sunken craft. He stands and regards it now, no doubt running over in his mind the possibilities that might pertain to Sunday night's events. Then he laughs, and cuffs himself with the heel of his hand upon his forehead. He returns to where the boat is moored, kneels down, and hooks out his old khaki rucksack; it contains his mobile phone and various other essential personal possessions, such as a *Kelly Kettle* and the wherewithal to make tea.

The short path that winds through the wood must seem familiar, although it was at dusk and then in darkness that he used it previously (apart from Monday morning, when he was somewhat under the weather). He takes his time, walking soundlessly over the mulched earth, alert for signs of life. The dense rhododendron shrub layer, however, affords little lateral vision, and he is restricted to watching the path ahead, and the oaks above, still hanging on to a good many russet autumn leaves, despite the best efforts of the storm. He pauses, hearing a sound, and then waits motionlessly as a little passel of Long-tailed Tits, already coalesced into their wintering flock, bob across the gap a few yards from him, one at a time, like candy floss in miniature, pink-and-white-and-black balls of fluff on sticks, each taking their chance, running the gauntlet of what must be a Sparrowhawk's feeding corridor. He counts and reaches ten – probably a single family party – and no more, as the soft purring contact calls fade and the flock flits away on its incessant quest for food. He might reflect that, were he to come back here in spring, how many would have survived through the winter: two, or three perhaps?

Moving on himself, he quickly gains the edge of the clearing in which stands Grisholm Hall. There is a path that leads up to the main door, but Skelgill cuts across the damp mossy lawn and makes a beeline for the nearest corner of the property. From here he follows the perimeter of the building, skirting the wing and turning back into the courtyard, around which the rear of the hall makes a u-shape. For a minute he surveys the ungainly edifice: the windows along the first floor are those of the landing and corridors that serve the bedroom wings. At the end of each of these, on the ground floor, there is a fire exit, and also on this level the likes of the library and billiards room. The kitchen is positioned in the central block; it has a door set on one side and two large sash windows. Skelgill aims directly for the furthest of these from the door. Pausing to tighten the straps of his rucksack, he clambers nimbly onto the sandstone sill and, bracing himself in rock-climbing fashion against the stone jambs, stands upright. He leans back to check briefly through the pane at his midriff, and then reaches above his head. Now his purpose becomes clear, for there is a half-inch gap between the top of the upper sash and the frame. He slides his fingers into this space, and tugs. Nothing happens, though a few brittle flakes of paint falling cause him to shy momentarily. With his arms almost fully extended, he has little muscle leverage to bring to bear. Now he tightens his grip with his thumbs, and performs a little hop. The sudden transfer of weight does the trick: with a squeal of protest the sash slides down about eighteen inches and, with a second sharp manoeuvre, he pulls and then pushes it to waist level. On Monday morning he might have been the worse for wear, but he still had sufficient wits about him to notice that the rather tired old window lacks a sash lock.

His route now takes him via a drainer onto the stone flagged floor of the kitchen, with a resounding clump of his boots. He stands for a moment, as though listening to the echo as it scouts about the house and returns with nothing to report. Apart from the obvious absence of any craft at the landing stage, he knows that there are no imminent bookings for the property, and that the agents have been instructed not to send in their cleaners until the police have cleared up their side of the case. So he can be confident that, small mammals excepted, he is alone.

He might be expected now to head directly upstairs and perform a thorough search of the bedrooms – most notably those of Rich Buckley and Bella Mandrake. He does indeed walk through to the central hallway, whence the main staircase leads to these chambers, but instead he does a rather curious thing. To one side of the chief entrance is an alcove used as a kind of robing area. Presumably provided for the benefit of guests, there are half a dozen pairs of partly perished green rubber wellingtons, a vase of furled golf umbrellas, and a series of old coats bunched together on a row of hooks – indeed among them is the long fawn mackintosh that Lucy Hecate must have borrowed when she went out to signal for help. Skelgill loosens one strap of his rucksack and swings it to the ground. Then he sorts through the coats and selects a weathered *Barbour* that is not so different in appearance from his own rather more scale-spangled version that lies in the bow of his boat. And now, apparently suitably attired, he backs against the front door and closes his eyes.

213

After a few seconds he opens them and walks across the hall in the direction of the drawing room. One of the double doors is ajar and he squeezes through the gap. Now he stands still and closes his eyes again. After a short while he reopens his eyes, takes off the jacket, and hangs it on the back of a nearby Windsor chair. Then he strides across the room and takes a seat on one of the sofas, beside the fireplace. He leans forward, elbows on knees, chin cupped in upturned hands, and remains deep in thought for some minutes. At intervals he turns to face various parts of the room, nodding his head as though he is acknowledging the invisible actors in whatever little scene is playing out. While the casual observer would be excused for thinking these are the actions of a madman, of course, what he is actually doing is retracing in his mind the events – as best he can recollect – of Sunday night.

This peculiar pantomime does not end here. Employing the same method – move, stop, close eyes, ponder, open eyes, move on – he returns to the hall, ascends to Rich Buckley's bedroom, descends to the drawing room, leaves the drawing room, pretends to exit the house and then re-enter by the locked main door, re-visits the drawing room, departs for the dining room and takes a seat at the empty table (where he has all manner of silent conversations with non-existent fellow diners and servers), returns once again to the drawing room, plays a game of invisible *Scrabble* (on this occasion allowing himself a triumphant fist-pump when he lays out his killer word, *bumfit*), and – finally – he goes up to 'his' bedroom, and indeed through all the motions that he can evidently recall – including actually *using* the toilet and, from a prone position on the bed, staring at the empty candlestick, out of reach on the occasional table beside the door, before closing his eyes for a final time.

Just when it seems he might genuinely have nodded off, his eyes spring open, he springs off the bed, and the springs emit a creak of relief. At apparently no time during this performance has he paid any attention to the detail of his surroundings. And now he trots downstairs, collects the *Barbour* from the drawing room, replaces it (rather reluctantly) upon its peg, slings his rucksack on one shoulder, and strides through into the kitchen. He vaults onto the drainer, clambers out of the open window, and hauls the upper sash back into place, leaving the same half-inch gap as before. He bounds down into the paved courtyard and, checking his watch, sets off at a jog back towards the jetty.

Arriving at the double, he skids to what looks like a surprised halt – but this is due to the unexpectedly greasy boardwalk, and not the fact that his boat has gone – for this time, *it is exactly how he left it*. He unties the painter and jumps aboard, his momentum transferring to the craft and causing it to float gently away from the pier. He does not, however, immediately take up his oars. Instead, he unfastens a pocket of his rucksack and extracts a small notebook with a pencil held in a band at one side. Flipping this open to a marked page, he stares for a moment at its contents. Beneath the word 'Grisholm' is a list, numbered one to ten. Against each number is a name. Number one is Rich Buckley. Number two is Bella Mandrake. And so on, through the members of the retreat, down to number ten, which is marked *D..Skelgill!!!* – and which appears to have been added as an afterthought. Numbers one, two and ten are crossed through. Skelgill tugs the pencil from its holder and – as if out of superstition as much as expedient – licks the tip. Then he scores out two more names.

*

'Ah, Daniel – I was beginning to think you were enjoying too much the fishing.'

Skelgill chuckles.

'Hans, it would be a nice problem to have.'

The older man grins sagely without revealing his teeth. Soon to reach the age of seventy, though looking exceedingly robust, he is of medium height, shorter than Skelgill, though stockier, with close-cropped grey hair, a pinkish complexion, wide-set heavy-lidded pale blue eyes with fair lashes and brows, a broad-tipped nose and protruding lips. This is Dr Hans Sinisalu, an Estonian of Russian parentage, erstwhile Professor of

Toxicology at the University of Tartu, Estonia. Having built his reputation on Baltic soil during the Soviet era, the lifting of the Iron Curtain found his specialist knowledge of the adverse effects of chemicals upon human beings to be in global demand. He travelled widely, working in Africa, Australia, the Far East and North and South America, before finally settling in the United Kingdom, where he was retained as a consultant to the British police, and appeared in many high-profile trials as an expert witness. Coincidentally a lifelong fisherman, a chance remark during a telephone conversation some ten years ago with the then Detective *Sergeant* Skelgill led to the discovery of their shared passion: most notably for *Esox lucius* (to use the lingua franca) – pike in English or *haug* in Eesti. It is Estonia's most widespread species of fish, and one that, unlike in Britain, appears commonly on menus. A conversation about this creature led to an invitation to fish in the Lakes that was in due course taken up and – to cut short a long story – eventually to the venerable academic choosing Borrowdale in Cumbria for the place of his retirement. Here he resides contentedly with his wife – a former zoologist of some eminence – in a small cottage, surrounded by its own grounds and with its own landing stage, in a secluded corner of Derwentwater.

'Come inside, Daniel – you look tired, if you don't mind my saying so.'

Skelgill grins.

'I love the way you Ruskies call a spade a spade.'

'I am Estonian, Daniel, and proud of it.'

Skelgill stops for a moment, and cocks his head on one side.

'Didn't we just play you at football?'

'You did – and you lost – although we "Ruskies" are not known for our gloating. It is our austere upbringing.'

The professor beckons to Skelgill and leads the way through the interior of the stone cottage. It has been tastefully converted to admit modern conveniences, such as central heating and a fitted kitchen, whilst retaining its original seventeenth century charm. There are exposed oak beams barely above head height, and walls of geometrically laid Lakeland slate. They enter a comfortable lounge, where stone flags give way to a deep-pile carpet, and from a log fire in a great stone hearth emanates the pungent scent of pine resin. The room has been extended, and a pair of French doors and their adjacent picture windows afford a magnificent view down to the lake, where Skelgill's boat can be seen moored at the little landing stage. A couple of wicker armchairs face this view, angled slightly towards one another, with a low oak table between them. Upon this is evidently laid a meal of some sort, beneath a square of fresh white linen.

'Annika has a yoga class in Keswick – she sends her best regards – she says she is sorry she will not be here to cook *verivorstid* – but she has prepared a cold lunch for us.'

Skelgill lowers himself into the seat as indicated, while the professor removes the cloth from the food: a selection of open-face sandwiches on thinly sliced black rye and white breads, a mixture of fishes and meats garnished with sliced cucumber, pickles and tomato.

'Looks delicious, Hans – tell her she's too kind.'

'I shall – now, please, help yourself – *jätku leiba*.'

Skelgill requires no second invitation and does as commanded. The professor pours them each a frothing beer – this a local Lakeland brew – which also meets with Skelgill's approval.

'I thought just a small one, Daniel – you will want to be keeping a clear head out on the water.'

Skelgill nods, chewing hungrily.

'That forms part of the questions I have for you, Hans.'

'Really?'

'Aye – but first I wondered what you can tell me about atropine.'

The professor glances sharply at Skelgill, though his implacable Slavic features register little or no change. He takes a small sip of beer and replaces his glass carefully upon the polished surface of the table, aligning it with the whorl of a knot.

'*Atropa belladonna* – your Deadly Nightshade – one of the oldest of poisons.' He gazes unblinking over the lake.

'Apparently Cleopatra considered it for her suicide – until she saw its effects on the poor slave upon whom she tested it.'

Skelgill's eyes widen.

'Did it not work?'

'It worked – but it did not look pretty. She settled instead upon the bite of an asp. Or so the story goes.'

Skelgill glances rather introspectively at the older man.

'My dog's called Cleopatra – I inherited her – the name came as part of the package.'

'But you are thinking of keeping both?'

Skelgill chuckles.

'Aye – this concerns a human poisoning – a *possible* poisoning.'

'It would not be the first – and of course you have an infamous case of atropine – the Edinburgh poisoner.'

'Edinburgh?'

Skelgill does a little double take, as though one more coincidence will give him a nosebleed.

'Two decades ago now – perhaps before your time in the police.'

Skelgill nods.

'What happened?'

'He was a scientist – an academic.' The professor bows his head in a rather apologetic manner, as if to acknowledge that evil prowls all walks of life. 'He was found guilty of trying to kill his wife.'

'Trying?'

'She did not drink all the poison.' He picks up his glass and raises it to Skelgill. 'It was insufficiently disguised in a gin and tonic – you see, atropine is intensely bitter. This is why so few children die by accident – the berries appear delicious – like polished black cherries – thankfully the taste is a deterrent. It is worse than sloes. Yet birds can swallow the fruit with impunity, and are an important vector for dispersal of the seed. And while insects are essential for pollination, there are even reported cases of atropine poisoning from honey, where the bees have relied heavily upon the plant – this is quite a variation on your heather honey that is so popular! Herbal teas have also caused accidental poisoning – when leaves of Deadly Nightshade are picked by mistake and incorporated into the crop.'

The professor allows himself a wry grin. Skelgill is silent for a moment; he chooses another sandwich.

'I've never seen it growing hereabouts.'

The professor shakes his head.

'I am no great botanist, Daniel – although I believe it is a species that favours chalk downlands.' He lifts a hand, correctly in a south-southeasterly direction. 'However, the chemical agent is commonly available in medical and scientific circles – it is used in many preparations. The Edinburgh poisoner simply ordered extra stocks of atropine sulphate for his experiments.'

Skelgill nods.

'So, you wouldn't have to use an extract from the plant?'

'The liquid form would be more convenient. How was the poison administered?'

'As you just touched upon – the victim was taking a medicine that contained atropine. But the concentration in the body doesn't correspond to the concentration in the pills.'

'What were the symptoms?'

Skelgill shrugs reluctantly.

'He was found dead some time later. No one knew he was ill. The actual cause of death was heart failure.'

The professor blinks a couple of times, though his features remain implacable.

'Atropine may lead to a coma before death. It is metabolised quickly and leaves no inflamed organs for the pathologist. In some circumstances it could be the tool for the perfect crime. Although it sounds like your people have detected a flaw.'

Skelgill nods pensively.

'We can't be certain – statistically – but there's grounds for suspicion. Not least because of a second death at the same place the following day.'

'Also by atropine?'

Skelgill shakes his head.

'Looks like an overdose of sleeping pills – but we're told something's awry, given the brand involved – also too weak a concentration.'

The professor regards Skelgill with an affectionate concern.

'It sounds like you have your work cut out. Perhaps I should undertake a little research and come up to your office.'

Skelgill shifts rather uneasily in his seat.

'This visit – it's... er, kind of unofficial.'

'Ah.' The professor nods slowly several times. 'But I may still give you advice – perhaps by telephone?'

Skelgill, too, nods – though with considerably more energy.

'Well, in the meantime – have another sandwich – I had a late breakfast – you still have much exercise to do – and your complexion is not as robust as I remember it.'

Skelgill raises his eyebrows resignedly.

'Maybe it's the weather. The sun's hardly shone for a fortnight. And I've been busy – I haven't been out as much as I would have liked.'

But the professor does not look convinced, and Skelgill perhaps feels obliged to elaborate.

'I wasn't too grand on Sunday night – felt a bit tired and dizzy – then I had a blinding headache on Monday morning.' He shrugs. 'I put it down to too much red wine.'

The professor is observing him closely – indeed, watching as much as listening to his words.

'Were you by any chance in the vicinity of those who were – shall we say – poisoned?'

Skelgill glances up in surprise, a sandwich mid-way to his lips.

'Aye, I was.'

'Then perhaps you were lucky.'

Skelgill seems unsure of how to respond to this insight, and in lieu of a better course of action he takes a large bite of the bread. The professor sips his beer in silence. Then slowly he intones a little ditty.

'Hot as a hare, blind as a bat, dry as a bone, red as a beet, and mad as a hatter.'

'What's that?'

'An old saying about the symptoms of atropine poisoning.'

Skelgill chuckles.

'Sounds more like me, flapping about on this case.'

The professor shakes his head.

'I think you will solve it, Daniel. Your record is excellent, no?'

Now Skelgill sighs guardedly and contemplates the platter and its remaining sandwiches, though with apparently diminished enthusiasm.

'The Chief doesn't set great store by past records.'

'She has a fiery reputation.'

'Don't mention the word *fire*.'

The professor tilts his head to one side, perhaps assessing the nuance in Skelgill's warning.

'But you have some thinking time.'

Skelgill glances up.

'I'm stalking a pike.'

'I am glad to hear it.'

For a moment Skelgill appears more animated. He gestures towards the lake.

'Hans – what's the biggest you've had out of Derwentwater?'

The professor contrives a somewhat confessional expression.

'Ah, Daniel – in five years of trying – and despite your trademark plugs – only nineteen pounds and ten ounces.'

Skelgill seems to fight back the urge to swallow – he has limited success and reaches for his beer as cover. The professor does not seem to notice his unease, and begins to reminisce.

'My adoptive home lake, as well – it is a long way short of my Bassenthwaite best, caught with your expert assistance – and, can you believe, less than a quarter of the Estonian record?'

Skelgill shakes his head – though now his expression is one of wonderment.

'I think I need a long weekend in the Baltic.'

'Catch your poisoner – and they will surely give you one.'

Skelgill raises his eyebrows rather doubtingly; as things stand, he shall neither solve the crime nor – when his bungled bet expires in the next thirty-six hours – be able to afford a holiday.

17. THE YAT

Thursday 9pm

'Guv – DI Smart has arrested Dr Bond.'

Skelgill, having casually slammed shut his car door and set off jauntily marching towards his waiting colleague, is visibly rocked by this howitzer of news discharged across the pub car park. His face rapidly falls in, when a second earlier it was dominated by a demob-happy grin (enhanced it seemed as DS Jones stepped into the moonlight to reveal a most un-detective-like outfit). Now he halts a yard or two short of the embrace that would befit the meeting of such an attractive young woman. Reduced to his more customary attitude of watchful sentry, he realises she is shivering.

'Come on, lass – let's get inside and sat down – then you can tell us proper.'

The hostelry, an old coaching inn that – while popular with those in the know, and renowned for its excellent food and generous portions – is one of those out-of-the-way places where couples of all descriptions can meet without announcing themselves to the entire county. Tonight, highlighting its isolation, a near full moon spreads a silvery shroud over the low building and its silent environs, a harbinger of the frost that will follow as the mercury falls further. In contrast, from the mullioned windows emanates a cosy glow, redolent of oil lamps and a roaring log fire – and indeed beyond the heavy oak door they are greeted by the scent of paraffin and the crackle of a blaze from the inglenook.

At this time of year the Lake District is largely reclaimed by its locals, and the cosy bar harbours a small contingent of quietly conversing regulars and their lazing dogs: Lurcher, Lab and Lakeland Terrier among them. A Border Collie rises and strolls over to inspect the new arrivals, but it is jerked back by a sharp *"That'll do!"* from a gnarled shepherd who nurses a half-pint of mild in a dark corner. Skelgill makes a little motion of the hand at waist level, and the old man responds with the faintest of nods. Otherwise their entrance garners little notice.

The regular landlady is not in attendance – though a female member of staff in her late twenties with spiked hair and a knowing smile eyes DS Jones with a casual interest. Skelgill orders a pint of bitter, and a *Martini-and-slimline* for his companion, and a mild to be delivered to the shepherd. They don't have a booking – but there is no need – and indeed rather than pass through into the deserted restaurant area they opt for a small round table close beside the fire.

For a few moments DS Jones continues to shiver, and Skelgill takes the opportunity to peruse the menu while she recovers her composure. However, she soon chuckles when he announces that he "can feel a black pudding coming on" – he is a man of habit when it comes to his stomach. She would no doubt predict that home-made steak-and-ale pie should follow as his choice of main course. After a minute he glances up and turns expectantly to the bar. He catches the eye of the young woman, who may have been keeping them under low-grade surveillance. She emerges to reveal a slim figure, trim in a tailored charcoal polo shirt bearing the pub logo, and tight-fitting black jeans of a satiny material. She knows she draws his eye and, with notepad and pen poised, she stands just behind and to one side of DS Jones. Skelgill becomes conscious that he is the object of attention of at least two varieties, and folds his arms rather defensively as he places their order. When the waitress departs he reaches for his jug and takes refuge in its depths until he seems to think it is safe to emerge. He bangs it down decisively upon the table.

'Not so smart Smart.'

DS Jones understands his meaning; she nods and gathers herself to speak.

'He got us to tell him everything we know so far, Guv – first thing this morning, that was – and then at the end of the meeting he just stood up, acting really cool – he said we couldn't see the wood for the trees – and he went straight up to the Chief.' She pauses to take a measured sip of her drink. 'The next thing we knew he was dragging DS Leyton out to go and arrest Dr Bond.'

'I bet he didn't say *we*.'

'Sorry, Guv?'

'I bet he didn't say *we* couldn't see the wood for the trees.'

DS Jones winces apologetically.

'You know what he's like, Guv.'

Skelgill's eyes narrow.

'I'm surprised he didn't take you with him, over to Bond's place.'

DS Jones lowers her gaze.

'DS Leyton got the impression that the Chief had decided he should accompany DI Smart – perhaps because of yesterday.'

'So you've not been involved in the interviews?'

'No, Guv – but DS Leyton is keeping me in the picture, where he can.' She leans forward, suddenly eager to please. 'And here's something to make you smile, Guv – Dr Bond is now demanding that you're put back in charge of the investigation!'

Skelgill shakes his head; his features remain stern, though there is perhaps the tiniest glint of jubilation in his eye.

'What's Smart's case?'

DS Jones intertwines and studies her fingers: it seems they provide an excuse to avoid eye contact while she is obliged to iterate the unwelcome opinion of her new superior officer.

'I suppose it's logical really, Guv. If the two of them *were* poisoned, then it looks like medical knowledge and access to the drugs are the key factors. Dr Bond stands out by a head and shoulders. Plus, if he gave them a medicine, they'd probably take it without question.' She pauses to brush away a strand of hair from her eyes. 'That's the line DI Smart is taking. Apparently he's pressurising Dr Herdwick to make a categorical statement about the concentration levels. And he's arguing that the complaint against you was as good as an admission of guilt. He wants you to provide a statement that Dr Bond was acting suspiciously at Grisholm Hall.'

Skelgill's face is implacable.

'Motive.'

He delivers this single word as though he considers it is a knockout blow. But DS Jones's reaction is one of sudden anxiety.

'There's something I haven't mentioned to anyone yet, Guv – I've only had it verbally – I heard just before close of play – and DI Smart had gone home.'

'Better fire away, then.' Skelgill casts about the table and then the bar room. 'I think we can safely say this conversation's off the record.'

'About Bella Mandrake's rejection letter – from Rich Buckley Publishing?'

Skelgill nods, though now he seems a little agitated.

'Have you told Smart?'

In turn, DS Jones looks more concerned.

'Er, no, Guv – I imagined you'd put it in your report – of your trip to Scotland?'

Skelgill forces an ironical grin. It would appear he is not intending to do DI Smart any unnecessary favours. Indeed, his sketchy initial draft contained little more than that Bella Mandrake was certainly a pen name for Jane Smith, and that Sarah Redmond had no intention of allying herself with Rich Buckley Publishing; but there was no mention, for instance, that the two women were not entirely unacquainted. The only cat that came out of the bag, so to speak, travelled back to Cumbria in his car.

'Aye – maybe I did – you know what my memory can be like.'

DS Jones nods, a little relieved, though guardedly so, for the adjective applicable to his memory is *selective*.

'Well – it gave me the idea to contact Constance Belgrave. I asked her to check whether the firm had rejected manuscripts from any of the other writers who went on the retreat. She said they didn't keep records of rejections, but that if the author had sent a cheque to pay for return postage – recorded delivery – then they would have the Post Office receipt and an entry in their ledger.'

'And?' DS Jones has only paused for breath, but Skelgill is quick to chivvy her along.

'Dr Bond, Guv – he had a manuscript rejected in February – nine months ago.'

Skelgill folds his arms.

'Anyone else?'

DS Jones gives a little shake of the head.

'No. No others. At least – as I say – not that there is a record of.'

Skelgill's gaze wanders away from his companion and drifts about the low-ceilinged room, eventually coming to rest upon a dusty glass cabinet, one of several fixed against the opposite wall. It contains an ancient stuffed and faded Polecat, its facial mask barely distinguishable; it looks like it must have been frozen in its snarling pose for the best part of a century. Whether contemplating its life and times distracts him, or even that its weaselly countenance recalls his nemesis DI Alec Smart, it is impossible to know, but when Skelgill finally speaks it is evident that his thinking has moved on some.

'You said Bella Mandrake was pestering Dr Bond for tablets?'

'That's right, Guv – maybe *she* upset him, too. I mean, what if he actually *is* crazy, Guv? DI Smart's going round boasting that he's caught the next Harold Shipman.'

'It's Smart that wants his head examined.'

Skelgill, however, looks determined that this *should* be the case, rather than absolutely confident that DI Smart is wrong. And the dark brown eyes of DS Jones, too, harbour a hint of doubt that Skelgill can be so sure.

'We've not found anything at Dr Bond's house, Guv.' She seems to perk up in delivering this information. 'I mean – by way of medicines that could have been switched at Grisholm Hall.'

Now, paradoxically, it is Skelgill that plays devil's advocate.

'Aye – but he wouldn't be stupid enough to leave that sort of stuff lying around – especially after your first visit. That'd be long gone down the Eden.'

DS Jones nods.

'I know, Guv – DS Leyton's calling at his former practice in Appleby tomorrow – to find out if he still has connections or access there. He might easily have kept a set of keys.'

Skelgill shakes his head.

'As far as Smart's theory goes, I still come back to motive. If Bond's a nutcase, why not kill all of them?'

'Perhaps he was planning that, Guv? Or at least as many as he could get away with. Imagine if he leaves a trail of apparently innocent deaths wherever he goes? Maybe there would have been more incidents – on this hiking trip he's got planned?'

Skelgill looks doubtful and reaches for his beer. He could mention Dr Bond's forthright remark at Grisholm Hall – about his attending to corpses in various hotels in which he has lodged – or indeed that the good doctor was among the most insistent that he should not attempt the swim that might have saved the life of Bella Mandrake. But he does neither.

'Jones – you're starting to sound like Smart. Constance Belgrave is more likely to have tampered with Buckley's medicine than Bond – and at least she has a motive, poor woman.'

Skelgill probably does not intend to sound severe, but now he rather glowers at DS Jones, and her elegant cheekbones appear to colour in the glow from the hearth. Her gaze becomes forlorn, and her full lips form the beginnings of a petulant pout. Skelgill, for once, seems to detect the impact of his mordancy; he reaches out, and with surprising gentleness brushes a knuckle against her cheek.

'Cheer up, lass – it's not over until the fat lady sings.'

DS Jones blinks and leans back in surprise and grins at this somewhat nonsensical remark. Then she nods in agreement, and seems to gain a new determination to support his cause.

'Guv – another thing I've been looking at is all the emails the attendees at the retreat have forwarded to us – from the untraceable Wordsworth company.'

'Aye?'

'We've got them from everyone except Bella Mandrake and Rich Buckley – Constance Belgrave still can't access his system, and she thinks he probably would have used a private email account, anyway. But the interesting thing is that they were sent on different dates. The earliest was to Sarah Redmond – by over a week. Then Angela Cutting and Dickie Lampray were contacted on the same day as one another – and after that it was another week before the novice authors received their applications.'

Skelgill does not react – in fact he glances rather impatiently towards the bar, as if he is wondering what has become of their food. Then, in a rather offhand manner, he turns his attention back to DS Jones.

'So – what can you read into that?'

DS Jones is eager to supply an answer.

'Well, remember, Guv – Dickie Lampray said he was surprised that Rich Buckley even went on the retreat? He said it couldn't be for the money – and that it was more likely he was interested in Sarah Redmond, since she was supposedly looking at moving to a new publisher.'

Skelgill scowls.

'She knocked the idea on the head as soon as I mentioned it.'

'But Buckley wouldn't have known that, Guv – or even if he suspected, from what we know of him, it's unlikely to have put him off trying.'

Skelgill still seems averse to any travel in this direction of thought.

'Lampray was wrong – Buckley did need the money.'

DS Jones nods, undeterred.

'That just made it all the more attractive for him, Guv. Sarah Redmond sells stacks of books.'

Skelgill frowns, but now – albeit reluctantly – he joins with her line of argument.

'So what are you saying – Sarah Redmond was bait to get Buckley to Grisholm Hall?'

DS Jones hesitates.

'Well... yes, I suppose so, Guv.'

'Aye, well... maybe she was.'

DS Jones's eyes widen at this response – but before she can invite Skelgill to elaborate, the young woman in black arrives to steal his attention – or, rather, the plates of piping-hot food she bears do so. The agenda becomes suspended while he takes up arms against his black pudding; DS Jones somewhat more demurely dips into her mushroom soup. And, when Skelgill speaks again, it is evident that a more pressing matter has surfaced.

'It was Smart that told the Chief about me and Angela Cutting, wasn't it?'

'What do you mean, Guv?'

DS Jones looks puzzled, but Skelgill has successfully employed his ambush technique, and the conscious adjustment she skilfully makes to her reaction is just not quite quick enough to conceal the honest reflex that precedes it.

'Jones – there's no need to be diplomatic on my account. You know me – if I'm caught with my trousers down – I'll put my hand up to it.'

DS Jones contemplates her consommé.

'I think it was, Guv.'

'Jones, you know it was. Did he show you the photo?'

She gives a little nod.

'Aha.'

'It's not what it seems.'

'I know that, Guv.' She meets his gaze; however, she does not sound entirely convinced.

'She was just getting me to taste her lobster.' (At this they exchange knowing frowns – lobster being such an extravagant dish that it clearly undermines his defence.) 'She'd insisted on trying my pie, and so I felt obliged. What I didn't realise was that she's a minor celebrity. I noticed there were folk staring at us during the meal – but I never twigged that we were being photographed.'

DS Jones glances surreptitiously about the pub. She leans a little closer to Skelgill.

'Guv – the old guy in the corner – the one you bought the drink for – don't be surprised if he's already tweeted our picture.'

'The Collie's heard every word we've said, that's for sure.' Skelgill laughs, and seems more relaxed, now that this little issue has been outed. 'I guessed straight away it would be Smart. The Chief's above that sort of thing. Tiger versus Grizzly's more her cup of tea.'

DS Jones grins.

'He's always looking at that website, Guv – he says it's important in our job to keep up with current affairs.'

'Aye, the emphasis on *affairs*, eh?'

DS Jones lowers her eyes; her long lashes lying like soft filigree fans upon her cheeks.

'I suppose so, Guv.'

Skelgill seems to be gathering himself to say something, but just then their starter plates are cleared and simultaneously replaced by their mains – an efficiency that might disconcert the average diner wishing to pause between courses, but which heartily meets Skelgill's approval – to the extent that he appears this time not to notice the waitress at all.

There is a small hiatus as they familiarise themselves with their meals. Skelgill has the house pie, and takes a moment or two to determine the most propitious angle of attack; DS Jones is more delicate, having opted for a lighter portion of scallops. The challenging upward trajectory of their conversation seems to have peaked. Instead their chatter slaloms through the rather haphazard landscape of the investigation. As Skelgill pointed out during his off-piste exchange with Sarah Redmond, brainstorming is a dangerous game, and can lead to all manner of seemingly plausible yet precipitous conclusions. With this evidently in mind, he takes care to stay within the markers of known facts. DS Jones, however, seems more prepared to explore the fringes of their knowledge.

'I was thinking, Guv – about the idea of Bella Mandrake being the killer?'

'Aye?'

'We know that she was left alone with Rich Buckley on the night before he died – and also that she was wandering about on the landing in the early hours.'

Skelgill shrugs.

'*Do* we know? We've only got other people's word for that. Neither Buckley nor Mandrake is here to deny it. And Buckley died the next day – the next afternoon. It's not like she slept with him that night and spiked his nightcap. He woke up and took in his breakfast tray. And if she paid him a sneaky afternoon visit and he copped a heart attack, she did a good job of dressing him up.'

DS Jones's eyebrows show a flicker of surprise at Skelgill's rather blunt assessment, though she nods reluctantly.

'It's just – the rejection letter – it's the one tangible motive we do have.'

Skelgill shrugs.

'Aye, maybe – but I think she was thicker skinned than she made out. There's a whole drawer full of rejection letters in her flat. Why let one more bother her? Why pick on Buckley?'

'You said it was particularly scathing, Guv?'

'Aye – but nothing worse than I get most weeks from the Chief – and look at me.'

DS Jones grins. In typical Skelgill style, this remark does not really make sense – but he has a way of concluding arguments with statements that can confound his opponent purely through their cryptic nature. Not that he is trying to baffle DS Jones – he simply appears unwilling to paint Bella Mandrake as the guilty party.

'But if it wasn't Bella Mandrake who killed Rich Buckley, Guv – then we're looking for two motives.' She screws up her face in a moment of frustration. 'Yet the MO is virtually identical.'

Skelgill grins in a sympathetic manner.

'You can see the appeal of Smart's theory.'

'I know, Guv.' DS Jones shakes her head ruefully. 'I was talking with DS Leyton – he's convinced that money's at the root of it somewhere – but that would surely cast suspicion in the direction of Dickie Lampray and Angela Cutting.'

Skelgill regards her shrewdly. He decides to add a little meat to the essential bare bones of his Edinburgh report.

'Sarah Redmond reckons that Dickie Lampray has some kind of scam going. Nothing illegal – but basically the author ends up paying for their book to be published. If Rich Buckley was strapped for cash – Lampray's deals would be the sort of thing he'd favour.'

DS Jones appears perplexed.

'But that would be Dickie Lampray killing the golden goose, wouldn't it, Guv? You said that yourself when we were discussing it on the train.'

Skelgill affects an indifferent shrug.

'Unless Buckley was squeezing him – for a bigger cut.'

For a moment, DS Jones ponders this idea. She begins to nod in agreement.

'Dickie Lampray played down the suggestion that Buckley needed the money – and he does seem to be struggling financially himself. And I thought he looked mightily relieved when you said we shouldn't need to bother him again, Guv.'

Skelgill grins.

'That might have had more to do with his dog-sitter, though, Jones.'

They exchange knowing glances, although this remark appears to take them into a little cul-de-sac, and neither of them adds anything more. After a moment or two, DS Jones raises a tentative finger.

'Actually, Guv – there is something about Angela Cutting – along possible financial lines.'

'Aye?'

'It's a bit of a long shot.'

'Shoot, anyway.'

'Well, I've been searching all of their names online – just to see what comes up. For her, you get hundreds of hits – not surprisingly, really.' (She flashes him something of an old-fashioned look.) 'But in her professional capacity – I came across some of her book reviews. Most of them are quite positive and constructive – but one recent one was really blistering – in fact it was so harsh that the review itself had been reported on.'

'Not one of Bella Mandrake's books?'

Skelgill's quip is intended to be flippant.

'No, Guv – but the novel was published by Rich Buckley.'

Now Skelgill raises an eyebrow.

'Let me guess – it must have been one of Dickie Lampray's authors.'

DS Jones shakes her head.

'I checked that, Guv – it's actually quite a well-known writer – with a different literary agent altogether.'

'So what's the story Jackanory?'

DS Jones folds her hands together, and assumes a patient air.

'You know how – inside book covers – they have all this glowing praise – and you never believe it – it's like it's been commissioned?'

Skelgill looks only vaguely engaged with this notion.

'Go on.'

'Whereas the independent reviews – in the Sunday newspaper supplements – they seem a lot more credible.' Her features are eager. 'Guv – a positive review from Angela Cutting must be worth a lot of money – to a publisher.'

Skelgill pulls a doubting face, although his next comment reveals that he is in fact following her line of argument.

'And Buckley stopped paying?'

'If he was in financial difficulty, Guv.'

Skelgill inhales slowly. He folds his arms and looks up to the timbered ceiling. Perhaps he is assessing to what extent Angela Cutting would be in need of money: her apparent lifestyle would suggest not – although to sustain it might require otherwise.

'What you say could be right.'

DS Jones looks pleased – but she knows this idea is still short of being a compelling motive. Indeed – even if she is right, it may be a fact with no bearing on the case whatsoever.

'DI Smart wasn't interested, Guv.'

Skelgill scoffs.

'Aye, well – why let the facts spoil a good yarn?'

'He said he'd have Dr Bond squealing by midnight, Guv.'

Skelgill looks at his watch and shakes his head.

'I'll drag a twenty-five pound pike out of Derwentwater between my teeth before Bond admits to murder.' His gaze wanders and settles now upon a display case that holds a crumbling plaster cast of a monster Eamont salmon. 'In fact I'll break the Estonian record, to boot.'

DS Jones is pensive. Skelgill's uncompromising view of DI Smart's chances begs the question about what makes him so sure. It is quite possible that personal enmity is clouding good judgement. To dismiss Dr Bond as the most likely culprit undoubtedly flies in the face of the facts. But Skelgill's allusion to his angling challenge now provides the opportunity to tack away from the choppy waters of the investigation.

'I take it you drew a blank today, Guv?'

Skelgill looks back at her in surprise.

'What? No – I caught a bucketful – just couldn't get through the jacks, though.'

DS Jones folds her arms on the table and leans forward. Her silky dress is close fitting, and the action accentuates her cleavage. She appears to have his attention.

'You'll have to translate that one for me, Guv.'

Skelgill blinks exaggeratedly.

'Jack pike – officially it's the male fish – they don't grow much above ten pound.' (He has the fisherman's habit of using the word pound as singular, irrespective of weight.)

DS Jones grins.

'So it's a female you're after?'

Skelgill grins ruefully.

'They're more of a challenge.'

'But the greedy little males keep stealing their dinner?'

'That's one way of putting it.'

Now DS Jones smiles with affected condescension.

'Lucky I had scallops and not lobster, then, Guv.'

'Very witty, Jones.'

18.
DERWENTWATER

Friday 8am

There are few places in England more beautiful than Borrowdale, and Skelgill must reflect that, when you live in the Lakes and fishing is your thing, all clouds have their silver linings. Not that there are any clouds to speak of this morning. The scene is pure chocolate box, a cobalt blue sky and a silver lake, and the glow of golden oaks as autumnal sunshine creeps like a warming blanket down the fellsides beyond Derwentwater's western bank and begins to draw a delicate mist from its mirrored surface. This deferred dawning obliges Skelgill reach for his wide-brimmed *Tilley* hat, as the sun crowns High Seat, king of the ridge that divides Borrowdale from Thirlmere. A few more minutes sees its rays flood Ashness Fell, raising the flat landscape into a relief of highlighted bluffs and shadowy crags.

It is the last day of October; Skelgill's final chance to win his bet, and to this end he has again gravitated to the southern reaches of the majestic lake, in the vicinity of Grisholm, well away from any disturbance that may emanate from jetties in the neighbourhood of Keswick. Already two hours into an expedition that began in the dark, and apparently none the worse for little sleep, he is alert and purposeful as he goes about the business of catching a pike. It being the cusp of the year, there is no one mode that is favoured, and thus Skelgill is pulling out all the stops. He has two rods rigged with dead-baits (steadfastly a winter technique), cast from the stern, the rods splayed like outriggers; a whippy fly rod (definitely a summer method), ready and waiting should he head for one of the shallower bays; and his trusty spinning rod – to hand – loaded with his most productive plug, known as 'Harris', after the manufacturer of the paintbrush, the handle of which forms the main body of the improvised lure. Plugging is the most reliable way to catch a pike, but also the most demanding. If pike fishing were horse racing, spinning would be a graceful flat stakes, fly fishing a relatively easy hurdle, and plugging an energy-sapping steeplechase. While the cast is no different to spinning – the aim being to achieve a good distance, in order to cover water that looks likely it might hold a patrolling pike – much greater skill lies in the retrieve. A plug vaguely resembles a small fish that bristles with treble-hooks. Once submerged it is intended to ape a distressed or stricken creature: one that is signalling its presence as easy prey. To achieve this effect requires a jerky retrieve, with erratic but coordinated movements of both rod and reel, and thus constant effort and concentration. For the novice angler – or even novice *plugger* – this soon becomes tiring, and half an hour's labour can lead to repetitive strain injury of the hands, wrists and arms. At this point, technique goes to pieces, and all hopes of catching a fish fade. But Skelgill exhibits no such fatigue, his metronomic cast and retrieve unflagging, as his grey-green eyes – reflecting the colour of the lake – scan the surface for essential signs of aquatic life.

But, in due course, he does halt. He has been watching an area of water with greater interest than any other, and now he spends some time and effort manoeuvring his boat into this very particular spot – one that, it must be said, is apparent only to his keen senses. Carefully, so as to minimise disturbance, he drops anchor, and counts the depth as he hands out the line. Derwentwater is a relatively shallow lake, but here he lies in about fifty feet of water. The boat settled to his satisfaction, he reels in the dead-baits, and is just about to re-cast the first of them when his mobile rings.

With a predictable expletive he winds over the bail arm of the reel and carefully lays the tip of the rod across the gunwale. Uncharacteristically (although purely to keep warm) he is wearing a scuffed and faded life-vest that normally serves as a seat cushion, and he has to burrow into its obstructive bulk to get at the handset in his breast pocket. Additional expletives from his repertoire are now required – but these are curtailed when he sees who is calling him. He taps the screen and lifts the phone to his ear.

'Hans.'

'Ah, Daniel – not too early, I hope?'

Skelgill shakes his head but does not answer directly.

'Hans, I can see your cottage from here.'

'And you are wearing your strange hat and an orange tank top.'

Skelgill squints across the water; the professor's cottage is a good half-mile away.

'You must have binoculars.'

'I was waiting until you stopped rowing – and before you made a cast – I appreciate there is never a good time to interrupt a man hunting a pike.'

'I'm always prepared to make an exception for you, Hans.'

'In that case, Daniel – I propose to meet you at my landing stage in one hour – I have something that might be of assistance to you in both of your quests – and, more pertinently, Annika is intending to furnish you with a flask of hot tea and some wholemeal toast.'

Skelgill chuckles.

'It's a no-brainer, Hans – I'll come now if it's all the same?'

*

Skelgill's boat, though unanchored, is becalmed at a spot close to where he took refuge during Sunday afternoon's tempest. Now, although a light south-westerly breeze has picked up, it does not trouble this mill pond-like reach in the lee of Grisholm. It seems the perfect location – and yet Skelgill does not fish. He sits unmoving on the centre thwart. Facing him on the bow thwart is arranged a series of items supplied by the kindly Sinisalus. There is the foil-wrapped toast, and an aluminium flask; there is what resembles a small rigid model of a

237

pike (about six inches long, it is coloured in the correct mottled greens, subtly lighter below and darker above, and where it lacks tail and pectoral fins there are gleaming treble hooks); and there is a sheet of lined paper, covered by neatly handwritten notes made in black ink.

A sleuth – even one knowing something of Skelgill's character – might be challenged to explain how he has gone this long and far, a good fifteen-minute row back across the lake (followed by a considerable pause for thought), without eating the toast, drinking the tea, and trying out the professor's prized Estonian lure, *"Beebi Haug"* ('Baby Pike').

The explanation lies in the notes. These comprise the concise – though expert – findings, analyses and musings of the professor, following on from as frank a debrief as Skelgill was able to provide prior to his departure yesterday lunchtime. The professor had few words upon handing them over, and instead left Skelgill to peruse them at his leisure – which he did the instant that Hans Sinisalu had left him apparently casting off from the little jetty. Now he takes up the page once more. It has three underlined sub-headings. The first two of these are, not unexpectedly, 'Atropine' and 'Benzodiazepine', but it is the third that has had most impact upon Skelgill. This is marked 'Chloroform'.

After a short while Skelgill carefully folds up the sheet, tucks it into his shirt pocket, and fishes out his own notebook from his rucksack. He locates the page headed 'Grisholm' and removes the pencil from its band. Of the remaining five names he methodically crosses out two. Now he stares at the list – though his eyes become glazed and unblinking, and it is clear that his mind is drifting from his immediate environs. With the pencil held between his index and middle fingers, he begins gently to brush the tip of his left thumb across his lips. He has full lips for a man – together about the width of his thumb – but now he parts them slightly as his breathing becomes more audible. After perhaps half a minute he seems to become conscious of what he is doing, he blinks suddenly several times, and withdraws his hand from his mouth, an expression of alarm creasing his features. He raises the notebook – and, with less certainty, slowly crosses out two more names. Now there is just one left. He looks away, towards the island – and makes several blind attempts to replace the pencil in its holder – but then some afterthought must strike him, and he inscribes a question mark against the first name he crossed out yesterday morning. Now he jams the notebook back into his rucksack, and fumbles in his pocket for his mobile phone. Hurriedly he brings up a number, and watches the screen intently until the call is answered.

'Hello?'

'Jones – can you hear me?'

'Sure, Guv.'

'You're really faint.'

'I'm whispering, Guv – DI Smart's just come into the canteen – he's beside the counter with DS Leyton – he'll want to know who I'm talking to.'

'Tell him it's your fiancé inviting you away for a romantic weekend.'

DS Jones is silent for a moment.

'That would probably get me in even more trouble, Guv.'

'Don't worry – I'll take the rap – but there's a couple of things I want you to check – as soon as you get a minute on your own.'

'They're scheduled to interview Dr Bond again in a quarter of an hour.'

'Have you got a pen?'

'Just tell me quickly, Guv – he keeps glancing over. Better if I don't write it down.'

Skelgill outlines his requests. As she feared, DS Jones is obliged to hang up before he can elaborate – but she insists she has the gist of what he seeks. Skelgill shrugs resignedly and returns his mobile to his shirt pocket. For the time being, machinations are out of his hands. But, thanks to his Baltic friends, he does have other distractions.

He inspects the Estonian lure, taking care not to snag himself on its evil-looking hooks. A barb in the hand is not worth two in the bush – in fact it means either an eye-watering DIY wrench with a pair of disgorging pliers, or complete abandonment and a trip to A&E at Carlisle General (not an easy drive, with a treble-hook embedded in one hand). The lure itself is a floating plug that dives to about ten feet when it is swiftly retrieved. It is designed as a replica of a small pike – not to scare off other species and leave the waters clear, but because big pike are cannibal. As the professor's sagely coined phrase goes, "It takes a pike to catch a pike".

Skelgill deftly replaces *Harris* with *Beebi Haug*. He wraps a piece of damp rag around the new lure, and, with all his might, tests the trace, knots and clips. If a big pike bites but gets away, he does not intend it to be with his friend's prized lure in tow. Now he weighs the rod with its new rig. *Beebi Haug* is lighter than *Harris* and will require a more energetic cast. He rises, and widens his stance in preparation, meaning to put his back into the action. He eyes the striated wind lane that trails off the southern tip of Grisholm, a feature that concentrates food and attracts surface-feeding fish (which in turn attract bigger ones from below). But, just as he lifts the rod above his shoulder, at the edge of his vision a red kayak slides into view. Then he sees there is an entire matching school of them, their occupants wearing standard-issue yellow life-vests and red helmets and the whole ensemble recalling the Spanish flag. He lowers his rod and watches. They must be coming up the lake from a boat-hire business not far from the Sinisalus' cottage; it does a good trade with a number of outward-bound centres dotted around the area. Skelgill counts eight craft – the leader is a male instructor, though it is hard to discern the other rowers' ages at this distance – and then there is one additional laggard, a couple of hundred yards behind the main group, although its unisex paddler sports an all-black athletic outfit and the kayak is a bright apple-green, and may be unconnected – or perhaps a second instructor catching up.

Although they are a long way from interfering with his fishing (or he their paddling, come to that), it is not clear at the moment whether their trajectory will bring them between him and Grisholm, or if they will pass behind the islet, out of harm's way.

While he awaits the outcome, he turns his attention to the warming picnic thoughtfully provided by Annika Sinisalu. While he has with him, as ever, his trusty *Kelly Kettle*, it can be a bit of a faff, and in any event far from safe to start a fire aboard a wooden-hulled boat. Thus the simple convenience of a flask, especially one freshly made and piping hot, can win the day. Indeed the rich brown liquid steams in the chilly air as he pours. Then there is the toast – now cooled, but no matter – he can dip it in the tea. He unwraps the foil; there are four thick slices – his legendary appetite goes before him – made up in two rounds. He extracts the first of these and pokes a rather grimy finger between the slices to inspect its contents. There is a generous layer of a pale creamy substance. It looks rather like stiff lemon curd, though the smell appears to baffle him. He might guess at some obscure Estonian delicacy, made from the roe of zander – but when one is angling, it is difficult to smell much other than fish. Undeterred, he takes a substantial crunching bite, and then grins approvingly as he recognises the taste.

It is about halfway through the second round of toast that lightning strikes, although Skelgill looks like he has broken a tooth. Eating – especially alone – is one of those peculiar activities, requiring little conscious effort and yet quite absorbing, which can bring on a sort of reverie – a *dwam*, as the Scots call it. And in such a place, pennies are known to drop. Mid-mouthful, Skelgill stops chewing and regards with some wonder the remaining piece of bread and honey (for the mystery opaque filling is *set honey*). He turns it in his hand, staring as if he can't quite believe what he is seeing. Of course, it is his mind's eye at work here, and actually he can't believe what he is thinking.

He sits upright and glances about. Perhaps switching into a more deliberative mode of reasoning, he recommences chewing, and swills down his mouthful with the half-capful of tea that remains. But he replaces the unfinished portion of toast in its wrapper, and carefully folds over the crinkled foil, as if to preserve some valuable evidence. It is clear his thoughts are racing – and his pulse, too, if his quickened breathing is anything to go by. His eyes dart about his surroundings – with no particular purpose, it would seem – until his attention is drawn once again by the kayaks. Without him being particularly aware, they have in fact passed behind Grisholm, and now, one after the other, they are beginning to appear beyond its northerly point. It takes under a minute for all eight red craft to emerge into view, and the mini armada paddles away on a course parallel to the shore of the lake. But now he continues to watch – not the flotilla, so much, but the tip of Grisholm. He watches... and he watches. Another minute passes... and then another. And then Skelgill reaches for his oars.

*

Skelgill's boat noses silently into the boathouse. He berths it alongside the apple-green kayak. He jumps out over the bow dragging a steel chain. This is fastened by a staple driven into the gunwale, and serves as an anti-theft device when the need arises. He slips the chain through a rusted iron mooring ring, and padlocks the loose end to the staple. He pats his breast pocket to confirm the presence of his mobile. Then he slings his rucksack on one shoulder and clambers out lugging his oars. He hides all three items in the thicket of rhododendrons at the back of the boathouse. Then he re-enters and unties the kayak, drags it to the end of the jetty, and pushes it out into the lake. It slides beyond the rocks at the entrance to the little harbour, and he watches until it begins to drift away. Then he sets off at a jog along the woodland path.

In its secluded clearing Grisholm Hall appears as silent and deserted as ever. Taking in this scene, Skelgill dwells beneath the sweeping branches of a Western Hemlock, one of the non-natives that provide the evergreen screen around the property. After a couple of seconds he breaks cover and makes a dash for the front door. He manhandles the large brass latch, and winces as it sends a hollow ring into the hall beyond. But the door is locked. Now he retraces his route of yesterday, keeping close to the building and ducking under each window that he passes. Reaching the courtyard, and treading softly on the mossy paving, he quickly tries the doors: that of the kitchen, and the two fire exits – but all three are firmly closed, and either locked or fastened from the inside. He stands, arms akimbo, and casts about, biting the side of his mouth.

The low autumn sun is angling across the courtyard, illuminating the first-floor corridor windows of what had been the 'Women's Wing' during the retreat. As Skelgill glances up something moves across the nearest window to the angle of the building. It is little more than a dark shape – but it can only be the top of a head covered by a black hat or hood. From Skelgill's position beside the kitchen door, he cannot see how far the intruder continues along the passage. But immediately he makes up his mind to enter the property. As before, he scrambles onto the windowsill – more nimbly without the extra effort required to counterbalance his heavy rucksack. He yanks down the upper sash – again it squeals a protest – to him it must sound like an air-raid warning siren – and he holds his breath and listens intently for a few seconds. But the kitchen is a good way from the bedroom wing, and there are potentially several closed doors between it and any eavesdropper. He determines that all is clear and clambers through the opening – this time taking care to land softly. His rubber-soled boots can be sneaky when needs must, and he silently crosses the flagstones all the way to the foot of the main staircase. From here there is worn carpet, although progress still requires care, as creaky risers threaten to betray his presence. On the central landing the doors of the four 'VIP' suites are all shut; but Skelgill makes directly for the interconnecting door that leads to the 'Women's Wing'. This has no catch – it merely swings on hinges and is returned to its position by means of a hydraulic closer. Just as he begins to pull it open there is a distinct sound from beyond – perhaps the hollow clunk of another door closing.

Cautiously he enters the corridor. Bright rectangles of sun spotlight each of the three bedroom doors – and all three here are shut, too. The sound, however, seemed to emanate from the far end of the corridor. Skelgill tiptoes along to the furthest door. This was the chamber allocated to Lucy Hecate. He pauses outside, leaning against the jamb and straining to listen, grimacing and breathing through bared teeth. After a couple of seconds he turns the handle – it squeaks alarmingly – and wrenches open the door. But the room is empty. He enters and quickly checks the en suite – but finds the same result. There is no obvious sign of disturbance, and he leaves the room and re-closes the door behind him. Then he pauses and looks broodingly at the narrow staircase that leads down to the fire exit. His next decision, however, is to investigate the remaining bedrooms. Using the same stealthy method, he works his way back along the passage, onto the landing, and into the 'Men's Wing', successively finding empty the rooms formerly occupied by Linda Gray, Bella Mandrake, Sarah Redmond, Angela Cutting, Rich Buckley, Dickie Lampray, Dr Gerald Bond, Burt Boston and – finally – himself.

In this latter room he pauses in the centre of the carpet and brings his hands up to his face, covering his mouth, with his fingertips touching the tip of his nose, in a kind of praying posture. He begins to rotate on the spot, and finds himself staring back at the door, and the small occasional table on which stands the candlestick. The *empty* candlestick. With a sudden realisation he homes in on this and strides across, snatches it up, and stares at it with alarm. Then he replaces it and turns to face the room. After a moment's consideration he rounds the bed and strides across to the window. The sun streams in here too and makes him squint. But in a second his eyes have widened. Down below, bordering the outside wall of this wing is an overgrown ornamental shrubbery – now an unkempt mix of dwarf conifers and azaleas and deciduous varieties of cinquefoils and St John's worts that have already dropped most of their leaves. And in their midst, bent over and obviously searching for something amongst the thick mulch, is the black-clad canoeist. The anonymous figure even wears black gloves and a black balaclava – of which Skelgill caught a glimpse. And the click of the door must have been, not a bedroom, but the closing of the fire escape as the intruder left the building.

Acting upon impulse – perhaps unwisely – Skelgill yanks up the bottom sash of the window. The resultant screech instantly alerts the individual below, who immediately turns and runs, raising their gloved hands to conceal what little of their face is visible.

'Stop right there – police!'

Skelgill's hollered entreaty is in vain. The person pays no heed and disappears from sight, darting first to the wall of the building, where there is a narrow shingle path, and then sprinting in the direction of the front of the house. Skelgill now has a decision to make. His quickest exit is via the fire escape at the foot of the stair outside his bedroom – provided it is operational – but this will bring him out on the wrong side of the wing. The kitchen window is further still, and will only deliver the same result – egress into the courtyard. Meanwhile a locked mortise renders the great front door impregnable.

Eschewing these options he rolls out onto the windowsill. To one side is the downpipe from the en suite bathroom. He lurches at this and just manages to get a grip with both hands. His legs follow and he swings into an improvised abseil brace position. Flakes of black paint and rust splinter from the pipe, and its brackets grumble alarmingly, but he doesn't hang about to test their stamina – he shins down like a native coconut harvester who has just met a giant python, and opts to jump the last six feet. He lands on his toes, but his outward momentum causes him to perform a backward roll into a Juniper bush. Perhaps propelled by its unforgiving foliage, he pounds in pursuit of his quarry.

The winding path to the boathouse is clear, although there are skid marks and ruts in the damp earth where the runner ahead of him took corners at speed. Arriving at the shore he finds the little harbour deserted, and for a moment his eyes flash with alarm and he scans the water – as if to confirm that the fugitive has not decided to swim for freedom. But then he hears a movement from within the boathouse. He is breathing hard, but he inhales deeply and gathers himself as if in readiness for the confrontation that awaits. But then there is a second sound – a voice – more of a sob, in fact. And he relaxes. For a moment he half-turns and gazes meditatively across the lake, and ruefully shakes his head – as if what he is about to do troubles him. He lets out the great breath as a kind of sigh and, rather like an automaton, he walks slowly to the boathouse, and steps across the threshold.

'You didn't find your scarf, then, Lucy.'

19. GRISHOLM

Friday 12 noon

By the time DS Leyton and DS Jones arrive with keys for Grisholm Hall, and a back-up team of constables and scene-of-crime officers, Skelgill and Lucy Hecate regard one another calmly from opposite sofas in the drawing room, beside a roaring log fire. The *Kelly Kettle* stands upon the stone hearth, and they each have an enamel mug of tea before them on the low table. It is of the builders' variety rather than Earl Grey, and Skelgill's third cup. Not surprisingly, therefore, he is relieved in more ways than one when a pair of WPCs arrives to assume responsibility for his charge. Solemn as ever, her pale cheeks streaked with the stains of what must be tears, Lucy Hecate casts one last mournful glance at Skelgill, and is led away. Skelgill smiles grimly. There is no sign of triumph in his eyes, and he excuses himself a moment later.

When he returns, he brings a jug of water and two mugs borrowed from the kitchen. And he seems to have perked up. He gestures to his sergeants to make themselves comfortable, and busies himself with recharging his contraption. As he rather audaciously steals embers from the grate, using his fingers as tongs, his somewhat bemused colleagues begin to offer items of news.

The first of these – that DI Smart has declined to accompany them, being determined to extract a confession out of Dr Gerald Bond, along the lines that he was a co-conspirator – raises a hysterical laugh from Skelgill. Indeed, from his kneeling position by the fire, he performs a truncated goal-scoring celebration.

The second is that DS Leyton has heard from the bank that handles the land agent's account. The cheque that was submitted as a deposit for the hire of Grisholm Hall has surfaced – marked 'refer to drawer' – and an investigation has revealed that it was written from a chequebook last properly used a month earlier in a small independent pharmacy in Covent Garden, and subsequently 'misplaced' by its unwitting owner. The eyes of the three detectives meet as DS Leyton utters the word *pharmacy* – albeit Skelgill's demeanour suggests this is not entirely news to him.

Thirdly, DS Jones also bears important information. This is in response to Skelgill's urgent telephone request. However, it is clear that events have overtaken this research and, for the time being, she holds her peace.

It is not long before Skelgill has brewed up more tea, to his somewhat idiosyncratic recipe (tea bag, powdered milk, sugar and boiling water, all in together), and placed mugs carefully before each of those present. *Carefully*, because also aligned on the table before them are several items, which appear to have been emptied from a small streamlined black fabric backpack, of the sort more often used by city commuters than outdoor junkies. Of course, it belongs (or belonged) to Lucy Hecate.

DS Leyton leans forward and squints at two clear jars placed beside each other. One is a miniature breakfast portion, the other a more standard retail size, although unlabelled.

'Honey, Guv? You've been having quite a picnic while you were waiting.'

Skelgill, leaning back against the settee and looking relaxed with his tea, narrows his eyes.

'It'd be no picnic if you ate that, Leyton.'

DS Leyton's eyes widen.

'Poison?'

Skelgill nods.

'Atropine – it's intensely bitter – like sloes but worse. That's why poisonings from eating the berries of Deadly Nightshade are uncommon.' (As their superior begins to pontificate along these lines, DS Leyton's jaw begins to drop. But DS Jones's reaction is more one of circumspect intrigue.) 'In order to disguise it, you need something very, very sweet. Such as honey.'

'Cor blimey.' DS Leyton gulps – but then a thought strikes him. 'But what about that bowel medicine, Guv – I thought that's what killed Buckley?'

Skelgill shrugs.

'What better way to make it look like an accident – than to plant some pills that contain the same compound?'

DS Jones sits forward, her brow now creased.

'But, Guv – there were the same tablets in Rich Buckley's office.'

'Aye – and when we search Lucy Hecate's flat I imagine we'll find a spare set of keys for it.'

'But, Guv–' DS Jones begins again to raise a query – but then she sees it. She stares at Skelgill, enlightened. 'She worked there, Guv.'

'Aye, she did.'

Now it is DS Leyton's turn to appear confused. He looks from one to another of his colleagues.

'I don't get this bit – what do you mean – she worked there – what, at the publisher's?'

DS Jones glances to Skelgill, anticipating that he will answer – but he gestures that she should explain.

'They employed students as interns – you know, unpaid work experience?' DS Leyton nods and she continues. 'So Lucy Hecate had a job there.' But now she holds out her hands in appeal to her boss. 'But, this is amazing, Guv – given what I found out this morning.'

Skelgill nods slowly.

'I know.'

'She told you, Guv?'

'What she wanted to – mainly about Buckley. And Myra.'

DS Jones shakes her head. DS Leyton is still looking bewildered. She turns to him.

'The woman you interviewed – Rich Buckley's widow – she's Lucy Hecate's mother. Lucy Hecate is the child that she had as a teenager and that was brought up by the father.'

DS Leyton is now getting the idea.

'But – wouldn't Buckley have recognised her?'

Skelgill is shaking his head. He takes over.

'Aye – as an ex-employee, perhaps. But in the family context he never met her. Lucy and the mother are estranged. That's part of the grand design.'

'The grand design?' This is DS Jones.

'Lucy got a job at Buckley Publishing. She knew who Buckley was, but didn't let on. The guy treated her like dirt – and worse – the extreme end of sexual harassment. While she was there she submitted a novel she'd written, under a false name. He ripped it to pieces. Meanwhile she found out what else he was up to – abusing her mother, women on the side – and she overheard his scheme to cut Myra out of his fortune. It was all too much for Lucy – and perhaps she saw it as a chance for reconciliation.'

'With her mother?'

'With her mother.' Skelgill brushes the fingers of one hand through his hair. 'With Buckley dead prior to the divorce, Myra would inherit everything. I don't know how Lucy planned to approach her – maybe as a fellow victim of Buckley – but she had some idea that she could pick up the reins of the publishing business.'

They are all three silent for a minute or so. Then DS Leyton pipes up.

'So this retreats company – that we can't find – it was Lucy Hecate?'

Skelgill is nodding.

'She set up a false email account – probably did it from an internet café to make it harder to trace – made all the offers of extravagant fees with no intention of paying.'

DS Leyton slaps a hand on his substantial thigh.

'And the stolen cheque, Guv.'

Skelgill flashes him a confirmatory glance.

'She's been doing part-time jobs in retail – one of them being a pharmacy.' He gestures towards DS Jones. 'As our colleague's research will confirm, Lucy Hecate's degree is in biochemistry.' (DS Jones nods as Skelgill continues.) 'So that's how she got hold of the chequebook – not to mention the various drugs.' He inhales suddenly, and then lets out the breath more slowly. 'One of which, I have yet to tell you about.'

DS Jones is eager to interject. She seems to miss the sense of gravity in Skelgill's final statement. Instead, she raises her hands with fingers spread, as though she holds an open book with the story now revealed.

'Suddenly everything falls into place, Guv. It's been driving me crazy trying to work out the connection between everyone on the retreat – and now we know it's Lucy Hecate.'

But Skelgill shakes his head decisively.

'Rich Buckley Publishing is the connection. Lucy Hecate joined up the dots – but the pieces were already in place. So she hatches a plot and collects all the contact details. I wouldn't be surprised if she's still got access to their computer system. She strikes lucky with Sarah Redmond and *bingo!* – Buckley signs up to the retreat drooling like Pavlov's dog. She hand picks a group of people that will give her the best possible cover if things go wrong – if Buckley's death is considered suspicious. People who know him in the industry – who might have their axes to grind – maybe they'll come clean, once they know they're in the clear. And a bunch of unsuspecting novice writers – all of whom you can bet have had manuscripts rejected by Buckley. She might even have written the rejections herself – spiced them up, like the one sent to Bella Mandrake. And enlisting the doctor was a masterstroke – almost. She even casually pointed the finger at him when I spoke with her in London.'

DS Jones has listened intently to Skelgill's thesis. She reaches to pick up her tea – so far untouched – and regards the floating blobs of powdered milk with some suspicion.

'Guv – what made you so sure it wasn't the doctor – you told me that before you got your breakthrough this morning?'

Skelgill gestures with one hand towards the entrance of the drawing room.

'If I walked in here, where would you expect my mobile phone to be?'

They each look puzzled, as though they believe it's a trick question. DS Leyton offers a conveniently dumb answer.

'In your pocket, Guv.'

'Exactly, Leyton.' Now Skelgill points towards the windows. 'So you wouldn't run off down to the jetty and shove my boat out into the lake, would you?'

'I dunno, Guv?' Skelgill frowns and DS Leyton corrects his answer. 'No, Guv.'

'But someone did, Leyton.' He nods several times. 'All along, I've been certain that someone untied my boat and let it drift away – knowing it had my phone aboard.'

'So, how does that exempt Dr Bond?'

'Because, Leyton, when I announced that it was safe in a dry bag in the hold, he wasn't in this room. Nor was Linda Gray, come to that.' He raises his arms in a reference to their surroundings. 'When I retraced my steps I realised that whoever wanted to keep me here, and make sure we stayed incommunicado – it wasn't Bond, and it probably wasn't Linda Gray. I reckon the boat was cast off when I went up with Bond and Dickie Lampray to look at Rich Buckley's body. It had to be one of the others – and given what happened to Bella Mandrake, it probably wasn't her either.'

Now both sergeants are looking expectantly at Skelgill. It is DS Jones who tentatively breaks the silence.

'Bella Mandrake, Guv – that *was* Lucy Hecate?'

Skelgill looks at each of his colleagues, then he points to a small self-sealing plastic bag that lies on the table next to the honey jars.

'I think we'll find that contains good old-fashioned extra-strong sleeping tablets – from the same apothecary in Covent Garden.'

DS Leyton is pursing his lips.

'Why, Guv?'

Skelgill shrugs.

'Unfortunately, she saw something – or, at least, that's what Lucy Hecate thought.' He shakes his head regretfully. 'Bella Mandrake made such a fuss – about evil forces – she might as well have signed her own death warrant.'

DS Jones is nodding.

'Was that why Lucy Hecate wanted to prevent you from calling for help, Guv – to kill Bella Mandrake before she named her?'

Skelgill seems a little unsure.

'Maybe.' He casts about the room and then apparently decides to make an admission. 'Look – I got some expert advice about poisons – an old chap I know from way back – he was a famous toxicologist.' He pauses to check their reactions, but neither officer appears in the least bit surprised that Skelgill has been pursuing his own private inquiries whilst on fishing leave. 'Apparently atropine disappears quickly from the human body. It leaves no inflamed organs and can be hard to detect. I suspect Lucy Hecate was hoping to put as much time as possible between Buckley's death and any proper medical examination. Leaving the drugs containing atropine was just a fall-back – but doubly smart to think of planting some in his desk to make it seem certain they belonged to him. Failing that, suspicion would shift to one of the others – with Gerald Bond first in the queue.'

Now DS Jones seems perplexed.

'But, Guv – it was Lucy Hecate who went out in the storm looking for assistance. That doesn't fit with the idea of creating a delay.'

Skelgill grins in a rather superior fashion.

'I doubt she was looking for help, Jones.'

'No, Guv?'

'No. I reckon she was intending to dispose of this stuff. The contaminated honey at least. It served its purpose – so chuck it in the lake. She had on a big long coat, and I believe this was hidden underneath it. Then she bumped into me and decided not to take the risk.'

'But why call out to you at all, Guv?'

'Because I spotted her first. She must have realised that if there had been an investigation, and some random fisherman later reported seeing her – and she hadn't cried for help – it wouldn't look too clever.

DS Leyton shakes his head.

'Must have been the last thing she'd have expected – running into a copper, Guv.'

Skelgill shrugs.

'She was cool as a cucumber. She sussed that all my gear was on the boat – and nipped back out and made it look like the storm had washed it away. It certainly bought her more time.'

'So *what* about Bella Mandrake, Guv.'

'I don't know, Leyton – I'm not sure if that was in Lucy Hecate's plan at that point. I reckon Bella Mandrake only started really playing up when I arrived – looking for attention.'

DS Jones raises a hand.

'Guv – why did you ask me to investigate Linda Gray's marital history – you said you'd eliminated her?'

'On the basis of the phone and the boat, I had.' Skelgill points to the smaller of the two jars. 'But Buckley was poisoned by the honey being switched on his breakfast tray. Linda Gray left that tray outside his door.'

DS Jones is nodding, though she is not yet completely satisfied with the explanation.

'But how does that relate to her previous marriage?'

Skelgill now looks at DS Leyton.

'Remember – Leyton found out that Buckley had been married twice before.' (DS Leyton nods to confirm.) 'I had to consider that she might have been one of those ex-wives – she was about the right age – if not the right type.'

DS Jones shakes her head.

'She was married to a farmer from Cleator Moor, Guv – for nearly twenty years.'

Skelgill grins.

'Give her a medal.'

His colleagues raise their eyebrows – but DS Jones is still eager to understand exactly what took place. She indicates with a hand the honey jars on the table before them.

'The breakfast tray, Guv – that could be what made Bella Mandrake suspicious? If she'd been in Rich Buckley's room when it was delivered – say she heard something – or even disturbed Lucy Hecate tampering with it?'

Skelgill nods.

'And if she did have a little liaison with Buckley – that might have kept her from saying too much about it.' Looking pensive, he drums the nails of one hand against his tin mug. 'Mind you – Lucy must have switched the poisoned jar back for the original – got it out of Buckley's room – that would be a second occasion when she might have been noticed.'

DS Leyton finishes his tea and grunts as he reaches forward with some difficulty to place it on the edge of the low table.

'But Lucy Hecate poisoned Bella Mandrake with these, Guv?' He gestures to the self-sealing bag.

'Aye – after putting me out of action.'

Both sergeants glance sharply at Skelgill. DS Leyton is first to speak.

'What do you mean, Guv – I thought you'd been on the old River Ouse?'

'Well, thanks for your vote of confidence, Leyton.' Skelgill's scowls severely at his subordinate, though his tone is forgiving. 'Since when has half a bottle of red had me keeling over?'

DS Leyton nods in a conciliatory manner.

'Good point, Guv – so what happened?'

Skelgill shifts in his seat and glances at DS Jones, and then about the room, as if he is composing a version of events that will suit his purposes. He folds his arms before he begins to speak.

'I think she slipped a sleeping tablet into my meal – although Linda Gray cooked it, Lucy served me with a second helping. We had this game of *Scrabble* after dinner – did I tell you I blew them all away?' (His sergeants nod enthusiastically, eager that he should press on.) 'Aye, well – and halfway through the game I started feeling like if I didn't lie down I'd fall asleep on the spot. I was first up to bed. Then that's what helped me narrow it down to Lucy.'

Clearly, this final sentence does not make sense, and both officers look like they want to ask Skelgill by what criteria he managed this elimination, but are afraid to ask. It appears he is not going to volunteer the answer, although his thumb drifts subconsciously to his mouth and he gently brushes his lips. That the truth concerns kissing, almost certainly means this aspect of his deductions will forever remain an official mystery. And just at this moment there is a sharp knocking, and a forensic officer sticks his head between the double doors of the drawing room. Exultantly, he brandishes a clear polythene bag that contains a white stick-like object.

'Found it, sir – almost exactly where you thought.'

Skelgill gives the thumbs-up sign, and the man disappears.

DS Leyton looks baffled.

'What was that, Guv?'

'A candle.'

'Come again?'

'The candle from my bedroom. My guess is it's got Lucy Hecate's DNA on the wick – from when she snuffed it out. Another little piece in the jigsaw if she decides to plead not guilty. I caught her looking for it today – she'd thought of everything.' He shrugs casually, perhaps aware of DS Jones's interrogative gaze. 'When I interviewed her – she even asked if we'd searched the island – she said she'd lost a scarf of sentimental value. What a nerve! All along she was planning to come back to get these things that she'd hidden in her room – plus the candle from the garden.'

DS Leyton looks perplexed.

'What was it doing there, Guv?'

Skelgill shrugs.

'That's down to you pair. You turned up at the crack of dawn on Monday – she probably wasn't expecting that we'd get help before noon. I reckon she realised the risk – tiny though it was – and nipped in here and lobbed it out of the window. I would never have thought of it in a million years – it was only because I noticed the candlestick was empty that my mind got working.'

DS Jones is watching Skelgill through narrowed eyes.

'Guv, why was Lucy Hecate snuffing out your candle?'

Skelgill looks momentarily cornered, but he has an ace up his sleeve.

'She chloroformed me.'

'What?' Both sergeants in unison utter this exclamation.

'Aye – belt and braces.' Skelgill now points to the last of the items on the table, a small brown bottle with a pipette cap. 'In case the drug wasn't working – I'd told them all I was a light sleeper – and I assume she didn't want to risk one of the strong ones on me. So she crept in and made sure I was out for the count. Remember my headache? Dizziness, confusion, fatigue – all the classic symptoms. I have it on the best authority.'

DS Jones seems willing to be convinced.

'So, Bella Mandrake, Guv – what do you think really happened?'

Skelgill shakes his head.

'Maybe Lucy will tell us in time. She could have switched the strong tablets for something Bella was taking anyway – or maybe dissolved them into her bedtime water. Then she sneaked back later and left the empty packet of the standard pills for us to find.' He pauses for a moment and leans back against the sofa. 'And you have to consider – if Bella didn't suspect any particular person, Lucy might have popped along to her room and offered her something that would help her sleep – Bella was drunk, remember. If she mixed them with a drink she could conceal a fatal dose. I don't doubt Bella was the gullible sort – and quiet little Lucy's probably the last person you'd put money on in a game of *Cluedo*.'

DS Jones now looks reflectively at her superior.

'Do you think she will plead guilty, Guv?'

Skelgill stares into the fire. The wood is burning down, there are fewer flames, and glowing embers nestle amongst a bed of white ash. A log slips and sends a little burst of sparks rushing up the chimney, a spirit escaping. He has been holding his breath while he considers this question, and now he sighs quietly. His response, when it comes, is somewhat obtuse – almost the answer to a different query, and one reflecting his torn frame of mind.

'Look – I shouldn't say it – Buckley probably got what he deserved. But killing Bella Mandrake?' Skelgill shakes his head. 'It's like going out deer-stalking and shooting a sheep.'

20. BEEBI HAUG

Friday 4pm

The day has remained clear and bright and, although the sun has set on Grisholm, its rays still illuminate Derwentwater's eastern shoreline and the fells beyond. The breeze has dropped, and the water is calm, as Skelgill dabs his oars and guides his craft out of the boathouse and into the sharpening air of the premature dusk. He sits on the centre thwart, facing DS Jones in the stern. It is time to return his boat to Bassenthwaite Lake, and she has agreed to accompany him to where his car and trailer await, to lend a helping hand on the slipway.

Skelgill appears pensive, as he has been on and off since the arrival of his colleagues. It seems the experience of arresting Lucy Hecate has left him with an uncomfortable wound. Sensing this, in making conversation, DS Jones opts for a lighter subject.

'DS Leyton tells me you've got a cat, Guv?'

Skelgill makes a tutting sound.

'Just temporary – I plan to repatriate it to Scotland.'

This statement does not sound very convincing, and DS Jones grins encouragingly.

'It'll be company for Cleopatra, Guv.'

Skelgill harrumphs.

'They haven't met yet – the dog's lodging with Sammy the Wolf this week.'

'Has it got a name?'

'I don't even know if it's a he or a she.'

'How about Anthony, Guv?'

'Very witty, Jones.'

DS Jones smiles.

'Well, at least cats look after themselves, Guv.'

Skelgill nods.

'Aye – if push comes to shove, maybe. This one wants tinned food, though. Last night I arrived back to three voles and a shrew lined up on the step.'

'That's its way of saying thank you, Guv.'

Skelgill shakes his head ruefully.

'Thing is – pets are all very well – good company and so on – but they cost a fortune. Vet's bills, kennelling, dog-walking and whatnot. Can you believe, some folk even pay for insurance?'

DS Jones nods sympathetically.

'What are you going to do about the bet, Guv?'

Skelgill scowls, as though he does not wish to be reminded of it. Restored though his professional pride must be – to have solved the case and proved wrong his doubters – there is surely a part of him that resents the forfeiture of half a day's fishing, and its corollary in financial terms. His reply is terse.

'Lose it.'

DS Jones frowns – she seems reluctant to see him give in.

'There's still time, Guv – when does the bet end?'

Skelgill is beginning to put his back into his strokes, now that they have cleared the harbour and are running up beside Grisholm's wooded banks. He cocks his head in lieu of an indifferent shrug.

'Midnight.'

'I don't mind staying out with you, Guv – if there's something I can wear to keep warm?'

Skelgill glowers disapprovingly.

'Jones – I've been out since six – I've tried everything.'

This, of course, is not strictly true. He was rudely interrupted by his subconscious, only minutes before he was about to test out the professor's loaned lure. And now his eyes fall upon the said *Beebi Haug*, which lies still attached to its trace, among the rods that are laid along the bottom boards, two on either side of the boat. Following his gaze, and perhaps reading the germ of thought that must take root in his mind, DS Jones makes a suggestion.

'I could fish, Guv – at least while you row back?'

Skelgill looks uncomfortable.

'It's not an approved method.'

DS Jones grins – she thinks he must be joking – that perhaps this must be a macho preserve, or something similar.

'Why not, Guv?'

'Trolling – that's what it would be – dragging a lure along behind the boat – that's not fishing – where's the skill in that?'

Now DS Jones smiles endearingly.

'Guv – it would be skill if I were doing it.'

Skelgill grits his teeth and grimaces as he pulls harder at the oars, fighting the urge to have one last dip at the challenge. Then he relents and stops rowing for a moment. He reaches down and slides his spinning rod out from beneath the thwarts. He flicks over the bail arm and tosses the lure past DS Jones into the water at the stern. Then he hands her the rod.

'Here. Let that run out, while I row for a bit. Don't want it too near the boat. Sit sideways.'

DS Jones does as ordered, and watches the line issue unchecked from the reel with each of his strokes. Skelgill is watching the water beyond the stern, and after half a minute he angles the boat through about fifteen degrees, perhaps so that the lure is no longer running in the wake. DS Jones, still staring at the emptying spool, suddenly makes a sharp intake of breath.

'Guv – should it be going this fast?'

'What do you mean?'

'Look, Guv.'

She rotates at the waist and brings the rod round so he can get a better view. The line is streaming off, no longer forming loose loops as it goes, but straight and almost taut. In Skelgill's eyes, there appears a tiny spark of hope.

'Turn the reel.'

'What?'

'Turn the reel!'

His barked command prompts her to act. She winds over the reel and re-engages the bail arm. A second later the rod is almost jerked from her grip, and it bends like a willow as an invisible force threatens to drag her over the stern.

'Guv!'

Her screamed entreaty must carry all the way to Keswick, but acting on what can only be instinct, pluckily she hangs on with both hands and drops to her knees on the floor of the boat so that she can brace against the transom. Skelgill has stopped rowing. For a moment he is transfixed. For there, no great distance away, a monster pike – a good thirty pounds – tail-dances on the water. And then he steps into the breach.

Releasing the oars he lurches forward and, not standing on ceremony, wrenches the rod from DS Jones. Then in one smooth sweeping movement, he stretches upright and strikes to ensure that the hooks are engaged. Feeling the full weight of the fish, the anxiety in his features dissolves into an expression of elation. As he enters the fray, he rocks and sways like the conductor of an orchestra, lost in the moment, engulfed by the maelstrom, fulfilled in employing the skills he has honed during a lifetime's dedication to his craft. While he is thus spiritually adrift, DS Jones contrives to crawl past him and take up the oars – and she seems to know to hold the boat steady, just a gentle movement against the direction of play. Within a minute or two Skelgill begins to make progress, and gradually wins back line onto the reel. It will not be too long before the magnificent creature – albeit temporarily – comes aboard to be photographed. His eyes flaming, his hair streaming, grimacing like a deranged Mongol warrior on horseback, Skelgill glances jubilantly over his shoulder at his companion. He calls out to her, loudly, as if a storm is raging about them.

'Jones – what do you know about Tallinn?'

'Isn't that Estonia, Guv?'

'Aye. It is.'

***

Next in the series...

CULT... OR OCCULT?
EVERY WHICH WAY, EVIL STALKS THE FELLS

A spate of vicious attacks upon valuable Herdwick sheep, the sudden disappearance of a foreign hiker, and the unexplained drowning of a woodland hermit – a series of apparently unconnected events – draw Detective Inspector Daniel Skelgill to the white-knuckle passes and isolated dales of deepest Lakeland.

As straws in the wind suggest there is sorcery afoot – and a connection to an equally sinister trade in human traffic – Skelgill and his team risk dire consequences as they strive to infiltrate the secretive ring and expose its evil perpetrators.

In the fifth Inspector Skelgill novel, the maverick British detective faces what is his greatest challenge yet, as he wrestles with an error of judgement that could leave his career – and his life – in tatters.

'Murder by Magic' by Bruce Beckham is available from Amazon

FREE BOOKS, NEW RELEASES, THE BEAUTIFUL LAKES ... AND MOUNTAINS OF CAKES

Sign up for Bruce Beckham's author newsletter

Thank you for getting this far!

If you have enjoyed your encounter with DI Skelgill there's a growing series of whodunits set in England's rugged and beautiful Lake District to get your teeth into.

My newsletter often features one of the back catalogue to download for free, along with details of new releases and special offers.

No Skelgill mystery would be complete without a café stop or two, and each month there's a traditional Cumbrian recipe – tried and tested by yours truly (aka *Bruce Bake 'em*).

To sign up, this is the link:

https://mailchi.mp/acd032704a3f/newsletter-sign-up

Your email address will be safely stored in the USA by Mailchimp, and will be used for no other purpose. You can unsubscribe at any time simply by clicking the link at the foot of the newsletter.

Thank you, again – best wishes and happy reading!

Bruce Beckham

Printed in Great Britain
by Amazon